Author photograph by Rebecca Ramage

Published by Ana Spoke, Melbourne, Australia
www.anaspoke.com

ISBN-13: 978-0994431219
ISBN-10: 099443121X

Book layout by www.ebooklaunch.com

This is a work of fiction. Names, characters, organizations, places, and events are either products of the author's imagination or are used fictitiously.

For Veronica

Table of Contents

Beats getting sued for slippery floors.

Debt is always negative, no matter how positively you try to look at it. The "minus" sign in front of your bank balance is a dead giveaway, despite what you might think about leveraging or whatever. It's even worse when it's a credit card or a student loan, and you can't even remember what you've bought or learned with it. Sure, the minimum repayments will eventually cancel it out, but by that time you will most likely have dentures and be peeing anywhere you damn well please.

That's what I usually thought about my student loans and extensive collection of overdue credit card bills. Yet on that hot, fated May afternoon I was in high spirits, not because I was on depression meds, but because I had a plan. Squirming in high heels and trying to discreetly pull sweaty polyester out of my butt I, Isabella Maxwell, was about to meet my destiny. It was as clear as the big blue sky above me that I was destined to be discovered.

Being discovered was my long-cherished dream. I didn't care what exactly I would be discovered for, as long as it meant a lot of money and at least fifteen minutes of fame. I'd always imagined it happening at the mall, or maybe a coffee shop. There I would be, laughing with my friends, young and carefree, throwing back my blond locks, when someone from "the industry" would happen to walk by. Something about me would stop them dead in their tracks and, after some small talk, they would offer me a contract for something amazing, definitely involving TV. They would say that I'm unique and special right in front of everybody, including Brad.

That dream became even more urgent after Brad broke up with me in February. We were high school sweethearts and had been dating for almost four years, so naturally I thought we were going to be together forever. I actually thought he was about to propose because he started to act all weird and nervous around me. Once, he went down on his knee in the parking lot and I screamed with excitement, but it turned out that his laces were loose, and I had to invent a story about a huge spider. Then a few days later, just before Valentine's Day, he messaged me "changed Facebook status". It wasn't how I imagined a proposal, a bit too modern for me, but a bad proposal is still better than no proposal.

I logged onto Facebook with shaky fingers.

"Single." Brad had changed his status to "single".

I didn't get it at first. I tried refreshing the screen a few times, until the tears turned the page into a swirl of blue and white. There had to be an explanation. Still crying, I pushed blindly at the phone buttons until I managed to dial his number.

"Sorry, babe," Brad said. "It's just that I'm about to graduate and get drafted by the NFL. You know that's my dream."

Brad was a football player in the same community college where I was studying for my liberal arts degree. He wasn't quite quarterback material, but he was tall and fit, and had amazing cheekbones.

"But, but," I cried. "It's my dream too!"

"Look, babe, once I'm in the League, I'll be dating actresses and supermodels. A girl next door just won't cut it in celebrity circles, you know. I'm doing you a favor."

It was over, but there was one more straw I had to grab. "But tomorrow's Valentine's Day!"

"Well, that's the thing. Your birthday's in a couple of weeks too. What's the point of buying you two presents when we're going to break up anyway?"

In hindsight, I have to admit that it was the most logical argument he's ever made. Still, at the time it didn't make sense to me.

"How can you do that, after all I've done for you? I did all your math homework for years!"

"Yeah," he said, "and all I got was a C-plus average!"

The breakup cut me hard, so hard that I could barely concentrate on my own schoolwork. All I could think about was that *I had to* become famous so Brad would come crawling back to me, begging me to take him back. In my daydreams, I tormented him with rejection but inevitably took him back. What can I say, I was in love.

Unfortunately, time kept passing by and still no agents or directors came out of the blue to offer me any contracts. I couldn't understand why, because I kept going to the mall and the campus, and even the trendiest, artsiest coffee shops, and I kept on laughing, maybe just a touch hysterical. I should have probably spent that time trying to develop some kind of talent, like acting or singing, but it didn't occur to me that talent was a necessary component of being discovered. None of the people from Jersey Shore had any talent, and yet Snooki was on every magazine stand, sporting either a massive engagement ring, or a baby, or both. Plus, I was already an awesome writer - every story I wrote got published in the school paper and my friends and family loved them. Sure, I was the editor-in-chief of that paper, but back then I had no clue about conflict of interest. I also kept a personal journal and planned to turn my notes into a novel one day, kind of like a new *Bridget Jones*. It was guaranteed to be a huge hit.

Looking back, I was probably depressed. I spent most of my time wallowing and ate very little, sustaining myself mostly with Red Bulls. When I wasn't dreaming of fame and fortune, I was stalking Brad on Facebook and Twitter, and Googling every possible combination of his name, nicknames, football team, and hometown. I also started obsessing over celebrity engagements and bump watches. It didn't even matter whether I knew who the particular famous woman was, or why she was famous. I wanted to know whether she was engaged or pregnant, how many carats or how far along, whether it was a flawless diamond, a boy or a girl, and just how delighted was the fiancée or the expectant father. I stayed up late every night, unable to tear myself from promises that Jennifer Aniston had finally confirmed a pregnancy.

With all that drama in my life, it was only a matter of time before I lost my job waitressing at Applebee's. My boss was a nice enough guy and ignored my tardiness for a while. He even bought my excuses of "horrible gastro" whenever I was late and "really horrible gastro" whenever I forgot to show up for my shift altogether. He finally had no choice when I dumped a bowl of French onion soup into a customer's lap while trying to check my phone for updates. I had no excuse - the customer was expecting a Caesar salad.

So it was sometime in late May when, unemployed, half-starved and depressed, I glimpsed a sign of hope. I just found out that despite my best self-destruction efforts, I managed to graduate from Capitol Community College, so I was celebrating the news with a sixteen-hour TV marathon and a family-sized bag of Cheetos. It was then, somewhere between the reruns of Buffy and MASH, that I saw the commercial that would change my life forever.

It started with a stock-standard montage of an office skyscraper and a boardroom business meeting. I was about to flip the channel, when the boardroom window exploded, as three men clad in unidentifiable black uniforms and armor swung inside, sending the unsuspecting business folk into screaming fits.

The camera cut to the leader of the SWAT team, who took off his uniform and helmet, revealing a business suit and a perfectly coifed head of graying hair. I immediately recognized him as Mr. Hue, the famous playboy billionaire. The businessmen and women stopped screaming and started laughing, shaking his hand and exclaiming, "Mr. Hue!" and "You rascal!" The other two militants continued to stand guard.

Mr. Hue turned to the camera, which moved in for a close-up.

"I'm Mr. Hue," he said. "You know me as the eccentric billionaire famous for crazy stunts, like going over the Victoria Falls in a barrel or hand feeding barracudas around my private island in the Caribbean." There was a rapid and spectacular montage of the hooting Mr. Hue jumping out of planes, off bridges, and into oceans of every shade of blue and turquoise.

"But did you know," said Mr. Hue, back in the shattered boardroom, "that I technically have a job as the CEO of Shizzle, Inc?" The montage resumed, now showing Mr. Hue surrounded by enthusiastic employees, talking and pointing awkwardly at business-looking documents.

"This job is very demanding," Mr. Hue's voice continued over footage of him in a hard hat, shaking hands with factory workers and pointing awkwardly at large blueprints. "It is only possible thanks to a dedicated team of personal assistants."

A team of nearly identical beautiful blond women smiled together for the camera. The montage continued with them running to and fro with business-looking documents and large blueprints.

"As Shizzle, Inc continues to grow, so does my team," said Mr. Hue, back in the boardroom, "and I am excited to announce the search for the ultimate Shizzle assistant!"

My pulse quickened, and my hand froze in the bottom of the Cheetos bag, where it was searching for crumbs.

"This nation-wide search will uncover the individual most deserving of making my coffee and answering my phone calls. Are you that special and talented person?"

"Yes!" I yelled at the screen and tossed the Cheetos bag.

"Are you ready to take on the world alongside the coolest and richest man in the southeastern states?"

"Yes!" I yelled with even more fervor.

He went on talking, something about terms and conditions, but I was no longer listening. I knew what I had to do.

*

Getting discovered would have been a lot cooler and easier than getting a job, but beggars can't be choosers, I thought. That was my plan, by the way - I was going to beg Mr. Hue, beg like he'd never been begged before. The way I figured, once I became a personal assistant to the guy who is constantly on TV and surrounded by celebrities, I would get discovered in no time. I didn't sleep until very late that night, updating my résumé, trying to put together a presentable outfit from my cheap and haphazard clothing collection, and grooming within an inch of my life.

Unfortunately, I wasn't the only one who had the same bright idea. Somebody famous once said that most of success is simply showing up, and the next morning it looked like the whole southeastern US had done just that. When I arrived at Shizzle, Inc headquarters bright and early at ten am, a line of thousands of wannabes snaked all the way from the parking lot, along the building facade, up the massive front stairs, and into the gaping mouth of the entrance. I took my spot at the end and tried to estimate how long it would take Mr. Hue to interview all those people, but gave up after I realized that it would be a very, very long time.

To my surprise, however, the line started to move relatively quickly and after a couple of hours I was already out of the parking lot. The sun reached its zenith, mercilessly smothering me and other global warming non-believers. I took off my jacket and draped it carefully over my head, trying to protect my fair skin without messing up my attempt at an elegant French twist. I was thirsty and exhausted, but my heart was full of stupid, unwarranted hope.

It was a beautiful day. Nearby, birds were busy plucking bits of cheerfully pink insulation from the dumpster and carrying them off to make cozy homes for their young. They seemed committed to family life even without the engagement rings.

"Can you imagine a pigeon announcing to his pigeon girlfriend that he was going to fly off and start screwing pedigreed white doves?" I asked a pretty redhead in front of me. The redhead looked at me like I was crazy and returned to studying her notes. I didn't have any notes, so I returned to studying my copy of *Star*.

The line slowed down around lunchtime. The redhead took a carefully wrapped sandwich from her insulated lunch bag, and I searched for loose M&Ms in the bottom of my purse. Then the line started moving again, even faster. When I finally reached the front doors, I saw why. Blocking the entry was a formidable group consisting of several security guards and an elegant middle-aged woman with a clipboard. The woman looked cool and sophisticated despite the heat, her dark hair arranged in a nest of wavy snake-like locks. The feminine look, however, did little to soften the steel edge in her eyes.

I watched in alarm as the middle-aged Medusa turned away most of the applicants on the spot. It seemed that only about one in fifty made it through the coveted doors. Coming closer, I could hear some of the exchanges.

"You can't reject me just because I'm a man!" protested a skinny and very unmanly youth. "It's unlawful discrimination!"

"It's only discrimination if you are a woman," Medusa said in a slight accent I couldn't place, as the guards dragged the skinny youth away. "Next!"

Other wannabes just burst into tears after being told that they were too fat, too short, too ginger, or too "eww" to fetch Mr. Hue's coffee. Suddenly I was no longer sure that coming down to Shizzle, Inc was a great or even a decent idea. I put my jacket back on and surveyed myself with the help of the phone camera. It was hopeless. My hair had defected despite the dozen pins and half can of hair spray. All my attempts at fixing the mess just made it look even more like a pigeon's nest. My makeup was practically gone, washed away by the hours of sun and stress-induced sweating. When it came to my turn to be judged by Medusa, I'd already turned to stone from fear and dehydration.

She looked me over like I was a heifer at a state fair. I desperately tried to think of something smart to say, to show how special and talented I was, but it was hopeless. We stared at each other in silence.

"Okay," she said finally and asked for my driver's license.

Still speechless, I handed it to her. I could hear a low rumble of shock behind me. Medusa gave me back my license and waved me in. I stepped towards the doors and was almost knocked over by a pretty blond girl rushing out in tears. I recognized her as one of the candidates who managed to get in just minutes before. The sea of rejected and still waiting hopefuls engulfed her. Everyone was asking if she got the job, but the poor girl just wailed. *She probably didn't get it,* I thought and walked inside.

It was the most impressive office lobby I'd ever seen, quite possibly the most impressive office lobby ever built. To start with, it was huge, easily large enough to park a mid-size passenger jet. It had a cathedral-like ceiling made entirely of glass panels in a spiraling design. The bright sunlight cascaded down onto the polished marble floors and reflected onto equally polished walls. Despite its humongous size, it contained hardly anything other than the reception desk and a few sculptures and plants.

"May I help you?" A woman's voice snapped me from my reverie.

I approached the sleek reception desk. Behind it was an elegant logo of Shizzle, Inc and two impeccably groomed secretaries.

"I'm here for the interview. Isabella Maxwell," I said and heard my voice echo in the background.

"Please have a seat," one of the secretaries said and went over to the full-length double doors off to the side. I looked around. It was not clear exactly where I could sit, as the only items nearby appeared to be abstract art pieces supporting vases of white flowers. I took a chance and perched on the edge of what looked like a huge stretching cat.

The secretary reappeared from behind the massive doors.

"Mr. Hue will see you now."

I jumped up and dropped my briefcase, reached down to pick it up, dropped my phone, then my sunglasses, and finally knocked over a vase. The heady scent of white gardenias filled the lobby. I shoved the phone and glasses into the briefcase and rushed towards the doors, mumbling "I'm so sorry!" over and over. I didn't yet know that the water from the broken vase had already spread in the same direction.

I slipped on the puddle, my feet sliding forward, followed by the rest of my useless body. The secretary jumped aside with a surprised shriek as I skidded through the door and across the office, crashing into an impressive desk.

There was a grunt of what could have been either amusement or disapproval. I scrambled onto my knees and peeked over the huge mahogany slab. Mr. Hue was lounging back on a throne-like chair, his feet crossed on top of the desk, a very large Cuban cigar clamped between his perfectly white teeth. There was not a single crease in his gray Italian wool suit. He looked every bit the dazzling playboy billionaire, the owner of Shizzle, Inc.

"Hi," I spoke in a barely audible whisper, rendered nearly speechless by the opulence of the office, his mere presence, and my comparative mousiness and general denseness. I felt behind me for a chair, unable to tear my gaze away from him.

"Fell me, me Miff Mawel, hot aches you infrared in a gob a whistle ink?" The cigar was obviously far too large to let him speak properly. He must have realized it as well, because he spat it on the floor and tried again, "Tell me, Ms. Maxwell, what makes you interested in a job at Shizzle, Inc?" He held onto his chin and fixed me with his gaze.

I did not expect this question, not in an interview. "Ahm, well, you know..." I looked around and blurted, "Your office looks amazing!"

He seemed pleased with my answer. "Yes. Indeed, it is the largest Shizzle office in the world." He slowly recrossed his legs, giving me a close-up view of the gray wooly crotch of his trousers. Then, suddenly, he swung his legs off the desk and leaned forward. "What makes you think you are qualified to work here?"

I certainly did not expect *that*. I froze, like a deer in headlights. Or a cucumber that gets shoved all the way back in the fridge and then you find it a week later, and it's all hard and gross. I tried to think of something, but the only thing that came to my jumbled and dehydrated brain was that he must've had his teeth professionally whitened, because you just can't get results like that at home. I looked down and noticed that I was still clutching my briefcase. The résumé! I reached in and pulled out a single page of double-spaced Arial 14 text. I held it out to him with a shaky hand. He took it, and without so much as a glance threw it down on the floor, where it promptly caught fire from the still-lit cigar.

I froze again, unsure of what to do. Luckily, the secretary rushed in with an extinguisher and a mop and cleared away the mess. By the looks of it, that kind of thing happened regularly here.

"I don't believe in formal qualifications," Mr. Hue said finally. "I got none, but I got billions."

I had nothing to say to that.

"What I want to know," Mr. Hue continued, "is whether you have what I call character. Are you clever? Savvy? Have you graduated from a School of Hard Knocks?"

I thought back to my community college honors classes and the Harvard law degree that I did in my spare time. None of my qualifications came from the School of Hard Knocks. Also, I don't actually have a law degree from Harvard. I mean, I do, but I printed it myself from a web template. But, like, on really nice paper, and I put it in a frame, so it looks all legit. Still, I had to admit to myself that I was indeed not qualified to work at Shizzle, Inc. My eyes welled with tears. I had to run away, as far away as I could from this perfection of rich mahogany and fine Italian clothing.

I jumped up, tripped over the leg of my chair and fell over for the second time in less than five minutes. This time, I did not have the strength to get up and just lay there until Mr. Hue walked over and stood above me.

"You seem to have a real knack for things." He looked down at me, deep in thought, and then appeared to make a decision. "You're hired!"

"What?" I couldn't believe my ears. I scrambled up to face him, but he was already back on his throne.

"Beats getting sued for slippery floors," he said to no one in particular. With that, he picked up a fluorescent pink marker from the desk, flicked off the top, and inhaled deeply.

"You start tomorrow."

Harden The Funk Up, no doubt!

I don't know how I managed to get back through the army of pissed off applicants and find where I parked, but the next thing I knew, I was behind the wheel of my Beetle. It was vintage, of course, and yellow - quirky enough for a future Pulitzer winner. I was driving down a street I'd never seen before. It was empty, and the windows of most houses were boarded up. Tumbleweed rolled by. I felt a growing sense of unease, like someone was watching me. It was just like the beginning of one of Stephen King's stories.

A wailing siren brought me all the way back to reality. The fuzz. Damn it. I pulled over and waited for the cop to stride over to my window. It took him a while, what with the swagger and all. I waited, watching a group of teenagers busily working on a car across the street. They seemed to be in the middle of changing its tires.

The cop dragged his nightstick over the side of the already dinged-up Beetle. Not a good sign. I rolled down the window and looked up at him. He was young and ridiculously good-looking - dark hair, chiseled face and aviator sunglasses, your typical new police recruit. He stared back at me, not saying anything, but I could tell that he was probing my body from behind the cool shades. For a moment I thought he was going to ask me out.

"May I please see your license and registration, ma'am," he said instead.

"Sure," I tried to sound nonchalant as I handed them over. "What seems to be the problem, Officer?"

He studied my license without reply, then scribbled something in his notepad. "You live at 842 Primrose Place?"

I nodded.

"What brings you to this neighborhood?" He handed the documents back to me.

I was about to tell him about my autopilot driving but bit my tongue. The taste of blood forced my face into a grimace. His eyes narrowed. "Step out of the car, ma'am," he ordered.

As soon as I was out of the car, he spun me around and pushed me against Beetle's hot metal. His body pressed against mine and something hard, probably a gun, poked into the small of my back. His hands slowly, oh so very slowly, went down the sides of my waist, hips, and into my pockets. He pulled out a pack of gum and a few coins.

"A pretty young lady like you might want to be careful around these parts." His whisper was hot in my ear. I wasn't sure what he was talking about, but it scared me. I shut my eyes tightly and waited for what was certainly coming next. Instead, he released me.

"I will escort you back to your house. Follow me." With that, he popped the gum into his mouth and pocketed my change.

I didn't say anything, just watched him swagger back to his cruiser and jump in through the window, Dukes of Hazzard style. There was the unmistakable sound of breaking beer bottles.

I got back behind the wheel, turned on the ignition, and watched as one of the hard-working youths rolled a tire across the street. The car they worked on was now sitting on blocks. The hot cop turned on his flashing lights and siren, and sped off. I hit the gas and struggled to keep up, as we weaved in and out of traffic, mounted sidewalks, and ran red lights.

Thankfully, it was over in minutes, because my house turned out to be just a few blocks away. As I pulled over at the front, knocking over garbage cans, the cop threw the cruiser into reverse. Tires squealed as he slammed on the brakes and came to a dead stop next to my Beetle. I looked over at him, waiting to be further reprimanded, but he just motioned to his eyes with two fingers, then pointed one at me, as if to say "I'm watching you." Then he slammed on the gas again and shot off in a cloud of smoke and burning rubber.

I sat behind the wheel, unable to move, unable to comprehend what had just happened. My gut told me that meeting the coolest man on Earth within an hour of getting the coolest job on Earth meant something besides an awesome coincidence. It was as strong and clear as knowing that your lucky numbers will one day win the state lottery jackpot.

*

I surveyed my shitty little house, delighting in the thought that sometime in the future, sometime very soon, I was going to move out of it and into something more suited to my self-image. It was old, but I doubt that it was a beauty even in its youth. The sagging roof seemed to weigh down the wooden porch, which itself was sinking into the piles of rotten leaves and scraggly azalea bushes. The lack of kerbside appeal continued once you passed the screeching front door and dingy hallway, revealing an oddly shaped living room utterly devoid of natural light, three small bedrooms, and a kitchen. The only distinguishing feature of the whole place was a cavernous basement with a dirt floor, the kind suited for cockfights or stowing away kidnapped victims. They say there is no place like home, but I've stayed in a Holiday Inn, and it's much better than home - the sink doesn't leak, and the sheets have hardly any stains on them at all.

The house was free, which greatly made up for its shortcomings in quality and ambiance. To be perfectly honest, I was actually squatting there with Tara. I thought it was okay - after all, everybody was doing it. The whole country was full of real estate that nobody wanted, and I'm pretty sure that on our street only Old Man and Married Couple paid either mortgage or rent. I even put the address on my driver's license, and Tara thought it was cool.

Tara's judgment of cool was highly questionable, though, considering that it sometimes led her to dubious decisions, like starting her own scented candle business. She was hard at work on it for months but had not yet sold a single candle, and the basement was full of stock. It wasn't all that surprising - the candles smelled terrible, kind of like a mixture of cleaning chemicals and pee. They didn't look good, either. Instead of glass jars, she poured them in pipes and even in pressure cookers, and instead of potpourri she mixed in nails and ball bearings. I guess it was to give candles an industrial look, but I personally wouldn't buy one.

Still, I admired Tara for her entrepreneurial spirit. It inspired me to start a couple of my own businesses, like the one where I called the customer service number on the back of every food package and complained about the quality of their products. I had refund checks and coupons waiting for me in the mailbox almost every day. Another one was applying for credit cards with introductory zero interest rates on balance transfers and shuffling around my debt. Mastercard sponsored my independence from Dad, which truly was priceless.

Anyway, Tara was not making her candles that day, but only because she'd been sick all week. I was getting worried about her because she even stopped smoking weed.

"Hey Tara, how are you feeling?" I tried to sound cheerful as I walked in and dropped my bag and jacket onto the already cluttered hallway floor.

"Not sure." Her weak voice drifted from the couch. "I can't feel my legs."

I rushed into the living room. She was shockingly pale, and her eyes were rimmed with red. I sighed with relief. At least she was smoking again, and it sounded like some good shit.

"What's that?" I nodded in the direction of a half-gallon Ziploc baggie on the coffee table. "Strawberry Paralysis?"

"No, it's new," she said and offered me the pipe. "Margaret Thatcher. Want some?"

"Maybe later." I know it sounds bad, but we only smoked weed because neither one of us was old enough to buy alcohol. "So, are you feeling better?"

"Yeah, heaps," she said, although she didn't look it. Tara was a pretty girl, but she detested personal grooming, which in her opinion was wasting water and destroying the ozone layer. Her short black hair was greasy and stood up on end as if she'd got licked by a friendly cow. She had way too many holes in her ears, chewed her nails, and dressed like a boy. I was pretty sure she was a lesbian, although I stuck to the "don't ask, don't tell" policy. She was also the coolest chick I'd ever known, spoke her mind, and had the kind of balls I admired in the West Coast rappers.

Tara took a drag, held it in, then let it out without a single cough.

She was sick. I mean, she was so cool, it was sick. Slang just gets confusing sometimes.

"How are ya?" she said, packing another bowl.

"Oh my God!" I shrieked and jumped about wildly. "I almost forgot, I got a job! I got *the* job - at Shizzle, Inc!"

"For shizzle?" She sat up straight, which was unusual for her. "You mean the global conglomerate of value creation processes?"

"Yes, the very one!" I plopped onto the couch next to her. "I start tomorrow!"

She didn't say anything, just stared wildly at her baggie of Margaret Thatcher.

"What's wrong?" I was confused. It was unlike her not to offer me a celebratory toke of the pipe.

"Nothing," she got up. "I need to make more candles." And just like that, she left, which was actually pretty normal for her. I made a mental note to tell her about Mr. Hue and Hot Cop some other time.

I sighed, went to my own bedroom and stared at myself in the mirrored closet doors. Blues started creeping in, replacing my earlier excitement. The girl in the mirror looked utterly incapable of holding down either a job at a major corporation or the attention of a ridiculously hot cop. Her hair was too blond, her breasts too large, and her lips too pouty. There was nothing even remotely original or quirky about her. I sighed again and flopped onto the bed.

My cell phone burst into a rendition of DMX's "Party Up", which meant that it was Harden. Harden was my other best friend, the one responsible for introducing me to all things rap.

"Yo, Slim Whitey, what up!" I said into the phone, feeling instantly better. Harden, a.k.a. Slim Whitey, was a cool dude to hang around. He was an aspiring DJ, and I had no doubt that he was going to succeed one day, even though his tastes in music ran a bit old-school. But then, if it weren't for him, I would have never known how cool Outkast were before they went mainstream.

"What up, Izz," said Slim Whitey. "By the way, it's not Slim anymore. Changed my name, yo."

"Again?" Harden had been constantly changing his name ever since I met him, which was in elementary school. Everyone called him

"Hard-on" and I knew that it was bad even before I understood why. His attempts to explain the Old English origin of his name as "the valley of hares" just earned him another nickname, Rabbit. Nobody ever dared to touch him because he was so big, but he was an easy target for jokes.

"Yeah," Harden said. "I had to. Can't be too careful with copyright infringement these days. Homeboy would have me iced, yo. Did you see his last video?" Eminem was Harden's idol.

"Which one?" I asked.

"The one where he's yelling and throwing gang signs, then shit explodes and peeps die."

"You gonna have to be more specific," I said.

"Anyway," he said. "I found this website that makes up rap names - it's the shiznit!"

"Oh yeah? So what are you called now?"

"Check this out," Harden suddenly became serious. "Which one do you like better - Harden Dawg, Har Den, Jiggy Hard, or Harden The Funk Up?"

Jiggy Hard was an ironic name for someone who was as jiggly soft as Harden, both literally and figuratively. The boy even saved orphaned baby birds and cried when they eventually died. Of course, I wasn't going to say that.

"Harden The Funk Up, no doubt!" I said instead. "That's cool, man!"

"Better than Bubba Sparxx, right?" He sounded pleased. He was really just a sweet kid.

"So what's Harden The Funk Up up to tonight?" I asked.

"Now, check *this* out!" Harden roared. "I got me a paying gig on the Wess Saide, you dig!"

"That's bitchin! Congrats, Slim! I mean, Harden The Funk Up!"

"Thanks," he said. "Wanna come represent?"

"You betcha! Text me the address," I said. "I gotta go get m'self purdy!"

"You're always purdy," I heard him say as I was hanging up. Such a sweet kid.

It took me an hour to get ready, most of which was spent picking up clothes from the floor and the side of the bed I didn't sleep on, then throwing them back down. Nothing quite suited the momentous occasion. It was ridiculous, not having the money to buy clothes that made me look like I had no money. I finally settled on a ripped up pair of jeans, a black t-shirt, and a gray hoodie.

I chose Snoop Dogg's money anthem for the ride over, to get myself out of the broke-ass funk and to celebrate the new job. It took some careful knee driving to get the iPod into the cassette deck adaptor and the adaptor into Beetle's ancient audio system, but it was worth it. I sang along to Snoop's masterplan, feeling equally righteous about my own earning prospects.

Beetle tried to ruin the mood by introducing a new sound into the usual cacophony of misfiring pistons, but I just turned the music up. Unfortunately, the smooth beats could not mask the screech of metal dragging along the pavement, or the shower of sparks trailing behind me. I pulled over, wrestled the offending automotive part from under the body and examined it in the dying light. I could not discern if it was essential or not, but the motor kept running when I separated it from the mothership, and there was no sign of leaking oil, or at least no more than usual. Just in case, I tossed the part into the trunk and drove off, thinking that the new job could not have come a moment too soon.

When I finally got to the place, Harden The Funk Up was in full swing. I could hear "Block Rockin' Beats" rocking the house all the way from the parking lot. When I stepped inside, however, the house was far from rocking. It was a sad little venue, which belonged to someone called Billy, as proclaimed by the neon sign over the door. Inside it was dark and hot, with just a few dejected patrons on cheap aluminum stools around the bar. Behind the bar, a middle-aged bartender moved about leisurely. Old street signs and other miscellaneous dusty crap were hanging from the ceiling. It was ugly, but not *Coyote Ugly*.

In the corner opposite the bar was Harden with all his equipment, looking cool in a pair of professional cans and a giant neon safety vest. He'd been getting ready for this for a while, and most of his money went into purchasing turntables, speakers, and flashing lights. Unlike me, Harden had a well-paying job hacking into corporate computer systems. Not to steal, or anything, just to test the firewalls and virus protection, but it paid a ton.

I waved my hands in front of Harden, trying to get his attention. He broke into a huge grin and pulled one of the cans away from his ear.

"Thanks for coming!" he yelled over the music.

"Wouldn't miss it! What's with the vest?"

"Cool, huh? Got it from my dad." Harden got a lot of things from his dad, including his fat genes. The two of them haven't been able to hug properly since Harden was a little kid.

I was about to ask why he chose the vest for his debutant appearance when the bartender came up. He was a mousy little man, but he looked massively pissed off.

"What's this noise?" he screamed over the music. The noise at that moment was something from The Bloody Beetroots.

Harden looked worried, so I decided to do a bit of PR.

"It's great, isn't it?" I yelled. "Nice little place you got here!"

"Who are you?" the bartender yelled in my face.

I decided not to let his rudeness get to me. "Just a fan," I yelled back enthusiastically. "Out on the town, ready to bust some moves." I busted a move to demonstrate my point.

The bartender looked me up and down, then shoved me aside and screamed at Harden, "Turn that shit down!"

"Hey!" I yelled at his back. "That's no way to treat your clientele! Ever heard that the customer is king?"

The bartender turned his ugly little face to me. "No!" he spat. "Never heard this here shit, either! Turn it down and put on somethin' decent or you're outta here!"

Harden obligingly turned the music down. Everyone in the place was looking at us.

"What's decent, oldies but goldies?" I asked.

"You got a mouth on you, little girl," the bartender stuck a creased finger with a thick stained nail into my face. "Better watch it, if you know what's good for you!"

Since I was several inches taller than him, it should've been funny. Instead, I felt the angry beast inside me rise and shake its chain.

"You know what's good for you?" I asked.

Then, before I knew what my own hands were doing, the angry beast took the bartender by the bony shoulders, turned him around and shoved him towards the bar. "Doing your job!"

I completely miscalculated the effect my angry push would have on the feather-light maître d'. He surged forward, stumbled, and toppled down to shocked gasps from everyone, including me.

*

"I'm so sorry," I said for the thousandth time, helping Harden load his stuff into his mom's van. "I have no idea what came over me! I had no idea that was Billy himself!"

"That's okay," Harden said, although he looked close to tears.

"Plus," I said, madly grasping at straws, "it's not like that was your target market."

"No," Harden sighed. "It's just so hard to break into the field. I was hoping to get a referral or something. Plus, you never know, somebody from the industry could be in the audience."

I seriously doubted anyone from "the industry" was among Billy's redneck patrons, but my heart sank. Harden and I shared the same dream and I had just cut him at the knees.

Then I remembered my own news. "You know what? I just got a job with Shizzle, Inc and betcha I can get you a corporate gig! How would a corporate gig sound?"

"Shizzle, Inc?" Harden's face lit up. "They do the most incredible staff parties! That's like, legendary, Izz!"

"Aight, consider it done," I said, even though I had no idea how it was going to get done. Sometimes you just have to believe the unbelievable, the point most recently proven by my new and amazing job.

I hugged him goodbye. "Do you want to..." Harden suddenly looked tense, "...you know, maybe celebrate? I can get wine coolers, or whatever you want. If you want to?" Harden just turned twenty-one, which was yet another reason why he was so cool.

"Oh my God! Sorry Harden, where are my manners? Of course we should celebrate, that was your first gig!"

"Kinda," he said and looked down. "Anyway, I'm glad you came.

You've been MIA too long, Izz."

I hugged him again, and he held me longer that time. I breathed in his aftershave and thanked God that there was at least one guy who wouldn't dump me to serve his ambitions.

I drove home, and Harden rocked up five minutes later with a load of beer and wine coolers in every flavor. He also brought in his equipment and set it up in the living room, starting the party off with Far East Movement.

"What's going on?" Tara emerged from the basement to see what all the ruckus was about.

"Getting slizzered!" I sang along with the band and handed Tara a beer.

We drank, danced, smoked weed and yelled along to the words of the songs that had words - we just yelled "Woo!" to those that didn't. I danced on the coffee table and jumped up and down on the couch until my legs gave out. I remember Harden forcing me to drink water and take aspirin, then covering me with a comforter when I face-planted on the couch. After that, I don't remember anything.

I'm a derby driver.

I was late on my first day at Shizzle, Inc. I overslept, I was hungover, and I could not find anything to wear. Literally. We got robbed overnight, the side effect of living in a lawless neighborhood and being drunk and stoned into a coma. The thieves took almost everything, including our clothes, dishes, and Margaret Thatcher. Thankfully, they didn't notice my bag in the hallway, where it was hidden by a pile of trash. Tara was mad as hell and kept muttering something about boobies and traps into her cornflakes, which she had to eat out of the box.

By the time I finished making something resembling a dress out of a tablecloth and Tara's supply of rope and duct tape, it was nearly ten in the morning. I found a pair of black shoes even the thieves did not want, painted the scuff marks with a marker, then jumped into the car and tore off down the street. I was secretly hoping that Hot Cop would stop me for speeding, but alas, no. He was probably sleeping off his own hangover.

I practically flew into the parking lot of Shizzle, Inc, hitting the brakes while turning the wheel hard to the left. Beetle objected with every rusty joint, but spun neatly into a tight space between two exec-looking Benzies, only slightly scratching one of them. I scrambled out, bumped the edge of my door into the other Benz, slammed the door shut in righteous anger, spun around and nearly knocked over Mr. Hue.

He was just standing there, looking even more glorious than before. This time, for no apparent reason, he was wearing a white captain's uniform with gold buttons. Another massive cigar was sticking out of his mouth, like a smoking tailpipe. Two tall, handsome, and super-fit bodyguards in black suits flanked him. They looked like identical twins, except one was even better looking than the other. I froze in my tracks and tried to smooth down my skirt, ashamed of being late and of the thought that, given a chance, I would totally do either one of the bodyguards.

"Hi?" I finally managed. I wanted to say something about "horrible, horrible gastro", but I just couldn't do it in front of the two hotties.

Mr. Hue didn't say anything, just kept looking at me with those piercing, all-knowing blue eyes. He puffed on the cigar, then took it out of his mouth and held it out with two fingers. A massive diamond sparkled on his outstretched pinkie. He let the cigar drop, then slowly ground it into the pavement with the toe of his sleek white patent shoe. I squirmed.

"Ms. Maxwell, isn't it?" he squinted at me. You'd think a billionaire could afford a pair of sunglasses. He would look good in a pair of aviators, come to think of it.

I nodded and swallowed hard. Here we go, I thought, fired before I even make it in on the first day.

"Nice to see you upright." His voice was authoritatively stern. He looked me up and down. "Gucci?"

I looked down in confusion. He had to be talking about my dress. "Ah, no...it's an up-and-coming boutique designer. Very exclusive." I cocked a hip and jammed a hand into my side the way starlets do on the red carpet.

"Oh." He seemed a tiny bit impressed. "I could not help noticing your driving skills this morning. Is that your car?" He lifted his chin in the direction of Beetle.

I looked back at my dinged-up yellow piece of crap. "Oh, that...Nah, that's just a derby car I was driving last night. In a derby. I'm a derby driver." I'm not a bad liar on an average day, but that morning I was on fire, fueled by fear and adrenaline. "Yeah, it don't look like much, but this baby packs a mean punch. Got twenty-five...hundred...horses under the hood. Nitrous...something. You know, the works."

As if in protest, Beetle's tailpipe coughed up a pathetic wisp of gray smoke.

Mr. Hue smirked. "I got a Bugatti Veyron in my garage, bet that would leave you in my dust."

I tried to casually put my hands in my pockets, but there weren't any, so I anchored my hands on my hips and looked him square in the eye.

"Are you sure?" I asked. "I wouldn't bet on it. This one here is modified to bejesus, and it ain't even street legal." I spat on the ground for further effect.

Mr. Hue considered that for a moment. "Walk with me," he said and took off across the parking lot in the general direction of the drainage ditch. The bodyguards and I tried to keep up.

"You didn't answer my question yesterday," Mr. Hue said. "Why do you want to work for Shizzle, Inc?"

I almost blurted out "To get on TV!" but stopped myself just in time. I had a feeling that, despite taking place in the parking lot, the discussion was somehow significant to my budding career. I tried to buy some time by pretending to catch my breath, which was not such a stretch.

"I want to make a difference," I said finally.

Mr. Hue slowed down. "A *real* difference?"

"Yes," I said, sensing that I was on the right track. "A *very real* difference."

Mr. Hue stopped. "I knew it!" he exclaimed. "You're the Shizzle type!"

I practically radiated relief.

"You never know where you might spot a Shizzle type," Mr. Hue went on. "I usually find them in exclusive bars, luxury resorts or private golf clubs, but every now and then one just walks in, like you did. You probably don't even know you're special, but you are."

I wanted to say that I'd always felt like I was special and just waiting to be discovered, and that maybe one day there would be a movie made about my life - but he pushed on.

"Are you an ideas kind of person?"

"Yes," I said, trying to sound persuasive. "I have lots of ideas."

"That's great," he said. "Can you tell me about one of them?"

I panicked. I did have lots of ideas, all the time, but lately most of them were about how to get Brad back. While they were all really innovative, I had a feeling that Mr. Hue was talking about the kind of ideas that result in profits, and not in marriages and babies.

"Well," I said, "there are so many, it's hard to pick one!"

"Okay," Mr. Hue said, "pick the most profitable one."

Damn it, I knew he'd say that. I was about to tell him how I was planning to score a large diamond ring, but then I remembered a story my Dad told us countless times.

"I once had this idea for Velcro, but I didn't have money for a patent, and then Velcro invented it."

"Wow," Mr. Hue said. "You are full of surprises, Ms. Maxwell, and it's very hard to surprise me." He fell silent, and I held my breath. Suddenly he grabbed me by the shoulders and looked deeply into my eyes.

"I was going to start you at the bottom, working your way up through the janitorial positions and such, but you have already proven yourself beyond my wildest expectations. I shall take you under my wing."

*

Mr. Hue made a sharp u-turn and headed back to headquarters. "As my protégé, it's imperative that you see all branches of the business. We'll start by visiting the factory."

It was all happening too fast. Once again, I struggled to keep up. "What, like, now?" God, being around him was exhausting. I had no clue that working was so strenuous.

We walked through the lobby, were greeted by security guys standing at attention, and got into the elevator. A young guy with a takeout coffee, who was already in the elevator, jumped out as if it was on fire. The twin bodyguards followed us in, and one of them pressed the button for the top level. "Is the factory in this building?" I asked, confused.

Mr. Hue just smiled enigmatically, and we rode up in silence. When the doors finally opened, we were on the roof, and I was staring straight at an Apache helicopter. *Holy shit.* It looked brand new and was equipped with all the standard missiles and rocket pods, plus what looked like a custom after-sale job.

"Hellfire?" I nodded towards the extra pod, incredulous.

"Yes." He choked with emotion. "Fitted with a thermobaric warhead. You have to be prepared for anything these days."

There was no pilot, and I expected one of the bodyguards to get behind the controls, but Mr. Hue dismissed both of them with a curt nod. Once I climbed into the passenger seat, I saw that there was no space for them anyway - the entire cargo area was replaced by the kind of speakers you would expect at a Skrillex concert.

Mr. Hue climbed in and started to flip switches. The instrument panel lit up, the rotor blades came to life, and a blast of "Rock the Casbah" from the back deafened me. Mr. Hue put on his harness and headphones, and I hastily did the same. Even with the headphones on, the roar was unbearable. I turned to close the door, but there wasn't one. I pulled harder at the straps of my harness.

"Ready?" Mr. Hue winked at me, then reached into a compartment and pulled out a book. *Choppers for Dummies.* On the cover, it had a cute cartoon of a cross-eyed stick man waving from a helicopter cockpit.

"Are you sure you know what you're doing?" I screamed over the noise. He waved me off authoritatively, and I heard his voice in my headphones, "Worry not, Ms. Maxwell, I am a qualified pilot." He rustled through the book. "I just need to do a pre-flight check."

I thought back to my law degree and tried to remember if the website had any templates for pilot's licenses.

"Tower. This is Big Bad D-O-G, S-H-I-double Z-L-E, you know me, fo shizzle my dizzle. Clear for takeoff. Confirm, over."

"Big Bad Dog, you are clear." A tired voice crackled through the static. "And may I remind you to use the standard language only?"

"Roger, tower. Big Bad D-O-G is set, over and out. And it ain't nothin' but a chicken wang!" He winked at me and the chopper suddenly lunged forward.

For a moment, it looked like we were going to take out the bodyguards, but they ducked down in a practiced fashion. We headed for the elevator shaft, but at the last moment the chopper shot straight up, twisting like a corkscrew. I screamed as the speakers concurred that "the sharif don't like it". No, not one little bit.

I managed to catch a glimpse of Mr. Hue, who was erratically poking at the control panel buttons and jerking levers. He had his tongue out and looked like a kid trying to fit a square peg through a round hole. I screamed again as we lurched to the left in a wide arc, but couldn't help noticing the view before me. It was magnificent, an endless sea of parking lots filled with cars of all colors. My leg dangled out, and I clutched at the harness with white-knuckled fingers.

Suddenly we were going down in roller coaster fashion, and I squeezed my eyes shut. My life flashed before me, or at least the good bits, and then we half-crashed, half-landed on something. The rotors slowed down, and I risked opening my eyes. We were not dead, just on the roof of another building. I unbuckled my harness with trembling fingers and staggered out. I could see the Shizzle, Inc headquarters a few hundred feet away.

I turned to Mr. Hue, who was lighting another cigar. "We could have walked here," I said in a shaky voice.

"Nonsense, my dear child," he laughed huskily. "This ride was tax deductible, and walking isn't." With that, he turned towards the exit, where another pair of genetically engineered bodyguards awaited us.

*

Once inside the factory, Mr. Hue ordered all workers to assemble for his address. The foreman tried to protest, citing something about O, H, and S, but Mr. Hue ignored him. He climbed into a cherry picker bucket and motioned to be lifted up until he almost hit the roof.

Eventually, a large crowd of disgruntled employees assembled before us. They were covered in soot, and many were missing digits and limbs. All of them were staring at us with open contempt. I backed away until I wedged myself in-between the two bodyguards.

"Check...check..." I heard Mr. Hue's voice, booming at us from the overhead speakers. "Hello, Detroit! Put your hands up!"

The crowd grunted unhappily. Someone at the back woo-hooed and shot up a hand, but was promptly smacked down.

Mr. Hue didn't seem to notice. "Colleagues. Employees. Temporary staff and illegal aliens. Today I would like to talk to you about the recent events at this factory." He paused dramatically. "As you know, the *New York Times* accused Shizzle, Inc of serious shortcomings in work safety." His voice was grave.

"Yet I see a whole army of supporters here in defiance of such accusations." The crowd murmured. "You have come to work at Shizzle, Inc out of your free will. Well, maybe not you, Gimp." He pointed at a man in the front row, who was wearing shackles and a collar. The man nodded. "But the rest of you deserve a workplace free of safety hazards. And I want to personally assure you that if such safety hazards were discovered, they would be immediately addressed, eventually."

"You said this last time," shouted an old man at the front. "And we still don't have the grinder guard!"

"If you need this guard so much, why don't you go work at Circuit City?" Mr. Hue replied.

Several people took off their aprons and walked away.

Mr. Hue continued with increasing fervor, "Run and you may live another day. And dying in a retirement house years from now, what would you give for another chance at a job with Shizzle, Inc?"

A few more people walked off, some of them children.

"So what if you work longer hours at a lower pay? That's what gives our customers cheap products they want. We may not give you job security or benefits, but we give you an opportunity to really immerse yourself in your work. Sure, some may say that the only reason you are here is because you got no education, skills, or in some cases, rights," he pointed again at Gimp, who uttered a long resigned sigh, "but I don't believe it. I know that because I've tried working alongside you at this facility, and I couldn't handle it for more than a couple of hours. I honestly believe you are here because you love your work. So go back to your workstations and feel good about what you do! Also, don't forget to join the new Shizzle Health Club while the membership is offered at the introductory $99 per month. It won't stay that way for very long!"

The remaining crowd dispersed as Mr. Hue was lowered in a theatrical fashion. I looked on, stupefied, while the bodyguards helped him get out of the safety harness. The foreman was back, complaining again, this time about plans and quotas. Mr. Hue told him to deal with it and turned to me.

"What do you think!" he said without a question.

"They all quit!" I blurted and immediately regretted it.

"Not all," Mr. Hue corrected me, brushing off invisible lint from his perfectly smooth suit. "Only the ones lacking in Shizzle spirit!"

"What?"

"The Shizzle spirit! It's a special quality that only Shizzle types have. You and I have plenty of it, while *those types,*" he waved his hand at one of the workers, "don't care about the company. They are only here for a paycheck." He headed towards the elevators.

"Isn't that why most people go to work?" I asked, following him. "For a paycheck?"

"Not me!" He said haughtily and turned to face me. "Are *you* here for a paycheck, Ms. Maxwell?" He squinted and studied me like a specimen.

"No, no!" I said hurriedly. "I am here to, you know, learn!" My heart was pounding. I was perilously close to losing that paycheck and any hope of ever getting discovered by one of Mr. Hue's celebrity friends.

"Didn't think so," he said, turning away. "I have a very good feeling about you, Ms. Maxwell."

I nodded and tried to steady my breathing. A dreadful feeling came over me, like picking up a Christmas present only to discover that it's soft and squishy, like Grandma's sweater or a bunch of socks.

*

By the time we finally made it back to the grand lobby of his office, Mr. Hue had his arm around my shoulders and was in the middle of telling me about his plans for the Middle East. Medusa and the impeccably groomed secretaries looked at us in astonishment.

"Eleanor." Mr. Hue beckoned Medusa. She approached with caution, probably expecting me to knock something over or set off the fire alarm.

"Yes, Mr. Hue?" she said in her fancy accent. She was definitely either British or French. Either that or she was from one of those new Eastern European countries with weird names.

"Please take Ms. Maxwell to HR for induction and call Mr. Warburn into my office. Oh, and have Mr. Warburn clean his desk - Ms. Maxwell will be taking over his position."

Somebody was getting fired because of me! I felt an unfamiliar sense of accomplishment and pride, mixed with a tinge of guilt. I told myself that Mr. Warburn was probably a young know-it-all prick.

Eleanor did not flinch. "Please follow me, Ms. Maxwell."

I looked back at Mr. Hue, but he'd already disappeared into his office. I made a mental note to express my gratitude later and followed Eleanor. We turned the corner, and I was about to try breaking the ice, when she spun around, her face contorted with either rage or a facial tick.

"Look," she said poking me in the chest with one perfectly sculpted and polished fingernail. "I don't know what you did to get promoted so quickly." She gave me a look that indicated that she had a damn good idea, yes she did. I didn't know what to say. "Mr. Warburn has been with this company for twenty years," she continued. "He gave up on his wife and family to be where you are now."

The young know-it-all prick in my head morphed into a sad little man with glasses and a bald spot. He was probably alone in his tiny and dirty bachelor kitchen somewhere, maybe even contemplating suicide. It was a horrible picture.

"That's what we call dedication to your work. Do you think you're going to last? There are hundreds of young Harvard lawyers out there ready to kill you for this job." She motioned down the hall, and I spun my head in horror, but thankfully, there were no lawyers there.

She returned her finger to my chest. "My job is already hard enough without having to babysit you," she continued, "so let's get this straight. Don't encroach on my territory and I will not have to accidentally push you down the stairs. My job is to answer his phone, organize his appointments, and remember his passwords. You will be getting his coffee, scrapbooking articles about his accomplishments, and making sure he *always* has enough markers. And most importantly, I will be the one to accompany him to the Gala next Wednesday.

Got it?"

With that, she turned her back to me and continued briskly down the hallway. I followed and flipped her judgmental back the bird. It made me feel a little better.

In the HR office, Eleanor introduced me to Manuel.

"Hello darling!" he squealed and kissed me on both cheeks, then held me at arm's length, admiring my dress. "I just love your style! Gucci?"

If the Shizzle thing doesn't pan out, I thought, I would have to try and get on Project Runway.

He did not wait for my response, instead throwing open the doors of a stationery cabinet next to his desk. "Let's get you set up with the basics."

With that, he pulled out a bunch of sticky pads, magic markers, a phone, and finally a Colt M1911. I wrinkled my nose at the gun. "A bit old-school, isn't it?"

"As old-school as stars and stripes!" Manuel looked offended. "Like you have something better?"

I pulled out my Sig Sauer P250 and held it up to him. Manuel's face lit up. I may not have that much money, but I take safety seriously. You have to, in this world we live in.

"Yeah, but you can't compare it to the Colt," he was smirking again. "It's just not as accurate."

There was only one way to settle this. "Where's your range?" I asked.

"Downstairs, in the rec room."

Nice! "Okay then, let's compare notes," I said defiantly.

"I'll take you up on that one day!" He beamed and handed the Colt over to me.

"Can I use it for personal protection?" I asked, trying to fit both guns into my bag.

"Yes, of course, we appreciate that carrying two guns may be inconvenient. Just don't go overboard." He handed me an extra magazine and a box of bullets. "Welcome to Shizzle, Inc!"

Next, I had to sign a contract, which, as much as I can recall, went something like this:

1. You shall have no other jobs besides this one. You shall not look for another job anywhere on the internet, or in Sunday papers, or in shop windows.

2. You shall not apply or even think about applying for other jobs; for Shizzle, Inc is your employer, and it is a jealous employer, punishing the children of ex-employees to the third and fourth generation of those who steal its client base, but showing love to those who grow its profit margin.

3. You shall not misuse the logo of Shizzle, Inc, for it is copyrighted and Shizzle, Inc retains really good lawyers who will sue the shit out of you.

4. Six days you shall labour and do all your work, but the seventh day is for rest at Shizzle, Inc, unless your manager requests you to come in anyway, whereupon you shall do so without excessive whining. For if six days are not sufficient to meet the quota, then all servants of Shizzle, Inc shall labor on until it is met.

5. Honor thy manager, so that you may be promoted within the pay band Shizzle, Inc has assigned to you.

6. You shall not:
    a. murder your manager under any circumstances;
    b. commit adultery with a co-worker, unless it's after hours, and you both had too much to drink;
    c. steal stationery;
    d. give false testimony against Shizzle, Inc. Refer to Clause 3 about the lawyers and the suing the shit out;
    e. covet your co-worker's cubicle;
    f. covet your co-worker's stuff, including but not limited to staplers, markers, chairs, company car, and novelty coffee mugs.

It was really long, so I didn't read much more after that, just kept signing until my wrist throbbed. There were lots of clauses, including intellectual and semi-intellectual property rights. There was also one that simply said, "We own you."

I spent the rest of the day at HR, filling out forms and question-naires, setting up my 401K and signing endless liability waivers. The only thing that kept me going was the promise of a paycheck at the end of the month and the mirage of TV-flavored fame. I certainly hoped it was worth the freedom I was about to give up.

*

Just before the end of the day, I managed to find a few minutes to thank Mr. Hue for the job offer and to check if he needed any coffee. He didn't want anything but asked how I was getting settled into my new role. He seemed in a great mood, like he was high on something.

"I feel bad about Mr. Warburn losing his job," I said.

"No need to feel bad," Mr. Hue said. "Over the years I've had to let go of many dedicated employees and even close friends. It's all in how you do it. I'm sure Tony and I will remain friends and will probably laugh about it in a few years, when we vacation together."

"Oh," I said. It made me feel a whole lot better. "Do you often go on vacations with your employees?"

"All the time," he said. "I also party hard with them at my man-sion. It's a major bonus of working for Shizzle, Inc. Of course, I could give them cash bonuses instead, but I'm sure they would agree that it's a lot more fun to use that money for spectacular parties. Plus, the tax deduction is good news for my accountant!"

"Wow," I said. "Can I come too?" The corporate life sounded like fun, not at all like the gray drudgery I imagined.

"Of course! Last year's Christmas Booze Up got us a noise abate-ment notice, and this year it will be even better! I am, after all, a connoisseur of parties, even more so than I am an expert on books."

"You are?"

"Yes. I not only thumb through them, I also write them," he said proudly.

I was genuinely impressed. Writing a book is a lot more classy than making a lot of money in business, unless of course you made a lot of money by writing books, and that's just, like, wow.

"What do you write about?" I asked.

"My life. A lot can be learned by studying my life experiences," said Mr. Hue. "My books chronicle how awesome I am and how much I help various causes. I'm currently writing the third one, entitled *The Secret to Becoming a Billionaire 3*. It's a guaranteed bestseller. My first two books *The Secret to Becoming a Billionaire* and *The Secret to Becoming a Billionaire 2* sold like hotcakes."

"So, what's the secret?" I asked, with a pen ready over my notepad. "Or is it secrets?"

"There really isn't a secret per se," Mr. Hue said, "but it makes for a better title and bigger sales. I do give some tips though, for example how to discourage a competitor or deal with business challenges, like union regulations or demands for fair pay. The modern business environment is a nightmare! In my books, I advise entrepreneurs to do business in countries free of workers' rights, although those countries are harder and harder to come by. The three books basically tell the same stories in different ways, but that's the key to market penetration! If the average Joe hears enough times that my company and I are the answer to saving the world, he'll eventually believe it."

"Oh," I said, disappointed that there wasn't a quick fix to my financial woes.

Mr. Hue was on a roll. He put one foot on a chair and leaned his elbow on the knee, looking vaguely like a well-dressed Captain Morgan. "Success in business comes down to hard work, a bit of luck, family and friends willing to lend you money, and being in the right place at the right time. It's no use being in the right place at the wrong time, or being in the wrong place at the right time. Wait, I have to record this!"

He pulled out a small recorder and narrated a rambling passage about the importance of the right place and time for everything, complete with an anecdote about climbing into the office window of the Minister for Foreign Affairs, thinking it was the Minister's daughter's bedroom.

Just as he was getting to the really kinky stuff, Eleanor appeared. "Mr. Hue, *she* is here to see you."

Mr. Hue seemed irritated. "What does she want?"

"She didn't say," Eleanor tilted her head politely.

"Never mind, I know it's money," Mr. Hue gave me an annoyed look. "That's the trouble with celebrities, for every million they make, they spend two. Tell her to wait."

Eleanor nodded and left.

"We'll have to continue this conversation some other time," Mr. Hue said. "I feel that we've made a lot of progress today."

I agreed. It all seemed to be going really well, even if I wasn't sure where.

*

On the way home I picked up my graduation cap and gown, then stopped by the mall to buy a couple of real outfits for work. I also got some dinner, effectively maxing out all my credit cards, but I wasn't worried. All I had to do was survive for a week on the kindness of my family and friends, then pay them back when I got my first fat paycheck. I stabbed a plastic spork into the sweet and sour chicken, looked at my phone and saw at least a dozen missed calls from Harden. I hit redial.

"Sorry, man," I said. "I had such a crazy day!"

"Are you okay?" Harden asked. "You seemed pretty out of it last night."

"Yeah, I was late for my first day of work this morning."

"Sorry!"

"Nah, it worked out great," I said through a mouthful. "I'm now Mr. Hue's protégé!"

"Wow, congratulations! What does that mean?"

"I don't know, actually, I haven't had to do any work yet. He just talks to me a lot. You should see their rec room! And I got a new gun!"

"Why do you need another one?" Harden was such a pacifist.

"Cause I need it! I have to protect myself, you know? I can get raped at any moment. You just don't understand."

"No, I don't," he agreed. "Nobody would ever want to rape me."

God, I was sick of him sulking about being single. I'd tried setting him up on dates and dragging him out to raves, but he barely talked to girls. It was pathetic.

"C'mon," I tried the old pep talk, "you need to give it a chance. I'm sure plenty of girls would jump your bones if you just talked to them."

"Maybe when I'm famous like Armin van Buuren," Harden said. "Unless you want to beat them to it?"

I laughed and suddenly saw a pair of aviators lurking over a newspaper a couple of tables away. They disappeared behind the paper, but not before I recognized the Grecian nose supporting them.

"Gotta go," I said into the phone, but when I looked up, the aviators and the paper were gone.

You've got nothing to worry about, unless, of course, you're an orphan.

I couldn't sleep the night before graduation, standing guard over my gown and cap. Thankfully, the neighborhood gangstas left us alone, probably because we had nothing worthwhile left to steal.

Finally, a bit of luck today, I wrote in my journal, after months of downward spiraling into the abyss of despair. God or Random Chance, or whatever else rules the Universe, truly works in mysterious ways. It takes away the love of my life and lands me on my butt in a puddle, before offering the sweet apple of opportunity. I can only hope that the apple is not poisoned.

I must have dozed off right before the sunrise, because I was shopping in JC Penny's with a shiny new credit card when loud knocks on the door woke me up. It could only be my parents, and they were, of course, several hours too early. Dad is always early, especially for any kind of event or public transport. Whenever I'd tried to convince him that a plane departing early, or even on time, would have to make the seven o'clock news, he would always reply, "And how stupid would you look then, on the seven o'clock news?"

I opened the door, and Dad barged in with bags, without so much as a kiss on the cheek. "Hi Mom," I said to my mother, who followed behind with more bags. "What's all this?"

My mother was stressed to the max, as usual. "Oh, sweetie, you know how much we worry about you. These are just a few things to hold you over." That, of course, meant that one of the bags was full of meds, and the other three of stuff they should have taken to the Salvation Army.

She scurried into the living room, where Dad was flipping

through the TV channels to find the CBS morning news. Luckily, the thieves gave up on dragging away our enormous, ancient TV set. They succeeded only in moving it a couple of feet, where it now sat, next to the square of slightly less dirty carpet. Without the news for more than a couple of hours, Dad would probably get withdrawal shakes.

"Why are you not dressed?" Dad said in his usual field marshal tone.

"Because it's seven am on a Saturday morning, and the ceremony is not until the afternoon!" I cracked my knuckles. It was on, like the seething Obamacare commentary on CBS.

"Do you really want to be late for your graduation?" Dad barked. "It's going to be years before you get a chance to go to a real university."

I had absolutely no intention of ever studying again, but, of course, it pissed me off. "How do you know that? Maybe I already got accepted to Harvard law!"

"Oh, sweetie, you are delusional!" Mom chimed in. "I have just the pill for that!" She tugged one of the bags open, and an avalanche of prescription bottles spilled out. Mom's faith in meds was so strong that the placebo effect alone would have her waking up in *The Matrix* if that's what the blue pill label claimed.

"It's Dad who needs pills!" I said and kicked some of the bottles towards him.

"I've never taken steroids!" Dad was furious. "I would have made it to the Olympics if I did!" He never made it past the wrestling team in high school.

"Who said anything about steroids? Methinks the lady doth protest too much!" I yelled, inwardly proud that my education was good for something.

Mom popped a pill into her mouth. "Dad's just worried about you sweetie. We all are."

"Yes, frankly we're amazed that you've managed to graduate from college without an illegitimate child." Dad's voice quivered. "We are so proud of you."

"Are you pregnant?" Mom asked.

"I'm *not* pregnant! Can't you just be happy for me for once?"

"We *are* happy for you," Dad was visibly confused. "I just said that, didn't I?" He turned to Mom for confirmation.

"Whatever!" I flipped Dad the bird in the pocket of my bathrobe. The old trick helped me calm down enough to remember. "And by the way, I just got a job with Shizzle, Inc! And not a janitorial position, either!"

Mom and Dad were speechless for a second. "You mean Sizzle, the BBQ place, right?" Dad asked.

"No, I mean Shizzle, Inc, the global conglomerate of value creation processes!" I was elated. Advantage Isa, old man.

Mom looked back and forth between us, waiting to back the victor.

"Isa," Dad sounded sad. "Your mother is right. You *are* delusional. There's no way you could land a job with Shizzle, Inc straight out of college." Mom's face lit up, and she went on rummaging through the bags. "I, on the other hand, almost landed a job there once," Dad said. "It's too bad that the interview panel took it personally when I pointed out what a poor job they were doing."

"Why would you be interviewing at Shizzle, Inc?" I asked. "You're a history teacher. Shizzle, Inc is not interested in history."

"I'm a *historian*! And *everyone* should be interested in history!" Dad yelled. The news blared on in the background, as Dad got onto his favorite high horse. "If people paid more attention to history, humanity would not repeat the same mistakes over and over again. Just imagine if that idiot Greenspan consulted with a historian, for example myself, on the dangers of excessively low credit rates. 'Why, Mr. Greenspan,' I would have said to him, 'it is very wise of you to consult with an accomplished historian on this topic. Let me explain how your idea of lowering credit rates is going to ruin this country...'"

"I'm Mr. Hue's protégé!" I yelled, in hopes of putting an end to his monolog. To my surprise, it worked.

"Really?" Dad asked, awestruck and not even trying to hide it. "Isn't he a billionaire?"

"He sure is!" I said.

"Does he have a historian on staff? He probably doesn't. Aren't you glad now you've studied history and not medicine or some other garbage?"

Mom forgot her pills for a moment.

"Isn't he single?" she asked. "You could marry him! That would be even better than marrying a doctor."

"I don't want to marry him, or a doctor!" I was getting to the end of my rope, and fast. "You didn't marry a doctor, so why do you constantly tell me that I have to?" My sister married a common male nurse, and for the last few years the pressure was on me not to make the same mistake.

"Your mother married a *historian!*" Dad bellowed. "If not for the foolishness of the general population, historians would be the most respected and well-paid professionals, not those human body mechanics who spend their days up to the elbow in blood and guts!"

Mom put her hands up to him in a pacifying gesture and cooed something about how he's a misunderstood genius, but Dad was too riled up. He puffed out his chest and continued to rant about doctors and their biological warfare against society. For as long as I could remember, Dad has not been to a doctor because, according to him, doctors are to blame for people getting sick in the first place.

I tried to interrupt him while thinking about how different my life might have been if Mom *had* married a doctor. Mom used to be a nurse but quit her job when my older sister Felicity was born. Officially, it was because she wanted to devote herself to the children, but I suspect it had something to do with Dad's relentless jealousy. She never went back to work, and while it was nice to come home to a house smelling of freshly baked bread, it put a strain on the family's finances. Our house was ugly, the family car was an ancient station wagon, and I was always wearing my sister's hand-me-downs. I was ashamed to ask other kids to come over to my room furnished with Salvation Army bargains and, as a result didn't have that many friends, except for Tara and Harden.

Despite our best efforts, Dad refused to stop his methodical condemnation of the health sciences. I was about to pull out my new Colt and start firing warning shots when the front door blew open. It was Felicity and her entourage. That was a shocker because she was usually late to everything.

"Sorry, I missed your graduation!" Felicity said, examining a wet stain on the front of her tight black jeans. "Back to diapers for you, little fucker!" she said to one of her twin five-year-olds, Tommy or Jimmy, I wasn't sure which. Neither one of them responded, as they were already busy kicking shit around the room.

"Hello, darling!" Mom screamed, as one of the boys kicked her in the shin. Dad fizzled, now that everyone's attention was turned to the newcomers. Felicity's husband Mark sat down on the couch and stared off into space as the twins continued their rampage.

"You're not late, the graduation isn't until the afternoon," I said to Felicity and kissed her on a cheek. She smelled like baby food and pee.

"Wasn't it yesterday?" She was clearly disappointed.

"Isa is going to work with Mr. Hue!" Mom said brightly.

"No way!" Felicity said. "Doing what?"

"I don't know," I said. "So far not much. I think I'm supposed to make his coffee."

"Get into the sales department," Felicity said. "Work like hell, save your money and retire early."

My sister worshipped the sales idol, probably because it gave her the kind of life I always wanted. Her childhood wasn't much better than mine, which is probably why she skipped college. She got a job instead, as a secretary at the local Toyota dealership, and then worked her way up to a sales position. She was a natural at sales, finding just the right way to talk to her customers. It also didn't hurt that, like me, she inherited our mother's legendary boobs.

"I don't know if I want to work like hell," I said. "I've only worked one day so far, and I'm exhausted."

"You have to work hard!" Dad jumped in. "If you try to make money the easy way, you'll end up in jail, just like your mother's ancestors!" He was obviously still hurting from Mom's doctor comment.

"Not *ancestors*!" Mom said. "Just great-uncle Charles!"

"Like you don't have any skeletons in your family closet," Felicity said to Dad. "What about the one who sold moonshine during Prohibition?"

41

"He was ahead of his time!" Dad said. "He was a genius, and he made a fortune, too. It's just too bad that his *wife* was a genius at wasting his money!"

"What are you saying? Are you saying Mom wasted your money?" Felicity snapped. Mom looked confused and hurt. She never fought with Dad, but she also didn't stop us from fighting on her behalf.

"No," Dad said. "I'm just trying to say that *my* ancestors were proud and honest people."

"Please!" I rolled my eyes. "Judging by your temper, they just as well could have been thugs, pillaging villages of other people's proud and hardworking ancestors!"

"At least they were not some witch-doctor shamans claiming to cure ills with magic potions!" Dad was back on his broken record. "They didn't try to bring about the rain season by getting high, having sex with virgins, and then demanding payment for their services!"

"What are you talking about, honey?" Mom asked.

Felicity was the first to give up. "I need a shot," she said and went into the kitchen.

"Oh, no, sweetie, you can't drink! You could be pregnant!" Mom dashed in after her. I heard the roar of a lion and a door slam. It was good to have sis backing me up.

"You have to have sex to be pregnant." Mark's voice startled us. He was a pathetic, lanky man, which sort of explained why we completely forgot he was even there.

Dad and I scoffed at Mark. It felt good to find something in common with Dad.

*

It took the rest of the morning to figure out who was wearing what, which car we were going to take, and where Jimmy was hiding. By the time we were ready to go, my sister was staggering drunk, Mom was in prescription la-la-land, and Dad nearly talked Mark into a suicide. I had to drive my sister's enormous Land Cruiser with everyone piled up in the back and the twins happily bouncing from lap to lap.

I parked, killed the engine and turned to the back.

"Okay, listen up. For some reason, this feels important to me. So you better behave and not make a scene." Mom mumbled something and offered me a handful of pills.

I ignored her, got out and ran for the gym-turned-celebration hall, where flags and streamers did little to hide drab walls and peeling plaster. The festivities were in full swing, and the class valedictorian had just finished her speech to the feeble applause, background rumble of "Boo!" and a few shouts of "Slut!"

I sneaked between the rows of graduates to an empty seat in the second row. The Dean took the podium and tried to introduce the next speaker, but I could not hear anything through the roar of "Boo!" and stomping feet. I was looking through the program, trying to estimate how long I would have to suffer through the speeches when the noise suddenly died down. I looked at others for a clue and followed their gazes until I saw Mr. Hue up on the stage.

He was just carried in by eight of his blond female assistants on some kind of an awesome stretcher decorated with a white canopy and silver tassels. He looked splendid in an all-white tailored suit, white shirt, and white tie. His assistants were equally stunning in matching white and silver dresses. Against the backdrop of the worn-out gym and the worn-out faculty in their faded gowns, they looked like a flock of angels.

Mr. Hue allowed a few frantic photographers to document the magnificent moment and then, as we held our collective breath, he took the podium. Below is the transcript of his speech, which made the news all over the country the next day.

Students. Faculty. Friends and family. Distinguished guests. Lesser-known guests. The pretty girl who was just talking.

As you may know, I've never graduated from college. But, as you must also know, that did not stop me from becoming the seventh-richest man in the Southeastern United States. And let me tell you, it's great to be a billionaire. Do you know what it's like to own an island in the Caribbean or a football team? Or to buy some community college a new library, just to have your name forever emblazoned in giant letters over its entry? No, you don't.

So you may ask yourself, "Why did I spend four years and thousands of dollars on a piece of paper?" Well, I can't help you with an answer to that.

But what I can help you with, is some advice. The kind of advice they didn't give you in business school. And definitely not in the liberal arts, or whatever other useless departments you have here.

Out there a whole new world awaits you, ready to give you a wedgie and take your lunch money. The world where you ask for a Perrier, but instead get Evian. The world where you performance-manage the employee who got you that Evian, and then the next day "The Enquirer" reports that you are an abusive diva with anger control issues. The kind of world where you may start a business with your best friend from your parents' garage, then make your first million dollars and marry your high school sweetheart, only to find that the kid is not yours, and then the bitch leaves you but takes half of everything you own. It's the world where you have little chance of paying off your college loan.

I know you think this is all just strong words and tough love. I promise you, it's not. But don't despair, generation Z. Even though you don't have much now, you will eventually inherit your parents' fortunes.

So take that gap year. Volunteer for a charity. Join the Peace Corps and save the whales or whatever. You just need to scrape by until your parents or that rich uncle kick the bucket. You've got nothing to worry about, unless, of course, you're an orphan.

Then you are screwed.

Needless to say, everyone was speechless. Then, after a moment of deafening silence, the gym erupted in a thunderous applause that brought the house down. Not the whole house, just a few ceiling tiles and bits of plaster, but it certainly added to the general hysteria.

The graduates rushed to the stage and carried Mr. Hue down, forming a mosh pit where he body surfed while the other speakers tried to read from their notes.

I was also speechless, but for different reasons. For one, I could not help but be a little turned on by Mr. Hue's brazen display of alpha-male power. On the other hand, if he saw me among the celebrating graduates, I would have a very hard time explaining how I managed to graduate from Harvard and a community college at the same time.

Thankfully, the chaos around me created a perfect cover. I was sneaking away, about to sigh with relief, when powerful hands yanked me up. I choked on a scream, as I stared at my reflection in a pair of super-cool aviator sunglasses.

*

Hot Cop took a swig from a flask and wiped his perfectly sculpted mouth with the back of his equally perfect hand. "Going somewhere, babe?"

Once again, I felt a strange mix of desire and fear.

"I was just going to say hi to my parents." I pointed to the bleachers, where Mom was waving madly at me. Next to her was Dad, absorbed in a newspaper. My sister was on the phone, Mark had his face in his hands, and the twins were nowhere to be seen. Hot Cop tightened his jaw, and I almost swooned at the sight of his neck rippling with muscles.

"But I'm not going anywhere now," I added in what I hoped was a seductive whisper, and suggestively leaned forward.

He did not seem to take notice of my seduction attempt or the motley crew of relatives. Instead, he got out his notepad and thoughtfully scratched something down while biting on his bottom lip. He looked a bit like Mr. Hue trying to operate a helicopter.

"Where were you last night?"

"Huh? At home in bed. And what's it to you?" I said haughtily.

He ignored my attitude, too. "Can anyone vouch for that fact?"

"No. I don't have a boyfriend, if that's what you're asking. I mean, I had one, but he broke up with me before Valentine's Day. He always hated all that Hallmark pressure." I was rambling, but there was no stopping it. "But it's not like I pressured him or anything. I'm not high maintenance!" I swallowed hard.

He stepped in closer and towered over me. "What about your roommate?"

"Ahm…I think she was out." I said and backed off. He stepped in even closer, and we shuffled backwards until my back slammed against a wall. He put his hand against it, blocking my escape, leaned in and took a long sniff from my collarbone up into my hair. I froze with longing and trepidation. He slowly moved away, a knowing smirk playing on his lips.

"Margaret Thatcher?"

I tried to say something, but only a weird gurgling sound escaped my throat. He put a finger to my lips, then pointed it at me, as if to say "I am watching you." I whimpered again, and he was gone, vanishing into the crowd.

"Ms. Maxwell," said a voice in my ear and I shrieked with surprise. It was Mr. Hue, just as I feared, flanked by the omnipresent guards.

"Who was that young man?" Mr. Hue asked.

I was about to tell him the whole story but then thought better of it. There was no reason for my new employer to know that I didn't pay rent, drove on autopilot, or got high on an herbal equivalent of the Iron Lady.

"Don't know," I shrugged. "A headhunter, I think. He was just offering me an extra ten grand to leave Shizzle, Inc. I told him to piss off."

Mr. Hue nodded gravely. "I see." He motioned to his guards, and one of them disappeared into the crowd after Hot Cop.

Mr. Hue turned to me. "It does not surprise me, Ms. Maxwell. You are one hot property." I blushed in humble acceptance of the compliment.

"I can't afford to lose you," he continued. "In fact, effective tomorrow, I'm doubling your salary."

I wanted to ask what my salary was since I still had not seen a written offer, but the statement rendered me speechless. Mr. Hue looked at me expectantly.

"What do you think, Ms. Maxwell?"

"Thank you, Mr. Hue!" I finally found my voice. "I won't let you down."

I was pretty sure that eventually I would let him down, perhaps even royally piss him off, but that didn't really matter as long as I collected a double of the unknown salary amount before then.

"Excellent. You are doing me a favor, Ms. Maxwell. I'm afraid that lately I feel disconnected from the new generation of Shizzle, Inc customers, and I have a gut feeling that you are the voice of that generation. How about we celebrate with a lunch," he said without a question.

"I'm supposed to have lunch with my family," I blurted and immediately regretted it.

"Superb!" Mr. Hue exclaimed. "I would be delighted to meet the parents who raised such an extraordinarily intelligent and capable young woman."

I wanted to say that I too would like to meet such parents, but instead murmured, "This way."

Mr. Hue walked confidently ahead of me. We made our way through the crowd of students and parents, which parted before us like the Red Sea. Almost everyone had their phone out, snapping photos.

A portly little guy, weighted down by several professional looking cameras, stopped us.

"Ahm, Mr. Hue," he bleated. "Such an honor...and whatnot. Just one little snap?"

Mr. Hue smiled generously. "Certainly," he said, grabbing me by the waist and bending down to paw at my knees.

"What are you doing?" I panicked and wriggled out of his arms.

"Oh, my apologies, Ms. Maxwell," he said cordially and straightened up. "It's just that I always hold a pretty woman in my arms when posing for a photo."

"Why?"

"I don't know," he shrugged. "Habit, I guess. I've been holding up girls for photos for so long that I don't even know how to pose without one."

The sheepish photographer looked at me pleadingly. Everyone else was staring as well, waiting for my response. It suddenly occurred to me that Brad might see the photos in the paper and that there could be a healthy dose of speculation about me being the billionaire's new girlfriend. If I were good enough for a billionaire, I should be good enough for an NFL wannabe.

"Oh, what the hell!" I said and threw my arm around Mr. Hue's neck.

He heaved me up with a considerable effort. "It pains me more than you," he said through clenched teeth. "My back's just not what it used to be."

I smiled and flung up my other hand and heels in an effort to look joyful. Cameras flashed, and I threw my head back in almost real rapture, ignoring Mr. Hue's groans and dreaming of the front-page headlines.

The only thing that marred my excitement was the dread of the imminent implosion of this dream upon direct contact with my family.

*

The disaster almost passed me by, as Mr. Hue headed straight for the exit, but unfortunately Mom must have seen us and reassembled the forces. Just as I started to relax, there they were - Mom, Dad, and sister with their mouths open. Mark was behind them, holding onto the wriggling twins.

I stepped in front of Mr. Hue. "Mr. Hue, this is my family," I said to him and pointed out the stunned members. "My Mom Candillia, my Dad Rupert, my sister Felicity, her husband Mark and their children - Tommy and Jimmy." I turned to my family and added "Everybody, this is Mr. Hue!" while attempting to communicate through crazy facial expressions a message of, "Just mention my school record, and you're dead!"

"How do you do!" Mr. Hue said cordially. "You can call me Mr. Hue."

Nobody said anything for a moment, and I tried to contort my face into an equivalent of "For the love of God, say hi!"

Then they all started speaking at once.

"So, you are a billionaire?" Dad puffed out his chest.

"You can call me Candy!" Mom said, blushing.

"Felicity Trooper, Toyota saleswoman of the year." Felicity handed Mr. Hue her business card.

Mark uttered a long pitiful sigh while Tommy and Jimmy continued their escape efforts.

"Lovely to meet you all," Mr. Hue said and dropped my sister's card on the floor. "I was just going to take Ms. Maxwell out to lunch to celebrate her promotion, and I would like to invite you all to join us."

"Who's Ms. Maxwell?" Dad asked.

"We would be delighted!" Mom shrieked.

Felicity clenched her jaw and Mark closed his eyes in quiet acceptance of this new torment thrust upon him by merciless fate.

I shuddered at the thought of taking another helicopter ride with Mr. Hue, but thankfully he opted for a more conventional transportation option: a fiery-red stretch Lamborghini. We all piled in, except for sis and her family. She was still obviously crabby about the business card incident and made some excuse of having to go back to her very important job. Mark seemed visibly relieved, but he missed out big time on the limo bar. Normally I don't drink that early in the day, but I had to down two glasses of French champagne to prepare me for the next stage of this nightmare.

We pulled in under the portico of an unfamiliar place which, to my horror, turned out to be the fanciest place in town, "Bonzhur Monami" something or other. A heavy cloak of dread enveloped me at the thought of having to use utensils, probably more than one. I'm more used to places that serve food between buns, in baskets, or on sticks.

"Oh, I love French cuisine!" Mom squealed. That was obviously a lie, since we always went to the same hamburger joints, but I let it pass.

The maître d' was all over Mr. Hue. He ushered us to the best table with a view of the garden, produced menus with a magician's wrist flick, and filled our glasses with sparkling water. There were a few other rich-looking people having lunch, but they all made a considerable effort to pretend that they didn't notice Mr. Hue.

Dad immediately got into the menu.

"Why aren't the prices listed? What kind of a scam is this?" he demanded.

I stared at my own menu, which could as well have been written in hieroglyphics. I sneaked a look around to see what was served on other tables, but could not recognize a single thing on anyone's plate. I looked over at Mr. Hue, but he seemed unconcerned, preoccupied with reciting his plans for the Middle East to my uncontrollably giggling mother. Dad jumped in with his own commentary on the Middle East, and Mr. Hue assumed the look of a curious explorer who'd unexpectedly come across a native tribe.

"I'm so sorry about my Dad," I whispered to Mr. Hue when Dad got distracted by the waiter trying to place a napkin on his lap.

"Nonsense," Mr. Hue said. "I'm quite enjoying this."

"Really?"

"Your father reminds me of my own," he whispered. "I'm not sure what it is. Probably the same lust for life and criticizing others. You know, he often told me I would not amount to anything."

"I guess you showed him when you made your first billion!"

"I wish," Mr. Hue said wistfully, watching my Dad wrestle with the waiter over the napkin. "He always maintained that I would have never made that billion without the millions he loaned me."

I was trying to come up with some kind of a clever response, when the waiter suddenly appeared at my side, asking if I wanted to order something that sounded like an "ontre".

I panicked. I did not know what an "ontre" was, let alone if I wanted one. I looked at the menu for inspiration, then at other tables, then back at the politely waiting waiter.

"Ahm..." I said, and then the inspiration finally struck. "I'd like some French fries!" Surely, they would have French fries in a French restaurant?

The waiter looked at me, then at Mr. Hue, who was now looking at me with that same curious expression.

"French fries!" Mr. Hue exclaimed. "Fantastic! Ms. Maxwell, you are the only person I know who would have the balls to order French fries in a French restaurant!" He laughed uproariously and snapped his fingers at the waiter, "You heard the mademoiselle!"

The waiter started to say something, but Mr. Hue raised one eyebrow and the poor guy scurried away. There were faint exclamations and the banging of pots from the kitchen. I felt the weight lift off my shoulders.

The rest of the lunch flew by. I was on a roll and ordered steak tartare, medium-well and served on a bun with cheese, lettuce, and mayo. The waiter no longer voiced any objections, and Mr. Hue continued to have a ripping good time. Dad told stories of how he could have started his own company which would have made millions, or perhaps even a billion, if he was not burdened by having to provide for his family. He continued talking while he ate his and most of Mom's meal, punctuating his monolog with precarious swipes of a steak knife. Mom didn't talk or eat much, just kept drinking champagne, never once taking her eyes off Mr. Hue. At one point, she even tried playing footsie with his leg, but I kicked her hard under the table, and she put her shoe back on.

We were all quite drunk by the end, and I remember only snippets of us leaving - Dad cornering the waiter, demanding to know how much Mr. Hue paid in a loud whisper, Mom taking Mr. Hue's arm and leaning on him for support, the popping and fizzing of champagne bottles in the limo.

We pulled up in front of the house, and my parents went inside, or rather, my Dad dragged Mom in while she continued to cry out some nonsense over her shoulder. I said "thank you" and was about to follow them when Mr. Hue took my hand.

"Ms. Maxwell."

"Yes?" I said, shocked. I felt an electric spark pass between us. Of course, it could have been static from my new graduation dress, made of the finest polyester money can buy. I looked at Mr. Hue. Maybe it was the champagne goggles, but I suddenly saw him not as a celebrity, but as a real man.

He'd lost his tie, his shirt collar was open, and his hair got tousled in a carefree, boyish way. He must have been very handsome once upon a time, and some of that stuff still clung to him in a George Clooney sort of way.

"I think you are a very special young woman," he slurred. "I have not met anyone as smart, bold, and full of life in a long time. You remind me of myself when I was young. I'm very happy that you decided to work at Shizzle, Inc."

He bent down to kiss my hand and lost his balance. The bodyguards caught him and folded him back into the limo in what looked like a well-practiced maneuver. Mr. Hue cried something that sounded like "Afiderzein!" from the back seat, and then he was gone.

After a moment of staring aimlessly into space, I made my way inside, where I was assaulted by questions from the whole family. Turned out that Felicity lied about working to avoid using knives and forks at a fancy restaurant. It was understandable, since we were both raised by the same pack of wolves. She wanted to know if Mr. Hue and I were officially an item. Dad wanted to know my salary while Mom kept asking if I noticed how Mr. Hue was looking at her during lunch. Mark stayed silent, curled up into a fetal position on the couch.

I was too drunk, tired and stunned to answer. Instead, I slid down on the couch next to Mark and stared into nothing, while trying to come to grips with the startling fact that Mr. Hue was in love with me.

Bitches be crazy.

I woke up in the middle of the night from a soul-crushing thirst. I was still on the couch, but Mark was gone, and so, it seemed, was everyone else. I pushed off the comforter and nearly tripped over a barf bucket, both undoubtedly left for me by Mom. That was sweet of her, considering that we were now caught up in some weird love triangle. The thought added a whole new flavor of bad into my already gross mouth.

I went to the kitchen, drained several glasses of tap water, and popped a few pills from the Mom-supplied stash. My head was pounding, and I swore never to drink again, hoping that this time I would last at least a week. On my way to the bedroom, I noticed a light under the basement door. Tara was working on her candles again. Suddenly I had to talk to her about Mr. Hue, and Hot Cop, and Mom, and the whole weird situation in which I now found myself.

I sneaked down the creaky stairs to the basement. Tara was hard at work, mixing up some evil-smelling concoction in a large vat. She didn't hear me because she was wearing her massive headphones. Even from a distance, I could hear the pounding of German techno. Techno instead of the usual Bob Marley, and the fact that she was working, meant that Tara was stone-cold sober.

I made a wide arc around Tara and slowly approached from the front. Knocking on her shoulder when she was thus engaged was guaranteed to get me a bloody nose. When she was not baked, Tara was jumpy and paranoid as hell. She was even paranoid about lighting her own candles. Once, during a lighting outage, I tried to light one. She started screaming, and then kept on screaming until I swore that I would never do that again. She later apologized and made a big deal about how the candle was a sample for a prospective buyer, but for a while it put a strain on our relationship.

I waved my hands at the edge of her field of vision, and she startled a little, but just turned off the music, slid the earphones down to her neck, and smiled.

"Hey, Isa, you're up early! Must've been one hell of a party - I heard your peeps arguing till midnight. Weren't they happy about you graduating?"

"Of course they were," I said. "It's just that Mr. Hue took us to lunch...and there was a lot of champagne..." I cringed at the memory.

She put down the bag of fertilizer and looked at me in disbelief. "Mr. Hue took you to lunch? The CEO of Shizzle, Inc?"

"Yes," I said and then blurted, "I think he's in love with me!"

Tara crossed her arms. "Really, Isa? What makes you think so?"

That might have been a perfectly reasonable question - after all, how often do billionaires fall in love with average busty blonds? Still, it got to me. I ached to wipe that smirk off her face, along with the fertilizer goo.

"Well," I said. "He just doubled my salary!"

"Congratulations," Tara said. "But I don't see how that means he loves you. How much was your salary to start with?"

"What does it matter?" I flustered but wondered the same.

"Nothing. Anyway, maybe he just highly values you as an employee?"

I scoffed at the suggestion. Truth be told, I always suspected that Tara thought she was hotter than me. She obviously could not stand the fact that someone found me attractive. Then I remembered.

"Well, it's not just him, there is also a super-hot cop that keeps following me around. Do you think he highly values me as a citizen?" I said with all the acidic sarcasm I could muster.

At the mention of the cop, all color drained from Tara's face. "Did he question you about me?"

Now, that cut me to the core. I remembered that Hot Cop did ask me about my roommate, but that was just a coincidence. I was not going to let Tara's paranoia ruin my newfound dream life.

"Stop being so jealous! Can't you just be happy for me?" I yelled.

"How can you be so selfish?"

I forgot that Tara was not in her usual half-baked and placid state. She puffed up like a blowfish, and her spiky hair seemed to stick up even more than usual.

"How can you be so dumb? Did. He. Ask. You. About. Me?" Her shrieks pistol-whipped my eardrums.

"No!" I lied. "Get it in your head - he is stalking me! Me!"

With that, I turned around and ran up the stairs as fast as my blinding headache allowed me. Tara kept screaming after me, something about "nincompoop".

"Who are you calling a turd?" I shouted back down the stairwell. "*You* are the turd!"

I ran to my bedroom, buried my face in a pillow, and cried myself back to sleep. They say you find out what your friends are made of when the going gets tough or something like that. *Well isn't it ironic*, I thought between sobs, *that Tara turned out to be made of shit.*

*

I woke up brooding late next morning. It was Sunday, and I had no plans whatsoever, so I just stayed in bed thinking about my various dilemmas.

Dear Diary, I'm so confused! The God of Random Chances is at it again, showering prospects on me like so many apples on Isaac Newton, but they leave me with more questions than answers. Should I date the billionaire or choose the broke but age-appropriate Hot Cop? Is it nobler to date a poor man? Am I noble? Do I want to be? And, most importantly, why is Tara being such a bitch?

I was not ready to talk to Tara about it again, at least not yet. The hurt feelings of last night didn't seem as immediate in the morning light, but it was important to give Tara an opportunity to admit that she was wrong, and that I'm hot enough to seduce billionaires and cops. I thought about calling my parents, but that was also out of the question. Dad would just use the opportunity to tell me one of those completely unrelated stories from his youth. Mom would probably try to convince me to choose the cop, but I could no longer trust her motives.

I picked up the phone and dialed my sister's number. To my surprise, she picked up.

"How are you feeling?" she asked. In the background, I heard the screaming twins and Mark's tired voice.

"Okay, I guess..." I started saying, but she butted in, as usual, "Have you slept with him?"

"What? When? I mean, no! Do you think I'm a slut?"

She laughed. "No, not at all! That's good, because to seal this deal, we need to embellish your assets, and since you don't have any assets per se..."

"Seal what deal? What are you talking about?"

"Mr. Hue, silly. Don't you want to marry him?" she asked, and then screamed to the side, "I'm on the phone!"

"Marry? I don't even know if I want to date him! That's what I wanted to talk to you about, you see..."

"That wasn't a question! Of course you want to marry him, we all do," she said and screamed, "Get it yourself!"

"Well, maybe *you* want to sell yourself, but I don't!" I said smugly.

"We all sell ourselves, every day," she said, sounding a lot older than her 23 years. "Don't make the same mistake I did, go for the highest bidder. Don't make me come there!"

"What?" I was thoroughly confused. Felicity had an uncanny ability to have several conversations going at once, but I could not match that particular talent, especially over the phone.

"He's getting on my nerves!" she said. I couldn't tell if she was referring to Mr. Hue, one of the twins, or Mark. "As I was saying, marry a rich man, so you don't have to be a working horse like me." There was a note of sincerity in her voice and a lot of fatigue. I knew she wasn't perfectly happy, but I had no idea that it was that bad.

Her frankness took me by surprise, but I persevered. "Isn't it nobler to marry someone your age, someone poor and ridiculously handsome, so that you can build a future together?"

She laughed, but there was a twinge of crazy in it. "Handsome fades, sweetheart! Look at Mark. Remember how he looked in his baseball uniform? And look at him now!" I heard Mark's weak protest in the background, which Felicity didn't acknowledge.

"Okay," she continued. "Let's discuss the terms and conditions. He will, of course, ask for a prenup…"

"He hasn't even asked for a date yet!"

"Not true, you've had lunch," she said. "We need to move fast here…"

"Butt out of my life!" I yelled. "I'm not going to marry him!" I gave the phone a middle finger. It made me feel a little better.

"C'mon, don't be such a nincompoop!" she said amiably.

That did it. "Stop calling me a turd!" I screamed at the phone and pushed the red button as hard as I could. She called back right away, but I turned the phone on silent with all the passion of throwing it against the wall. I wasn't going to do *that*, of course. If my sister was right about anything, it was about me not having many assets.

*

I flopped back onto the bed, fuming. I needed advice, badly. It occurred to me that, technically, both Tara and my sister gave me advice, even though it was not the kind I wanted to hear. Then it occurred to me that maybe what I needed was a male perspective. I tried calling Harden but got only his voice mail.

I thought about the other males in my life. Dad was out of the question. Mark and I hardly ever spoke, and I did not have his mobile number anyway. I even thought about asking my high school counselor, but remembered how he turned every problem into a discussion about my relationship with my father.

I thought about Brad - not that he would have been willing to talk to me about my problems. He never was. I sighed and let my thoughts loiter around the memories of his body…his strong arms, his chest, and the faint trail of hair that went from his belly button, over the ripples of his lower abdomen, down *there*. My thoughts went *there* and refused to return or consider any other issues at hand, even after I tried to smother them with a pillow. I nuzzled the pillow, thinking that at least Brad would happily have sex at a moment's notice. He wasn't a very good lover, but he could certainly go the distance. After thirty minutes of his enthusiastic jackhammering, I sort of didn't want sex for a while. I sighed, realizing that I had not had any sex, good or bad, for nearly four months.

I was still lost in my x-rated memories when I heard beeping outside. I peeked around the curtain and watched a van back into the driveway next door. A young black man in a t-shirt and jeans got out of the driver's seat, went around to the back, and opened the garage door. I watched as he lifted the van's doors and began to carry boxes into the garage. *One of those men with a van*, I thought, although the van was clearly a rental. He looked like a wholesome, hardworking young man, and I suddenly thought that he could be the one to give me the unbiased advice I so desperately needed. He didn't know me and I was never going to see him again. It would have been better if he was really old and wise, like Morgan Freeman, but he was a lot better than nothing.

I put on a pair of jeans and a t-shirt, checked in the mirror that I too appeared hardworking and wholesome, and sneaked out the front door. There was little danger of running into Tara, as she was probably sleeping off a hard night's work, but I didn't want to take any chances. I walked casually to the van.

"Howdy," I said, also very casually.

The young man stopped and put down the box he was carrying.

"Howdy," he said, and his face crinkled in a smile. He was surprisingly handsome, kind of like a young Tiger Woods.

"I live next door. My name's Isabella, Isa for short."

"Nice to meet you, Isa," he said, offering his hand. "I'm David." I was expecting Tyrone or something like that, but David seemed to fit his athletic physique.

We shook hands. He had a good, wholesome grip - not too hard and not too weak. It made me relax and then I remembered why I was there.

"Can I help you?" I asked. You can't barrage someone you just met with questions, it's better to do something nice for them first - any nincompoop knows that.

"Sure!" He smiled even more heartily. "If you can carry in that toaster, it would be great."

I grabbed the toaster, he picked up the box, and we went through the garage into the kitchen. It was much larger and nicer than ours, with granite countertops and a huge double-door fridge. I whistled appreciatively.

"Nice place," I said. "Must be some rich folk moving in?"

He laughed. "I just bought it."

I was speechless for a moment. "No kidding? How can you afford it? I mean, you're so young and..." I almost said *black* but stopped myself just in time, "...good looking! Your eyes are very...brown!"

He laughed again. "Need some help getting that foot out of your mouth?"

"I'm so sorry!"

"Nah, that's alright. I'm used to being underestimated; you grow a thick skin after a while. Plus, success is the best revenge, isn't it? Look at me, came from the ghetto and now I'm buying up all the white folks' houses. This is number four. Not bad, huh?"

A self-made black man. He couldn't have been more perfect! I put the toaster down on the countertop, and thus, considering my part of the deal done, barraged on.

"David, you seem so smart," I started with a quick suck-up. "Can you help me with a question?"

He seemed flattered. "Shoot!"

"My housemate, Tara, is being a real bitch. I don't know what to do!"

He shrugged. "Bitches be crazy."

That made a lot of sense. Encouraged, I pressed on. "Also, you see, my boyfriend dumped me, and I was so depressed, and now all of a sudden there are two men interested in me. One is young, ridiculously handsome and probably poor, and the other is much older, only sort of decent-looking and stinking rich. I don't know which one to choose!" I looked at him hopefully.

He seemed taken aback with the question. "Why do you have to choose?"

"Well, I can't marry both of them!" Maybe he wasn't that smart after all.

He leaned against the wall and crossed his arms. "Why do you want to get married anyway? You're so young, how do you know either one of them is right for you? Maybe it's neither? Maybe it's someone else entirely?"

Now it was my turn to be taken aback.

"Someone else?" I asked. That thought had not crossed my mind.

He shrugged. "You never know. It could even be someone right under your nose. Someone you didn't consider before."

Suddenly, it all made sense. I felt a red-hot blush creeping in. I'd never dated a black man, but the thought *had* crossed my mind. I snuck a peek at his crotch, but it was hard to tell with the baggy jeans. One thing for sure, it would so totally show Brad.

"Do you want a drink?" David asked. I caught myself still staring at his crotch, preoccupied with a fantasy of introducing a black boyfriend to my freaked-out parents.

"Oh, no!" I said, tearing myself from the imaginary shouting cross-fire about retribution. "I can't drink in the morning! Plus, I drank way too much yesterday, and I will probably never drink again, ever."

"Right," he laughed. "You need the hair of the dog. What bit you last night?"

"Champagne."

"Okay," he said, looking through one of the cardboard boxes. "I have a bottle of Moët. What do you say I put it in the freezer? I can show you the rest of the house while we wait."

It was hard to say no. He took me on a tour of the three bedrooms, the formal dining room and the living room opening out onto a deck framed by garden beds. It was beautiful, the kind of house where I could raise a family of interracial children while writing my novel about ethnic tolerance.

He paused before the basement door.

"Look," he said. "You seem open-minded, so I hope you can handle this."

"I am extremely open-minded," I assured him. "I just graduated from a liberal arts program."

He looked at me for a moment, as if about to say something, then opened the door and flipped a light switch. I followed him down a flight of steps. What I saw proved that the community college did not adequately prepare me for life's surprises.

"Wow!" I said, looking around the room.

"It's not finished yet," David said apologetically. "The walls are going to be covered in burgundy velvet, and I'll hang that there rack from the ceiling." He pointed at a huge cast-iron grid, complete with ropes and chains, which was leaning against the wall.

Next to the grid was a large vintage chest of slim drawers, like the ones in old architects' offices, designed to house stacks of blueprints. In one corner was a padded burgundy leather bench, equipped with a multitude of straps. Two more benches, each with a different configuration of angles and straps, were shoved into the other corner. Fixed to the wall was a polished wooden rack, full of really long and skinny pool cues. A pile of straps, bars and clips was on the floor next to them, and unpacked boxes occupied the rest of the floor. The room smelled of oiled wood and leather, and something else, like old sweat.

"What do you think?" David asked nervously. "If you don't like it, we can go, you don't have to…"

"I love it!" I said enthusiastically. Dad, of course, would not approve of someone pumping iron in the basement, but I was a lot more accepting of people trying to chisel a perfect body. "This explains how you got to be so fit!"

He laughed, relieved. "Oh, it's a cardio workout, all right."

"Is this your hobby, or do you train for a living?"

"Well," he said, "I make videos and sell them on the Internet. Pays a lot better than working for the man."

"Is that a Pilates Reformer?" I asked, pointing at one of the benches.

He laughed uproariously. "No," he said, "but a couple of hours strapped into it, and you're guaranteed to be reformed! Wanna give it a try?"

I nodded, and he pulled the bench out, away from the wall. Then, just as I was about to lie down, my phone informed me that it was about to lose its mind up in here.

"It's Harden!" I said. "Sorry, but I have to take it!"

"Who is Harden?" David asked. He seemed frustrated. "I thought you said that you don't have a boyfriend?"

He tried to say something else about the joys of his burgundy leather Reformer, but I mumbled another apology and ran out.

*

"Harden!" I yelled into the phone. "Thanks for calling me back!"

"No problems," he said. "Thanks for calling me in the first place! I think that was the first time you've ever…"

"I need your help," I interrupted, heading home across the front lawns.

"Sorry! Sure, what is it?"

"You would not believe this! You know how Brad broke up with me, and I was all devastated and thought nobody would ever love me again?"

"Why would you think that? Wait, are you getting back together?" Harden did not sound happy. He never approved of Brad, probably because Brad never approved of him.

"No. At least, not yet. Anyway, you know how I told you that I'm now Mr. Hue's protégé?"

"Yes?"

"Well, I think Mr. Hue is falling in love with me! He took me on a helicopter ride, and then he took my whole family to lunch, and then we got drunk, and he tried to kiss my hand. Oh, and he was so jealous when he saw this hot cop talking to me. Oh, yeah, this cop, he's really hot, and he stopped me, but I wasn't speeding or anything, and then he escorted me back to the house with sirens, and now he's stalking me, and Tara is super jealous!" I paused to inhale.

"Wait! What are you talking about?"

"Mr. Hue, of course! And Hot Cop! I can't decide which one I should date, but I should decide real soon, or they might find out about each other and then I wouldn't be dating either one of them!"

The line went dead. "Harden? Harden!" I yelled.

"I'm here," he said.

"So? What do you think?"

"I don't know what to think, Isa. I don't know this hot cop, but I've seen the billionaire dude on TV, and he's old. I can't believe you're even thinking about dating him. He must be fifty, at least."

"So what? Fifty is the new forty, and forty is the new thirty, so it's not that much of an age difference. Plus, he's really smart and writes books. Maybe he's a little strange, but it could be because he's a genius."

"Genius? You mean a billionaire?"

"What are you trying to say?" I knew what it was, but I needed to hear him say it before I tore him into pieces.

"C'mon, Isa. Why would someone young and beautiful like you be interested in an old fart like that Hue?"

"He's not a fart! And I'm interested in him because he is actually really interesting." I tried to imagine Mr. Hue with all his books and gray hair, minus the money and power, but Harden wouldn't shut up.

"So would I suddenly become more interesting if I won the lottery?" He sounded angry and hurt. "Maybe people like you wouldn't notice my gut so much and notice my musical talents instead!"

"What do you mean by 'people like me'? I can't believe you can be such a jerk, Harden! You're just jealous!"

The line went dead again. I yelled for a few seconds until I realized that Harden had hung up on me. That was also a first in our relationship. The next time he called I was going to lay into him like he'd never been laid into before.

The phone buzzed in my hand, and I angrily pushed the green button before realizing that it was my sister.

Cool Auntie Isa.

"ARE YOU HOME?" Felicity asked without as much as a hello.
"Yes, but…"

"I'm coming over," she said and hung up.

I sat down on my front steps, trying not to faint or have a stroke. I was angry at Harden for being such a jerk and dizzy from low blood sugar. I'd had nothing to eat since the hedonistic lunch nearly twenty hours before.

My sister pulled up just a few minutes later.

"Hey," I said weakly, but she didn't seem to notice, unloading the twins and bags from her monstrous SUV.

I came up closer. "Hey," I said again. "I'm glad you're here. I really need to talk to you…"

"Oh, hey, Isa," she finally noticed me. "Thank God you're home. Can you watch the boys for a couple of hours? Thanks! You're a gem!"

She dropped the last bag on the ground and ran around to the driver's door, yelling instructions over her shoulder. "There are books and toys in there, make sure they wear hats in the sun, I'll be back in a jiffy, no sugar or TV, thanks so much!" She jumped in and took off in a sharp u-turn, tires screeching.

I just stood there, weak from hunger and fear of watching the twins all by myself. This had never happened before, as Felicity was paranoid about leaving them with anyone without childcare experience or at the very least credentials in lifesaving and CPR. Tommy and Jimmy watched me with equal apprehension.

"Hi guys," I said, trying to sound cheerful. "Looks like it's just you and the cool Auntie Isa today! Are you guys hungry? I sure am!"

"Mom says that if we don't listen, we'll grow up to be like you," said one of the twins, the one in a blue t-shirt.

"Does she?" I said, making a mental note to add this to the list of grievances for my next fight with Felicity.

"Yes, a lot," said the one in the green t-shirt. "We don't want to grow up to be like you."

"Why not?" I asked. "I just graduated from community college!"

"We know," the one in the green t-shirt said gravely.

"Okay, then who do you want to be when you grow up?" I asked.

"A dinosaur!" they said together.

I picked up the bags and ushered them towards the door. "Why would you want to be dinosaurs? They have short arms and can't even scratch their butts!"

They laughed hysterically at this and went inside willingly. I felt a lot more capable for the moment.

"Jimmy," I said, and the one in the blue t-shirt turned around. Good, I could tell them apart for the day. My sister claimed to be able to do it somehow, but even she dressed them in different clothes. It was mostly for liability reasons, to make sure the right one got the spanking for biting another kid at the playground.

"If not a dinosaur, then who would you want to be?" I asked Jimmy, dropping the bags by the door and going into the kitchen.

"I want to throw rocks," Jimmy said.

"I don't think there's a job throwing rocks," I said opening the fridge. "Don't you want to be a fireman or something?"

There was nothing in the fridge, except for a half-carton of eggs, half-carton of milk and a stick of wilted celery. I took out the eggs and milk and bumped the door closed.

"No," Jimmy said solemnly. "Mommy says you have to do what you love, and I love throwing rocks."

I couldn't argue with that logic.

"I'm gonna make you guys an omelet!" I said, looking around for a pan and spatula. After a minute or two of searching, I gave up and decided to boil the eggs. The twins wandered off, and I remembered the books and toys. It was dangerous to leave them unoccupied.

"Let's read a book!" I said, rummaging through one of the bags.

"Let's not," Jimmy said. "Let's watch TV."

"No," I said slowly, as if to a child. "Mommy told me not to watch TV with you."

"That's okay," Tommy said. "We won't tell her."

"Yes," Jimmy said. "Let's watch HBO!"

"HBO is not for children," I said. "And anyway, I don't have HBO."

"I definitely don't want to grow up to be like you," Jimmy said.

"Well," I said, ignoring the last comment, "while you are still only five, I decide what you get to do, and I say that we are going to read a book."

"I want my Mommy!" Jimmy cried. He wasn't a very good actor - I could totally tell that he was faking it. He was, however, inspirational enough to get Tommy to join him. I pressed my lips into a thin line and put my hands on my hips. You have to be strict with kids. It's a battle of wits, and it's important to set the rules from the beginning.

They wailed on and on, getting red in the face. After a few minutes real tears appeared, and their high pitched screams started to get to me.

"Fine!" I yelled. "Fine, stop it! I will let you watch TV if you promise not to tell Mommy."

Magically, the tears disappeared, and they both nodded happily. I left them in the living room with *The Simpsons* and went back to the kitchen.

When I returned with peeled boiled eggs and two glasses of milk, they were lounging on the carpet watching Itchy and Scratchy cut, saw and blow each other to pieces. I thought about asking them to wash hands, but decided against it, lest there be another screaming fit. They probably needed some germs for their developing immune systems anyway, since my sister was a clean freak when it came to child rearing.

"Here you are!" I said, feeling like a domestic goddess.

They eyed the spread suspiciously.

"Mommy cuts eggs into pieces," Jimmy said.

"No problem," I said brightly, went back to the kitchen, got a knife, and chopped the eggs into chunks.

"You didn't do it right," Tommy said. "Mommy cuts them long."

"You ruined them," Jimmy confirmed. "They're all ruined."

"Look," I said and put a chunk of an egg in my mouth. "They taste the same."

They stared at me. I was pretty sure that Mommy was going to hear all about the egg disaster.

"Okay, fine," I said, eating the rest of the eggs. "Just drink your milk."

They picked the glasses up with both hands and drank some, looking very cute.

"Does it have luck-toss?" Jimmy asked, wiping his mouth with the back of his hand.

"What?"

"We can't have luck-toss," Tommy said. "Mommy says we're special."

"Oh, lactose!" I said, feeling superior in my knowledge. "I didn't know that. What happens if you drink regular milk?"

"I poop my pants," Tommy said and drank some more.

I snatched the glasses from their hands. "Hey, let's not risk it, okay?"

"I'm hungry," Jimmy said.

"Me too," Tommy concurred, and I sensed the onset of a tantrum. Thankfully, a light went on in my head.

"Let's go to McDonald's!" I said, and we went outside, with the boys whooping and cheering.

I strapped them into Beetle's backseat, but they got the seatbelts unbuckled as soon as we drove off. Only the threat of turning around and the promise of getting real Cokes got them to sit back down.

I pulled into the drive-through queue behind at least four cars, or maybe even more - it was hard to tell with the hedge obscuring the view. It would have been faster to go inside, but I insist on my God-given right to be served without leaving my car. Supposedly in Australia they even have drive-through liquor stores, which I find hard to believe. If that were legal, we would've been first to implement such a genius idea.

The wait gave me some time to find enough coins hidden in Beetle's nooks and crannies, and to sort out the menu.

"What do you want?" I asked the twins, who were bouncing up and down on the backseat in anticipation.

"Happy Meal!" they yelled in unison.

"And a Big Mac!" Jimmy added

Tommy immediately wanted a Big Mac too.

"No," I said, "that's too much. How about a salad?"

They looked at me like I was insane.

"I want a McFlurry with Oreo cookies!" Jimmy yelled, redoubling his jumping efforts. Tommy immediately wanted a McFlurry too, but with M&Ms.

"No," I said, "they have sugar. Your Mommy said no sugar, and I have already promised you Cokes. Plus, the McFlurries have ice cream, which has luck-toss, and I don't want either one of you pooping your pants on my watch."

"But Mommy *always* gives us ice cream!" Jimmy whined. He really was a terrible actor. "And apple pies, I want an apple pie!"

I tried threatening them with turning around, but several cars had lined up behind us, plus I was nearly fainting from hunger. The aroma of frying grease and caramelized sugar rendered me defenseless, so when we finally pulled away from the service window, the backseat was full of bags, boxes, and plastic cups. The boys were quiet for once, and I tore into my own Big Mac like a lioness into a zebra's hind. I had to drive extra carefully to avoid getting the burger juice on my t-shirt.

I was inwardly congratulating myself for getting the situation under control when the tide turned again. It started with a mild disagreement over the ownership of the last French fry and quickly turned into a tug-of-war over a frozen Coke. The Coke popped open and spilled everywhere, setting off yet another tantrum. I felt like my head was about to pop, too.

Luckily, we were just driving by the local park, and I spotted a playground.

"Who wants to climb on that thingy?" I asked, pointing to something that looked like a tower covered in a giant spider's nest.

"Me, me!" they screamed, instantly forgetting the fight. The only reminders of the near-brothercide were giant tears, still clinging to their rosy cheeks.

I had barely come to a stop when the boys opened the door and raced for the playground, their little legs fuelled by sugar and caffeine. By the time I made it to the tower, they were at the top, dizzyingly high above the ground. I wondered if swinging on the ropes like a couple of wild monkeys was okay, since Felicity did not provide any specific instructions on safe play. It reminded me about the hats, which were still at home.

"Don't tell Mommy that we forgot the hats, okay?" I yelled at them.

"Okay," Jimmy yelled down, "but then I want a Strongarm!"

"You already have strong arms!" I pointed out.

"No," he rolled his eyes just like his mother and climbed down a little closer to make his point. "It's a Nerf Strongarm! It's a gun, and it shoots darts, and they really hurt!"

"I want one too!" Tommy said.

"That's blackmail!" I protested.

"What's blackmail?" Tommy asked.

"I will tell Mommy about the hats!" Jimmy said. He had the concept down pat.

"I don't have any money right now!" I said. "How about you get them for Christmas, okay?"

It took a bit of convincing, but they agreed to layaway my debt until Christmas, on the condition that I add to the ransom a robot puppy called Zoomer. I agreed, since I seriously doubted that a robot puppy had been invented, or at the very least available for sale under such a dumb name.

The boys soon grew tired of the ropes and moved on to a wooden castle-like structure. Several kids were already playing on it, and a small group of bored-looking parents gathered nearby. I decided to join them.

"Hi!" I said to a woman of indeterminate age, dressed in mommy jeans and a t-shirt covered in handmade appliques.

"Hi," she said pleasantly. "Are those your boys?"

"Kind of," I said, proud of the co-ownership of a couple of humans. "They're my nephews. I'm only twenty."

"Are you?" perked up one of the dads. "Do you come to this playground often?"

A woman, obviously his wife, stepped in between us and started talking to me. I could tell by the way her husband withered that it was a well-used tactic.

I was in the middle of bragging about my new job when I was interrupted by ear-piercing shrieks. Just behind us, the kids were in a standoff. Jimmy and some other boy were exchanging sloppy punches while a bunch of agitated pre-schoolers jumped up and down around them. I could tell that Tommy was just waiting for his brother's command to join in the tag team.

"Stop it!" I screamed and pulled Jimmy away.

"He started it!" Jimmy hollered while the other kid declared the same to his mother, the jealous wife. There was a bit of back and forth about who started what, until a prim-looking little girl intervened.

"He kicked Billy," she said, pointing at Jimmy. I didn't expect such a cute little kid to be a rat. When I was young, we had an honor code, but I guess times have changed.

"Are you sure?" I asked her.

"Yes," she said. "Billy was playing nicely, but this boy kicked him." She pointed at Jimmy again, looking like a little bitch.

The other parents were staring at me, so I had to act quickly.

"Did you kick Billy?" I asked Jimmy.

"I kicked him in the stomach, but then I said sorry," Jimmy said.

"Oh," I said to the parents, relieved. "He'd apologized already!" I turned to Jimmy and added, pointedly, "Don't do it again! You can't use violence to solve your problems, we're not Nazis or Russians!"

Jimmy went on whining about the other kid starting it, but I no longer listened, suddenly aware of the hatred emanating from the parental group. They continued staring at me, and it felt like they had come in closer, even though I didn't see them move. Their grim faces took on the pallor of murderous zombies.

"I think you should leave," said Jealous Wife. Her husband didn't try to defend me.

"Why?" I asked. "Don't they do this all the time? Maybe they can, like, learn conflict resolution skills or something?"

"I don't think so," said the woman in mommy jeans. "We don't want our children to be subjected to bullying."

"No," Jealous Wife agreed. "Your boys must have learned this anti-social behavior from someone," she raised her eyebrows at me. "Our children learn only from positive role models."

"Aren't you overreacting?" I said, even though it was apparent that resistance was futile. I was outnumbered and the twins were probably already plotting a revenge attack.

"Bullying is a serious problem!" yelled another woman, who had so far kept quiet. Her face was red, and I could see an angry vein pulsing on her temple. "It's people like you," she added, pointing an accusing finger at me, "who try to sweep the childhood violence under the carpet. You are responsible for our children growing up with mental problems, substance abuse, and bad grades!" She clenched her fists, and I winced, getting ready to duck.

"I'm sorry, I didn't mean to, you know, sweep," I pleaded. "Jimmy is a very sweet boy, honestly! He's learned his lesson." No matter how scared I was of the zombie parents, I was even more scared of the spawn of Satan and of what it would do if dragged away from the playground.

"I can't take a risk of my son's impaired academic performance as a result of this incident!" Jealous Wife put her arm around Billy, who clung to her like a moron. "Take your nephews elsewhere!"

Angry tears started to swim in my eyes, and I hated my stupid eyes for betraying me.

"Okay," I said, trying to remain stoical. "We will go."

I collected the twins and dragged them towards the car, feeling the hateful stares burn into my back. The boys were hollering and trying to break free, but I persevered, praying for my sister to come and save me. Getting them into Beetle was like packing two weeks of vacation gear into one suitcase. I succeeded only after promising to add a Lego castle to the Christmas list. It didn't, however, stop them from bawling their eyes out for at least ten minutes. Then, suddenly, they were quiet. I looked into the rearview mirror, and there they were, asleep, with tears still clinging to their cheeks.

I pulled up in front of my house, uncertain of what to do. One thing for sure, I wasn't about to wake them up. I looked at my phone. It was nearly five, which meant that I'd spent almost four hours alone with them, and yet there wasn't a single missed call or even a message from my sister.

I tried calling her, but there was no answer. One of the boys stirred, and I drove off, terrified that he might wake up. I was prepared to drive circles around my block just to avoid dealing with another tantrum, but then I thought of a better idea.

*

When I pulled up in front of my sister's house, her SUV was in the driveway. I marched up to the front door and unleashed an angry barrage of knocks.

"Open up! Felicity! I know you're in there!"

When she finally opened, I could tell she was drunk. She was way too relaxed.

"Hey!" she said nonchalantly.

"Don't you hey me!" I said, fuming. "Why haven't you picked up your offspring? Why aren't you answering your phone? Are you drunk?"

"Sor-ry!" she slurred and pouted. "I put the phone on silent, so sue me! Where are the little monsters?"

We carried the sleeping boys into their room and tucked them in. They didn't wake up, only groaned when we pulled off their shoes and ketchup-stained clothes. We paused in the doorway on the way out. The twins looked like angels, bathed in the glow of the late afternoon sun peeking through the window blinds.

"I love them so much when they're asleep!" Felicity's voice quivered.

"Are you okay?" I said, unsure if I should hug her or leave while I still had a chance.

She closed the door, and I followed her into the living room. The blinds were down there as well, and a candle was burning next to an almost finished bottle of wine and a pack of cigarettes. Felicity topped up her glass and offered me some, but I opted for a glass of water.

"What's going on?" I asked, as Felicity lit up another cigarette and leaned back on the couch. "What was the rush, anyway? Did you have to go to work?"

"No," she said. "I'm sorry, Izz. I think I had a midlife crisis or something."

"What?"

"You know, a mental breakdown. Like when you suddenly think that selling the house and running away is a really, really good idea?"

"You wanna sell the house? You should wait a couple of years, with the market the way it is…"

"That's not the point," she interrupted me with a sigh. "It's just that I'm caught in this American dream, and it's not all it's cracked up to be!"

I looked around and thought that she was a bit selfish. Her house was huge, she had a great job, a husband that did her bidding, and two healthy boys that were well on their way to ruling the world with iron fists. I told her that, in slightly milder terms.

She laughed bitterly. "You know what I've realized today? That I pay for all that with my life! I have less than twenty years left of being hot, and what am I doing with that time? Working, cooking, cleaning and wiping shit! By the time the day's finished, I have no energy left for myself or anything fun! I can't remember the last time I've had sex!" Her face screwed up, and she uttered a heartbreaking sob.

I put my glass down and hugged her. I kept on hugging while she let it all out, bawling about the mortgage, the idiot boss, the first hair she found on her chin, and how, despite all the hard work, she was going to end up alone after Mark died from lack of exercise, and the ungrateful twins abandoned her.

I had no idea what to say, so I just kept on petting her hair. In the back of my mind, I couldn't help but think that all her problems could be solved with money. A measly million would let her pay off the mortgage, quit working and get laser treatments. Plus, when she got old, it would mean a younger lover and the sons constantly hanging around, worried that she would write them out of her will. I didn't say any of it to her, but later, sitting up in my bed, I wrote "self-made millionaire" in my journal. I stared at the words for a while, doodling a flowery frame around them, thinking it was no longer just for myself.

Outstanding!

I was excited to go back to work on Monday, not only because I was another day closer to that fat paycheck, but because I would get to hang out with adults, who were normal and sober to boot. I didn't yet know that nothing was ever going to be normal again.

I knew, however, that something was up as soon as I walked in - everyone seemed even more hurried and hyper than usual, running back and forth with folders and coffee cups. I caught a benign-looking guy in half-flight.

"What's going on?"

"Don't you know? It's the monthly communication meeting!" He pulled his sleeve out of my grasp and disappeared.

By the time I got to the main hall, it was standing room only, but the bodies parted before me, everyone elbowing each other and whispering. Undeterred, I kept walking until I ended up in the front row, which was suspiciously empty.

After a few minutes, the general chatter suddenly died down and the corporate jingle of "Shizzle, Shizzle, we are the best!" started playing. The back doors opened, and everyone got up, like at a wedding or something. I stood up as well and was just able to make out Mr. Hue walking through the crowd, shaking hands. He was slowly making progress towards the front, exclaiming now and then, "How's it going, ol' chap?" and "Outstanding!"

He was barefoot, dressed only in a robe. The bodyguards behind him were dressed as usual, in matching black suits and sunglasses.

"How's it going, ol' chap?" he said as he shook the hand of an old man in big funny glasses next to me.

Old Man tried to hold onto his hand. "I must speak with you at once about the share price!"

"Outstanding!" Mr. Hue beamed, as the bodyguards pushed Old Man back.

I was next. I was anxious about what he was going to do. Would he kiss me in front of the others? Would that be sexual harassment?

Mr. Hue took my hand. My heart skipped a beat, but he just boomed "Outstanding!" in my face and moved on.

I watched him ascend the stage. The crowd was cheering like mad. The jingle ended in an explosion of applause and confetti. Mr. Hue motioned for everyone to sit down and suddenly it was dead quiet.

Mr. Hue was silent for a moment, staring thoughtfully at the floor. I waited with bated breath until he looked up and smiled enigmatically.

"My friends," he said. "Yes, I said it. Each and every one of you is my friend, and I hope you all consider me your friend as well." He smiled humbly, and the auditorium erupted in applause.

The assistants at the front put down the APPLAUSE cards, and the ovations died down.

"You may have noticed that I'm wearing a simple robe today," Mr. Hue continued. "Of course, I'm just as much of an industry captain in this robe as I am in one of my Ralph Lauren suits, but it shows how down-to-earth I can be. I am simply a man, like any of you, except for the women. Sometimes I need to scratch my balls, just like an average Joe."

He scratched his balls through the robe to demonstrate the last point. The audience laughed appreciatively. I couldn't wait to see where he was going with that.

"No doubt you've heard the rumors of Shizzle, Inc planning to outsource your jobs to a third-world country with cheap labor rates and non-existent work safety requirements." He put his hands out to pacify the ensuing low rumble.

"I'm here today to tell you that it's absolutely and positively not true. In fact, it hurt my feelings." He screwed up his face a bit, and we all read "Awww" from the cue cards.

"And in any case, what is outsourcing, if not a helping hand extended to our less fortunate brethren?" he said. A young man next to me took out his phone and started flicking through Seek.com job ads.

"Sure, it may result in a temporary collapse of a vitally important service, but that's a small price to pay for making a difference."

He had to make another short pause until the noise died down.

"In any case, all that is theoretical mumbo-jumbo, and I'm not any good at theory," Mr. Hue continued. "What I've learned, I've learned by doing stuff. And what I've learned is that we are in the business of doing stuff. And when you've decided that the essence of your stuff is people, and making a difference, and above all, ethics, then you really are in business. Business is about getting things done, but not always about profit. Sometimes it's about non-profit, and sometimes it can be about massive losses. But it's always about progress."

The room rumbled on. I couldn't quite follow Mr. Hue's speech, but I was impressed. He looked so powerful up there, commanding the crowd with the help of his minions. I thought back to what Harden said and tried to imagine Mr. Hue without his personal army, money, or power. It wasn't possible. Even his robe looked like a million dollars.

"Shizzle, Inc has many faces," Mr. Hue carried on with his soliloquy. "We are a manufacturing company, a service company, and a transportation company. We are an ideas company, and that means a huge risk-taking company. We are leaders in co-creation of value proposition, specialists in cool colors, shock values, and buzz. We have many faces, but I'm now looking at the most important faces - yours. Above all, Shizzle, Inc is a people company!"

I clapped until my palms were stinging, thinking how bright my future looked at that moment. Sure, what he said didn't make much sense to me, but it had to make sense to others. After all, the man made billions saying those things over the years. Whatever his secret was, I was determined to find it out. I decided to start by asking for something more important to do than serving coffee. That seemed as good a plan as any.

"Just a few announcements to finish off," Mr. Hue said after we quieted down. He took a small notepad from his back pocket. "We have a birthday AND a long service award today!" he smiled broadly.

"And it's the same person! Can anyone guess who it is?"

"It's Tammy!" somebody said from the back.

"I'll give you a clue," Mr. Hue said. "She started working here as a secretary thirty years ago, and she is still a secretary. Anyone?" Nobody else offered a guess.

"Okay," Mr. Hue said. "I will give you another clue. She gained a kilo for every one of those thirty years! Am I right?" He laughed uproariously. I looked around, trying to guess who the fat birthday girl could be.

"It's Tammy!" Mr. Hue exclaimed and the happy birthday song started playing. We all sang along, as a heavyset older woman labored up the stairs. She didn't seem too excited about accepting flowers and a card from Eleanor.

"So you see," Mr. Hue said and put his arm around Tammy's shoulders, "we here are a family. And a family sticks up for each other, no matter what. Remember that when members of the media approach you." He hugged Tammy closer, although she did not seem at all grateful to have the attention of a world-famous celebrity.

The speakers started blasting "We are family! I got all my sisters with me!" as Mr. Hue descended from the stage and started making his way back out of the hall. I gathered all my courage and followed him.

"Mr. Hue!"

"Excellent!" He continued his decisive walk without turning back or even slowing down. I sprinted after him.

"Mr. Hue," I said, struggling to keep up without bumping into his bodyguards or anyone else. "I just wanted to thank you ever so much for hiring me and for the lunch, and for being so inspirational!"

"Outstanding!" Mr. Hue said to a young woman, who seemed to recoil in fear.

"I just love it here!" I continued gushing. "I hope to get a chance to contribute to the greatness of Shizzle, Inc..." I narrowly avoided the doorjamb as we walked out of the hall.

Mr. Hue bee-lined for the disabled bathroom. I would have walked straight in after him, but the bodyguards stood sentry at the door.

"I thought that maybe I can write copy for the company website,"

I yelled at the door, hoping he could still hear me. "I didn't get a chance to tell you that in college I was the writer and editor of the weekly circular. It was called *Weekly Voice Examiner,* and I got the subscriber list up by seventy-five percent!"

Inside the bathroom, a hand dryer turned on. "Of course, it was only three extra people!" I tried to yell over the noise. "See, it was four, but then I signed up my boyfriend Brad and my friend Tara, and also Mr. Todd, the English professor! Mr. Todd even said that it was really good and asked me to come over to his house one night for a reading."

The hand dryer stopped. Mr. Hue emerged from the bathroom and stared at me.

"But then his wife came back early from a work trip…" I trailed off under his hard gaze.

"Ms. Maxwell," Mr. Hue said finally, "your tenacity is remarkable. Your achievements are equally impressive. Walk with me."

He didn't have to ask - by then I was already used to half-skipping everywhere after him.

"We have a problem, Ms. Maxwell." He continued talking and walking straight ahead. The bodyguards, like a couple of well-trained sheepdogs, corralled him in the direction of his office.

"Shizzle, Inc sales are lagging this year. We hired the supposedly best consultants, but all they did was criticize our products, suggest that our marketing campaign was directed at a wrong target group, that our pricing strategy was unreasonable, and so on and so forth. You know what I mean?" He directed that last bit to me. I had no idea what he meant, so I contorted my face into something between delight and disgust.

Mr. Hue nodded. "Exactly. I am glad we are on the same page." I exhaled with relief.

"I thought this may need an out-of-box approach, but I was not sure who on my staff is sufficiently out of the box to take it on."

We arrived in his office, and he took the throne seat. The bodyguards dissolved into the shadows and I wondered if I should sit down. Or stand at attention. Or sit down and look relaxed. I finally sat down, crossed my legs, and leaned back.

Mr. Hue did his signature move of resting his chin on his knuckles and glaring at me. I panicked and tried to put my chin on my knuckles, but my chair did not have armrests for me to rest my elbow. I moved to the edge of the chair, placed my elbow on the table and got my chin roughly to where it should've been.

Mr. Hue watched my antics with deep concentration. "You, Ms. Maxwell, are as out of the box as I have ever seen. When I look at you, I don't even know where the box is!" He shook his head in a mock rebuke. I smiled coyly.

"I was hoping for a twenty-five, maybe thirty percent improvement in sales. But since you have a track record of seventy-five percent, you get the job!" He pushed the intercom button and bellowed, "Eleanor!"

Eleanor materialized soundlessly at his side, "Yes, sir?"

"Get the Kutcher and Associates file for Ms. Maxwell. And book a meeting in the conference room tomorrow for the whole unit. Ms. Maxwell is going to present her marketing strategy analysis."

I nearly choked. Tomorrow was tomorrow, plus I had no idea what he meant by a "marketing strategy analysis". Come to think of it, I didn't even know what a "marketing strategy" was.

"Certainly, sir," Eleanor said as if that was not at all a huge deal. "Will there be anything else?"

"Yes, I'd like a skinny latte, a *Vogue*, and a pack of highlighters," he said and put his feet on the desk.

Others took this as a sign to leave the office. I hesitated, as I felt that I had not sucked up to him nearly enough. I also wanted to ask him who this Kutcher was, and if he was related to Ashton, and if so, would I get to meet him, as he was a total babe. Then Mr. Hue gave me this look, and I cleared the hell out of there.

Eleanor was already waiting for me with a smart-looking folder in her hands.

"This way, Ms. Maxwell," she cordially waved her hand.

As we walked along the corridor, I could not help but think about how my life was changing for the better. My future at Shizzle, Inc looked bright. Success is all about who you know, and I now knew the seventh-richest man in the Southeastern US. It was mind-blowing. Even Eleanor was starting to show me some well-deserved respect. I was lucky to have on my side a woman with so much insider knowledge of the company, someone who could show me the ropes and whatnot. It was about time I pumped her for some information.

"Eleanor," I asked. "What's Mr. Hue's first name?"

"He's a dick," she said.

I was about to ask if she meant "Richard" or "not a nice person", but then she said, "Here we are."

My jaw dropped. We were in the doorway of what I could only hope was my office. Of course, it was nowhere near the size of Mr. Hue's lair, but it was still huge! A wall of glass framed a spectacular panorama of the city skyline, draped in a dreamy gray smog. I walked in slowly, as if in a dream myself.

"Is this...is this mine?" I managed.

Eleanor smiled with her mouth only and said, "Yes, of course. Mr. Warburn cleared his desk already."

"Oh," I said and sat down on the desk chair, which looked like it came from the future. It was surprisingly comfortable. I ran my fingers over an equally futuristic keyboard. "What is he doing now?"

"Applying for unemployment benefits, I imagine," Eleanor said, this time without even a hint of a smile.

"Oh," I said again and suddenly felt guilty about the sad little man in glasses. "Did you say he has a family?"

Eleanor closed the door gently, came up to my desk and suddenly slammed down her folder. I jumped back in my chair with a pathetic squeak. Eleanor put her fists down on the desk and leaned forward.

"Don't you play this game with me," she almost spat on my face. "I'm onto you."

"I'm not playing a game!" I whined. I'm usually quite good at fighting, but only with people I know. This was uncharted territory, and it seemed bipolar.

"Well played," she countered. "The best way to play the game is to announce that you are not playing the game while playing it!"

I thought it was best to keep my mouth shut.

"I know your type," Eleanor continued. "A dumb little slut, here to sleep your way to the top."

I squeezed my lips together even tighter.

"That's fine by me, as long as you stay out of my way and remember that I'm the one going to the Gala with Mr. Hue."

I nodded vigorously to indicate my wholehearted agreement with this arrangement. It seemed to satisfy her. She shoved the folder closer to me and left.

I hate to admit it, but the whole ordeal shook me to the core. I mean, you go through life armed to the teeth and feeling pretty badass, and then all it takes for that illusion to shatter is a skinny little woman with a psycho gleam in her eye. It dawned on me that I had no comeback to her "dumb little slut" comment, and it really burned me up.

I decided to distract myself by looking through the folder. It contained a thick, official-looking report and a cover letter. The letter was short, so I read it first. It summarized the same points Mr. Hue already told me about - Shizzle, Inc products were shit and the marketing campaign was a waste of time and money. I opened the report and started leafing through its pages, but it just made my head hurt. There were lots of really dense descriptions and chart after chart, all seemingly concurring that Shizzle, Inc had no idea how to make or market its products. It was hopeless.

I tried to cheer myself up by thinking about the worst possible thing that could happen if I couldn't complete the analysis. That strategy backfired, as I imagined myself thrown out of the front doors straight into a crowd of loitering paparazzi. I imagined the headlines: "Girl's Strategy Ruins Bluechip" and "Plummeting Sales Lead to Layoffs". All of the stories featured my security badge photo, in which I looked like a terrified chipmunk. Those stories would show Brad nothing other than that he was right in dumping me.

I pushed the scary thoughts away and turned to the only savior I knew - Google. As I typed "marketing strategy" into the search field, a warm and cozy feeling enveloped me. I tried to think what I would do without Google and pushed that thought away, too.

I went to the Wikipedia entry first. It explained that a marketing strategy is "a process that can allow an organization to concentrate its resources on the optimal opportunities with the goals of increasing sales and achieving a sustainable competitive advantage". I didn't understand any of that but copied it and a few more sentences into a new Word file. *Writing an analysis could be a lot like writing a school paper*, I thought, as I continued searching and copying. In a matter of minutes, I had an impressive pile of very impressive-sounding words. All that was left to do was to rearrange and thesaurus them until it was no longer plagiarism. I could even add quotes from the Kutcher dossier. Easy-peasy!

I was feeling so confident by then that I couldn't resist doing just one last little search. I typed in "Brad Suckling". I know, a horrible last name, but all I wanted at the time was to be Mrs. Suckling. What can I say, I was in love.

Unfortunately, there was nothing new, so I spent some time scrolling through his old football team photos. He looked amazing in his uniform, and the black war paint made his chiseled cheekbones look that much more chiseled. I sighed, wished that he hadn't blocked me and my entire family tree on Facebook, and signed off.

Jokers are wild!

I felt exhausted but accomplished by the time I got home. Tara was watching TV.

"How was it?" she asked as if nothing happened. That's what makes us such good friends - we can have a hair-pulling catfight one day and then paint each other's nails the next.

"Great!" I said, plopping on the couch next to her. "What are you watching?"

"Master Fat. It's new. Seriously, though, it's the best show ever."

"Looks like a cooking show," I said. "Please tell me it's not another cooking show?"

"It's not. I mean, technically it is, but it's more like Survivor and Biggest Loser in one. The fatties have to cook whole banquets, but they have to be on a diet and can't even taste anything they make."

"You're kidding."

Her eyes sparkled with excitement. "And that's not even the best part! It's fun enough to watch them suffer, but then every now and then one of them crashes and burns! It's like NASCAR!"

As if to prove her point, one of the supersized girls threw down her pan, flipped the judges the bird, and shoved a fancy cookie in her mouth. She was immediately disqualified and told to leave, but she just kept eating more cookies. Security came in and tried to escort her out, but she evaded them with surprising agility while throwing and eating random ingredients from other contestants' benches. She was also yelling at the judges between mouthfuls, but most of it was bleeped out. Another contestant folded under stress and started eating cookie dough, and then one of the judges lost it and started screaming at both of them. We almost died laughing as the guards who were trying to control the rampage slipped and fell on puddles of melted butter and candy sprinkles.

"Oh my God, you were right, it's even better than that other show," I said. "You know, the one where the celebrity has-beens do diving tricks and hurt themselves badly?"

"I know," Tara snorted. "Just when you think there's nothing good on TV, they come up with this awesome stuff."

On the screen, the guards caught up with the saboteur contestant and tackled her into the pantry. They re-emerged in clouds of flour, covered in colorful smudges. The girl was crying. I didn't expect that.

"Oh no," I said. "She's crying!"

"Oh my God," Tara said. "I've got to tweet this!"

She reached for her phone. I kept watching as the guards led the dejected girl out of the room. Her stats and smiling profile picture were on display. Some other contestants were crying as well and, suddenly, so was I.

"What's wrong?" Tara looked up from her phone in alarm.

"She thought...she could," I sobbed. "Look...how happy she was..."

"What?" Tara looked at the screen. A montage of the contestant's previous achievements was still going. "What are you talking about?"

I wiped the tears with my sleeve. "That poor girl probably thought she won the lottery when she got on Master Fat," I said. "But look where it got her!"

"It got her on TV!" Tara said. "We should all be so lucky!"

"Lucky? Look at her!" I managed to say between sobs. "She's crying, aaah! Because they're torturing, aaah! And mocking her! That's going to be meee! I have no idea what I am doiiing! I feel so faaat!"

"Don't be ridiculous," Tara said. "You're not fat!"

"Yeah?" I said through the tears. "But I *feel* fat! Are you saying that my feelings are wrong?"

"No," Tara said carefully. "I'm not. Come here," she said and wrapped her arms around me.

I sobbed into her shoulder. It was oddly gratifying.

"You are a beautiful, hot, and smart girl," Tara gently stroked my hair. "You will manage the new job and the boss. Everything will work out."

"Thank you," I mumbled into her neck.

"No problem, kid. I love you."

I stiffened. "What?"

"I'm here for you."

"No, the other thing." I pulled away.

She let go of me. "I love you. You know, like a girlfriend. You know what I mean?"

Whoa. She said "I love you" twice. That was, like, so gay. I pulled further away. "Girlfriend?"

"Yeah," she shrugged. "You're my best friend."

"Aha," I said, and then a flurry of images filled my head. Tara and I snuggled up on a camping trip, looking up at the stars. Getting drunk on spring break and waking up on the beach sleeping next to each other. That one time she brushed against my boob in the hallway. How could I be so blind?

"I have to go to bed," I said. "Big day tomorrow."

"Okay," Tara said and turned back to the TV. "Sweet dreams."

Well, I thought, *that certainly clarified a few things.* Who would've thought that all this time Tara was sweet on me! I went to my bedroom, shell-shocked. The room was a complete mess as usual, but now I had the great new excuse of working full-time. I took off my dress and looked at myself in the mirror. There was no big change there to explain the sudden influx of love interests. I turned sideways and sucked in my stomach. Not too bad. If I were ever going to turn lesbian, I would totally go for myself. Now that I was thinking about it, if I were ever going to turn lesbian, I would probably go for Tara, too. I thought about at least spreading a rumor that we got together. That would really show Brad.

I climbed into bed and snuggled in with two pillows and my phone. I checked email, Facebook, Twitter, Tumblr, Instagram, Flickr, LinkedIn, and Pinterest. There was still nothing new about Brad. Was he purposefully in hiding? How could he not be tagged in a single photo? It was encouraging, though, because there was absolutely no way a new girlfriend would not post a snapshot of them together. I googled public announcements and marriage records, then thought about it, and searched death records as well. Nothing. It's like Brad fell off the face of the Earth.

I looked up. The merciless clock said that four hours had passed and that it was bedtime for working girls.

*

I dreamed that Mr. Hue was God and that I was his henchman, like an archangel or something. Mr. Hue was seated on a cloud, glorious in a white and silver robe. I prodded along a never-ending row of sinners before him, while he yelled out nonsense, like "Jokers are wild!" and "More caviar!" It was supposed to let me know which sinners went to hell and which were forgiven, but I had no idea what he meant, so I just let everyone go to heaven. I was sweaty, and my wings were itchy, but I could not reach far enough back to scratch them. Just as I started wondering if I would be better off serving Satan, I noticed that Mr. Hue was now wearing an enormous top hat. We were having high tea with Eleanor, White Rabbit, and the bodyguards around a huge table piled up with empty cups, saucers, and multi-tiered cupcake stands covered in dry icing. There were cockroaches everywhere, jauntily running between the plates. Mr. Hue made a joke that I didn't get, but Eleanor, the Rabbit, and even the cockroaches burst into such hearty laughter that a pile of dirty dishes collapsed, sending shards of china flying everywhere. Nobody even moved to pick them up, instead continuing with their hysterical, high-pitched squeals.

"I'm not cleaning up this shit!" I screamed and woke up. My alarm clock was going off, and I punched it in the face. I felt hungover, even though I had nothing to drink the night before - or at least didn't have any recollection of drinking.

I poured two cups of coffee down the hatch and stood for a while under a hot shower, thinking about how much it sucked to be working. Luckily, I also remembered that working meant getting paid. The thought gave me just enough juice to get going.

I was driving down the highway in a half-stupor, mindlessly following the custom license plate of a Volvo in front of me, when something in the rearview mirror caught my attention. It was a cherry-red jacked-up truck with double back tires and a massive bull bar. It was on my tail like the IRS, so I numbly waved for it to over-take. It didn't.

I looked up from the blinding chrome trims to the driver, who seemed strangely familiar. I leaned closer to the rearview mirror to try making out his features. The guy sported shaggy Beatles hair, a bushy mustache and a pair of aviators. He reminded me of the cops in that Beastie Boys video, "Sabotage". The aviators also reminded me of Hot Cop and without thinking, I did the "I am watching you" sign with my fingers into the mirror.

The effect was immediate. The driver slammed on the brakes, veered to the left, overcorrected, rode the shoulder, and finally took the exit to a cacophony of squealing brakes, honks, and a few warning shots. I put my hands back to ten-and-two, smug in the realization that Hot Cop was most definitely stalking me. I wanted to call Tara but decided not to. The poor girl was already so jealous of me, in more ways than one. I sighed. Heavy is the burden of one involved in a love...what was it? Pentangle? For God's sake.

Those pleasant thoughts evaporated as soon as I entered the front doors of Shizzle, Inc. The stress was nearly palpable. Busy office workers were running around like the cockroaches in my dream. The "Monday-itis" and "I wish it were Friday!" jokes only added to the déjà vu feeling.

Eleanor intercepted me halfway to my office. "Good morning, Ms. Maxwell. Are you ready for your presentation?" She looked almost happy to see me. Kind of like a hungry hyena spotting an easy kill.

I followed her into the boardroom, which was already full of staff drinking coffee and talking about their weekends. Nobody said hi, although I noticed that a couple of junior associates put a little too much effort into not noticing me and talking loudly about the barbe-cue at Mr. Hue's house. I found an empty chair and tried to concentrate on my presentation notes.

The meeting finally started when Mr. Hue arrived, about ten minutes late. He also talked about the barbecue, picking on those staff members who had drunk too much, and those who hadn't drunk enough. I thought back to our lunch on Saturday. Turned out I was smart to match him glass for glass in the champagne marathon.

"Now, let's get down to business," Mr. Hue announced after the barbecue banter was sufficiently exhausted. "As you know, last week we ran the national search for my new personal assistant. Ms. Maxwell here was chosen from thousands of seemingly qualified applicants, so let's make her feel welcome!"

He made me stand up, and everyone applauded, which made me feel very uncomfortable.

"Ms. Maxwell has already shown some initiative by volunteering to review our marketing strategy."

Everyone stared silently at me. I was hoping the silence was a sign of respect, although in Eleanor's case it was probably contempt.

"Over to you, Ms. Maxwell." Mr. Hue waved his hand at me.

I stood up and smiled at the group. Nobody smiled back.

"Marketing strategy," I started reading from my notes, "is a procedure that can let a company distillate its capitals on the peak chances with the goalmouths of cumulative actions and attainment of a maintainable modest benefit." I'd done a lot of thesaurus work on the text to make it sound all complicated and technical.

"Marketing strategies," I continued with a bit more confidence, "are important behind marketing plans intended to seal market wants and spread marketing objects."

Everyone was still staring, but their facial expressions had changed. I could not tell if they were amazed at the depth of my analysis, or if they could tell I got it all off Google.

"Tactics and objects are usually verified for quantifiable consequences," I pressed on. "Usually, marketing strategies are industrialized as multi-year tactics, specifying precise movements to be talented in the present day."

There was fidgeting and whispering in the audience, barely perceptible, but enough to make me panic. I kept reading, but my confidence had evaporated. I looked at Mr. Hue for encouragement, but he was preoccupied with his phone.

Eleanor was smiling, which panicked me even more. I started talking faster, desperately wanting to reach the end of the damned presentation.

"In conclusion," I said, breathless, "a good marketing strategy should be gaunt from marketplace investigation, with emphasis on the correct creation combination in instruction to attain the all-out income possible and withstand the commercial."

I sat down, breathing hard, like a figure skater waiting for the judging results. I was afraid that at least one of my judges may not be fair in her assessment.

"So what should we do with the current marketing strategy?" Eleanor asked, smirking.

"Ahm," I said. "Change it?"

There was dead silence.

"Okay," I said. "If there are no further questions..."

"I have a question," said a young man at the back of the conference table. I could tell he was a total dick just by looking at him. I mean, his collar was turned up like he was auditioning for *Grease, The Musical.*

"Yes?" I said, trying to stay calm.

"So what you are saying," Grease said slowly, savoring his words, "is that the time-honored strategies and rules no longer work in our new complex reality. Are you also asserting that emotionally offending the consumers may essentially result in a higher risk-to-benefit ratio?"

My brain blew a fuse.

"That's true," Mr. Hue mused. "Today's consumers are crankier than ever, especially when shit hits the fan."

Grease, encouraged, pushed back in his chair. "I'm not sure if you understand that introducing arcane stimuli into the already attenuated market niche may sabotage the old-school thinking behind the traditional strategy." He glanced at Mr. Hue. "This would require refined marketing acumen."

I did not understand any of that either, but a gut feeling told me that what he said was not at all a compliment. I put my right hand behind my back and extended the middle finger as hard as I could. It had an instant calming effect. Once my brain was back in service, I noticed that Mr. Hue had not responded to Grease and was instead studying him like an insect. There was definitely something going on . there.

I grasped at the few words Grease said that I understood.

"Funny you should mention the old-school thinking," I said, "because your entire marketing strategy is built on that kind of old shit."

I felt a pang of intense regret, as I watched Grease snigger. He opened his mouth, ready to strike me down, but then Mr. Hue piped in.

"Wait, Thomas, let Ms. Maxwell explain her point."

I didn't actually have a point per se, but Mr. Hue's keen interest encouraged me to go with the flow.

"Take Twitter, for example," I said. "I had a quick look at the Shizzle, Inc feed yesterday. It's about as interesting as my grandpa talking about his socks. All you do is tweet about how great Shizzle, Inc is and how everyone should buy your products. Why should they?"

Mr. Hue nodded, and I felt another intense pang, this one of delicious hope.

"If you have so much acumen," I continued, pointing at Thomas, "then why haven't you figured out that this marketing strategy is a real buzzkill?"

"A what?" Now it was Thomas's turn to look like an idiot.

"Let me break it down for you," I said. "I've spent at least ten thousand hours on Facebook and Twitter, and this 'Look at me! Buy me!' shit just don't cut it, okay?"

"I've spent at least ten thousand hours in the marketing industry..." Thomas began, but Mr. Hue cleared his throat, and the poor guy choked on his last words.

"What Shizzle, Inc needs," I said, "is some fresh game."

Mr. Hue beamed at me.

"I...I don't understand..." Thomas looked at Eleanor for support, but she pretended not to notice him.

"Damn skippy," I said, high on adrenaline and endorphins. "I ain't got beef with y'all, but y'all be buggin'. I got juice and mad skills to get dead presidents, y'all know what I'm sayin'?"

The entire room stared at me like I was an alien from the future or something.

"Shout out to Mr. Hue," I finished and sat down.

Everyone turned to Mr. Hue in dead silence. He got up slowly and brought his hands up dramatically. For a second, I thought that he saw through my bluff and was about to point me out as the buggin' busta, but then he brought his hands together in a slow clap. Then again, and again. Soon everyone else clued in and began applauding vigorously. Even Eleanor and Thomas reluctantly joined in.

"Thank you, Ms. Maxwell," Mr. Hue said, and the applause died instantly. "Shizzle, Inc does need some fresh game and mad skills to leverage its marketing advantage in the attenuated marketplace. Your ideas are hip and cool, and hip and cool have always been the bedrock of our success here at Shizzle, Inc!"

I put on my best humble smile and nodded thoughtfully.

"Juice," Mr. Hue said to himself. "We definitely need juice."

There was that mad gleam in his eyes that I'd come to love, because it most likely meant another doubling of my mystery salary. I tried to estimate how much that might be, but I'm terrible at math without a calculator or at least numbers. Anyway, it had to be a lot more than I ever got before.

"Congratulations, Ms. Maxwell," Mr. Hue said. "You're promoted to the Account Manager position, effective immediately."

Eleanor gasped. Everyone else stayed silent.

"Furthermore," Mr. Hue continued, "you are now in charge of the Yomama account."

I felt my jaw drop.

Mr. Hue smiled approvingly. "I knew you were special from the start," he said, "but this presentation proved that you truly are a Shizzle type."

In the ensuing silence, I could hear the gentle hum of air conditioning and another sound, like a deflating balloon. I looked around for the source and saw Thomas collapsing and sliding down in his chair. Mr. Hue jerked his chin in the young man's direction.

"Thomas, make sure you hand over the account to Ms. Maxwell ASAP." He turned back to me. "Yomama Kabushiki Gaisha representatives will be here tomorrow to negotiate the terms of the merger. I know it's short notice, but I'm sure *you* can handle it!"

He put his hand out for a high-five. I slapped it obligingly, then put my palm up for the "down low". Mr. Hue slapped my hand, and we finished with simultaneous finger guns, pointing and beaming at each other. It was eerily reminiscent of the commercial that got me into all this, and I stifled the impulse to call Mr. Hue a rascal.

When I turned back to the others, however, nobody seemed amused. Everyone was staring at me as if I was a newly discovered animal species, possibly violent and most definitely venomous. I smiled broadly to indicate my good intentions, but all I got back was a few whimpers from the still-deflating Thomas.

"Well," Mr. Hue said. "As much as I would like for you to stay for the rest of the meeting, Ms. Maxwell, you have a lot of work to do. I suggest that you and Thomas get cracking on the Yomama handover. I'll have to show you pictures of my latest tropical island brouhaha some other time."

I nodded, gathered my notes, and headed out with a confident stride befitting a newly minted Account Manager. Thomas was already at the door. He was trying to turn the knob, but his hands were shaking too badly. I reached out and opened the door for him with the friendliest smile I could manage. He took one look at my face and whimpered harder.

We walked slowly down the corridor. I was starting to understand why Mr. Hue chose me to take over the account. Thomas kept pinching himself, glancing furtively in my direction, and every now and then uttering a muffled sob. He was a pale likeness of his arrogant former self, obviously a troubled young man, quite possibly manic-depressive.

"So," I said in an attempt to break the uncomfortable silence. "Yomama, huh?"

A hysterical giggle escaped his lips. He gave me a crazed look and picked up the pace.

I matched his stride. "What do they want to merge?"

Thomas didn't answer; he just groped at his hair. This made it stick out, giving him the look of a full-on madman. He quickened his pace even more and we speed-walked down the hallway like a couple of wannabe champions nearing the finish line.

Thomas burst into his office and started grabbing folders and flinging them at me.

"Here you go!" he finally found his voice. "Handover! Of! Yomama! Merger!" He grabbed a bulging three-ring binder, read the label and laughed hysterically, "Financial statements!"

He slapped the binder down on top of the stack of paperwork already in my hands and breathed heavily into my face. "It took me a year to prepare this deal, but I'm sure *you* can handle it by tomorrow!" He threw his head back and uttered a wolf-like howl of laughter.

I stood frozen, unsure of what to do or say. Finally Thomas fizzed out, went back to his desk, and put his head down on his arms. I made a mental note to discuss this behavior during his professional development review and walked out.

I barely managed a few steps when Eleanor caught up with me, snarling like a pit bull.

"You..." she said, out of breath, "you..."

"Isabella," I reminded her.

"I'm onto you!" she seethed, pointing an accusing finger in my face. "I knew you were trouble from the get-go, all innocent and baby-faced. I thought you were just trying to shag a billionaire, or maybe get a cushy job filing your nails."

She paused and took a ragged breath. "But you have bigger plans, don't you, *Ms. Maxwell?* Clawing your way up the corporate ladder, one dead body at a time...well, just remember that the higher you climb, the farther you fall!"

She slammed a fist into the palm of her other hand in demonstration of my imminent spectacular downfall. I squirmed, looking around for help, but the hallway was deserted. Everybody was probably still looking at Mr. Hue's island slide show. I clutched the Yomama files tighter, as if they could shield me from the attack.

"And one more thing," Eleanor continued. "If you think he will take you along to the Gala, think again. I have worked far too long and too hard to let you take my place. I will keep my promise!"

She raised her hands up, looking past me, as if talking to a ghost. Despite the obvious madness, she looked stunning - statuesque and intense, kind of like a dark-haired Evita.

"Yeah, okay," I managed to say. "I got it. No Gala."

Eleanor returned her attention to me and made the "I am watching you" sign. It made me wish desperately for Hot Cop. Surely he could arrest her for something.

*

I lugged the pile of files to my office, dazed and confused. I had so many things to worry about in addition to my bipolar co-workers. On the one hand, I was ecstatic to be promoted to Account Manager. On the other hand, I was concerned that Account Manager may have to be responsible for things. What kind of things, I didn't have a clue.

I sat down at my desk and got to work leafing through the files. The concern turned into a worry, and then the worry turned into a full-blown panic. The pages contained nothing but numbers. Rows and rows of numbers, some in bold, others highlighted in color, although I could not discern the significance of either. There were footnote comments, which were of no help, as they mostly referred to "metrics", "balance sheets" and "cash flow". I myself was only familiar with the good ol' U-S-of-A system of pounds and yards, and could not even balance my checkbook. I did like the idea that Shizzle, Inc had so much cash that it would flow, like a river or a flash flood. I wondered again about my salary and how big it would have to be, now that I was Account Manager.

"Getting the hang of it?" Mr. Hue's voice snapped me out of my daydream in which I was diving into a pool full of gold coins. He was leaning casually in the doorway, jacket unbuttoned, one hand thrust into the pocket of his finely tailored slacks. He looked stunning, like he'd just came back from a photo shoot for the Rolex that was gracing his wrist.

"Oh yeah, but it's a lot of material to get through in such a short time!" I said, starting to prepare my blame strategy.

"Don't worry too much about the details," Mr. Hue said dismissively. "Just convince the Japanese to pay more for their stake in Shizzle Cola. It requires your fresh ideas and know-how more than this accounting nonsense!" He winked at me.

I winked back, loving just how in tune we were. Maybe we were destined to be together after all. We had so much in common. For example, I've always liked alpha males, and he liked being one.

Technically, he still had not said anything about dating me, but I was fine with taking things slowly.

"You know," Mr. Hue said, taking a chair and swinging it round, "I usually go with my gut instinct on business decisions. I've been known to disregard whole volumes of painstaking research in favor of a hunch. Take this Shizzle Cola idea. Everyone told me that I was crazy to go into the already crowded cola market. They told me that it tasted like shit, had too much sugar, and was dangerously high in caffeine. But here we are, about to sell it to Yomama for a fat profit."

He sat backwards on the chair, looking cool, definitely younger than his fifty years. I thought Harden was way off the mark in calling him an old man.

"If you only knew how many times I've asked my management team 'why didn't we invent Twitter?' It took some convincing, but they finally warmed up to the idea, and we launched Shizzer. I wish I could tell you it was an overnight success."

"Was it?" I asked, thinking that I never even heard of Shizzer.

"No."

"Why not?"

"Lack of spirit," Mr. Hue said firmly. "I have personally tried to in-fuse Shizzer with the kind of entrepreneurial spirit we value here at Shizzle, Inc, but it was not to be. As a matter of fact, this is often the case. It's hard to infuse all your businesses with the spirit when you own over a thousand subsidiaries!"

"Wow," I said and scribbled "1,000 subsidiaries" in my notepad.

"But it doesn't matter," he continued. "When you own that many, you can just let a few fold and write them off on taxes. I'm gonna let you in on a little secret." He leaned in conspiratorially.

I leaned in too, eager to learn every bit of the money-making wisdom he had to share.

"It's deceptively simple," he said, "but if everybody used it, we would not be in this economic mess right now. It boils down to this: buy low and sell high."

I raised an eyebrow. It seemed a more sophisticated response than my usual "huh?"

"Yes, that's all there is to it," Mr. Hue nodded. "For example, right now is the best time to buy property. Then all you have to do is strip it bare, sell all components of any value, slap your brand on it, spin-doctor, subdivide, and sell again."

My head was buzzing with this new knowledge. I was afraid I'd forget the formula, so I quickly jotted down "strip-spin-subdivide-sell".

"You don't have to write it down," Mr. Hue said. "It's all in my new book that's coming out in a couple of months. I'd finish it even faster if I could find a decent second ghostwriter for the project."

He stood up and so did I, mesmerized.

"I'm glad we've had this chat," he said. "It's not often that I get to banter with my employees. They are just too scared to speak their minds around me, even though chitchat is essential to any business. After all, if there was no chatting, where would I get my brilliant ideas?"

I nodded, thinking that I should mention this to Mom, who often said that I talk too much and that my loose tongue would get me in trouble one day.

"Let's get this wrapped up tomorrow," Mr. Hue said, adjusting his perfectly smooth jacket. "Then we'll have something major to celebrate at the Gala!"

"What's this Gala about?" I asked. "Eleanor mentioned it, but..."

"The Gala, Ms Maxwell, is our annual event of celebrating shizzling accomplishments and raising funds for Shizzle Kids. This year it's a special anniversary, thirty years since the establishment of Shizzle, Inc!"

"You've managed to accomplish all this in just thirty years?" I swept my arm around my luxurious new office.

Mr. Hue seemed emotional. "You wouldn't believe how many people have criticized me over the years for becoming so rich so quickly," he said, pacing the office. "What they don't understand is that I'm only doing it to help others. Every time they write an exposé on the millions I've spent on a new holiday home, or a safari trip, or a Gala, they forget that I'm doing it for the poor."

"You are?"

"Yes," he paused and raised a finger. "They forget that it's those lavish parties that raise money for my many charities. It's my lifestyle that supports the Shizzle brand and attracts celebrities to poverty-stricken countries. It's the only way to help the poor."

I scribbled down "rich + celebrities = good for the poor". Mr. Hue was silent in thought, so I felt compelled to comment.

"Do you know a lot of them? Celebrities?"

"Do I know them?" Mr. Hue asked mockingly. "I not only know them, Ms. Maxwell, anyone who's anyone in the world is my close friend."

"Really? Is Mick Jagger your friend?" I asked.

"Yes, a very old friend indeed."

"Wow! The Dalai Lama?"

"Good friend."

"Bill Gates?"

"Rich friend."

"That's unbelievable! Do you know Putin?"

"Yeah, but he's not as tough as he'd like you to think. I once asked him over for a game of Russian roulette, but he declined. Such a wuss."

"Wow," I said. "Do you know Justin Bieber?"

"Who?"

"You know, this boy singer who drinks too much and takes his shirt off."

"Oh yeah, might have to let him go, now that his new album flopped."

That killed the conversation for a moment.

"Do you help others, like the homeless, or only the poor?" I asked to fill the silence.

Mr. Hue considered my question. "To me they are the same, poor or homeless, who are basically homeless poor. You've got to listen to the issue, then listen to the nature, and then put the power back in their hands."

"Oh. What do you...I mean, how do you do that?"

"Just give it to them," Mr. Hue said. "They'll take it. God knows, they steal stuff all the time. Unfortunately, it's the nature of doing business - once you become wealthy, you have to start giving some of your wealth to the poor, preferably kids or issues that are on the news.

If you don't, people won't like you, and that's bad for the business."

"How can people not like you?" I asked, genuinely surprised.

"Oh, you wouldn't believe it," Mr. Hue said. "It comes with the territory. Everyone constantly criticizes me for having too much money, for spending it, or not spending it, or spending it wrong. Take the example of helping the poor. Some have said that I should just give my money directly to the charities, without the extravagance and expense of fundraising Galas. What these people don't understand is that without the celebrity-studded Galas there would be nothing to write about in the newspapers. And who would that help?"

"The poor?"

He chuckled. "You still have a lot to learn, Ms. Maxwell. Give a man a fish and you will feed him for a day, but throw a huge party with celebrities, and your brand will go on to provide that man with two or even three fishes."

I wanted to ask about how Mother Teresa managed to help the poor without any Galas, but then remembered that I was on his payroll.

"Wow," I said. "Did you write that?"

"Yes, I did," Mr. Hue said, and his eyes got misty. "You wouldn't believe how many people have cried, thanking me for all that Shizzle, Inc has done for them. You can read all about it in my books."

I nodded enthusiastically.

"It's hard to believe that thirty years have passed since I set out on my own to follow the path to greatness." Mr. Hue continued.

"Wow," I said again and jotted down "the path to greatness".

Mr. Hue smiled approvingly. "I'm glad to see that you are taking notes. It's one of the key secrets to success in business, as described in one of my books, or maybe in all three, I can't remember now. I myself keep a notebook handy." He took a small pad out of his pocket and showed it to me.

I smiled back, slightly dubious about the importance of taking notes. I've been writing things down for years and still had nothing to show for it.

"Perhaps I am getting old," he said and held a hand up at my protest, "but it pleases me that the new generation is there to join me on the path." He paused and added, "By the new generation I mean you, Ms. Maxwell."

"Oh," I said. "Thank you, Mr. Hue!"

"No need to thank me," he replied, but his smile indicated that in the future I will need to thank him a lot, and often.

"Speaking of joining, I would like for you to accompany me to the Gala. It will be good for you to see that aspect of the business as well."

I gasped in horror, which Mr. Hue mistook for appreciation. "I'll have Eleanor arrange something appropriate for you to wear," he said. "The Gala is quite a conservative affair."

With that, he walked away, leaving me breathless. My pulse and blood pressure went through the roof as I saw a slow-motion flash-forward of Eleanor pushing me down the stairs. There was no way I could go to the Gala and live to tell about it.

Just as I was imagining Eleanor cutting my brake lines and getting a bead on my forehead, there was a scream and the sound of breaking glass from the lobby. I shrieked and practically catapulted from my chair. *This can't be good for my health*, I thought, grasping my chest to keep my heart from jumping out. Then it occurred to me that it, whatever it was, could be an excuse to take some stress leave and avoid the looming Yomama and Gala disaster. Thus encouraged, I skulked down the empty hallway towards the muffled voices.

I peeked around the corner and saw that a crowd had formed at the edges of the normally empty foyer of Mr. Hue's office. In the middle of it was Eleanor. She was clutching a briefcase to her chest, her usual sleek updo disheveled, her normally flawless makeup smudged. At that particular moment, she was more Courtney Love than Evita.

"Okay!" Eleanor announced to the assembled. The bodyguards positioned themselves behind her, ready to take her out at a moment's notice. Mr. Hue was nowhere to be seen.

"Okay," she said again. "Now, who's coming with me?" Nobody moved or said anything.

"C'mon," she said a little too enthusiastically. "You know you want to leave this God-forsaken place. I know I do! Seventeen years of dedicated service, ignored and unappreciated, is just about enough, thank you very much!"

She turned around, looking for confirmation, but everyone averted their eyes.

"C'mon," Eleanor said, a little less enthusiastically. "Anyone? Thomas? Thomas, where are you?"

I looked around myself, but Thomas wasn't there. He was probably still having a tantrum in his office. The phone rang, and the receptionist answered it in her usual pleasant tone, "Shizzle, Inc, how may I help you?"

"You can help *me*, Suzie! Help me defeat this stronghold of evil!" Eleanor yelled and held out her hand, still clutching the briefcase with the other. The beams of light from the glass ceiling lit her up like a mythical prophet, as she proclaimed, "Come! Join me!"

The crowd started to disperse, looking at their phones and watches.

"This is embarrassing," Eleanor stated the obvious. It truly was cringe-worthy. I would have totally come with her, or would have at least pretended to, if she hadn't threatened my life on at least two occasions. It was that heartbreaking to watch.

"Okay," Eleanor said, deflated. She turned to walk out when Suzie said "Of course!" into the phone.

Eleanor whirled around. "Thank you, Suzie! Thank you, I knew I could count on you..."

Suzie ignored her and continued talking.

"...to be a royal bitch!" Eleanor screamed and made a lunge for the reception desk. The bodyguards finally decided to intervene and caught her mid-flight. I could not help but be impressed, as they effortlessly carried the kicking and screaming woman outside.

"I will see you all in Hell!" was the last thing Eleanor managed before disappearing behind the entry doors. I shuddered at the thought of ever seeing her again, under any circumstances.

"Finally snapped, huh?" said a nearby balding man to his colleague, a chubby, Cupid-like man with a baby face and a full head of curls.

"About time, if you ask me," Cupid replied. "I would have snapped myself if she didn't go soon. She thought she ran this place. You know that she once called security on me because I stepped too close to her desk? Said that she might have *sensitive materials* on her monitor. Can you believe it?"

"Well, she could have been pre-selecting boss's porn, for all you know," Baldie said, and they both guffawed.

"Excuse me," I got the courage to ask. "Do you know what happened?"

They turned, and their eyes lit up, the way all aging or chubby men's eyes do when they first see me.

"El Witch quit because the boss is taking the new girl to the Gala instead of her," Baldie said and extended his hand. "I'm Greg."

"Isabella," I said and shook his hand.

"Hey," Greg said. "You are not by any chance *the new girl,* are you?"

"Ahm...I don't know," I said. "I mean, I could be. I'm a girl, I'm new, and Mr. Hue did ask me to accompany him to the Gala."

"Wow!" Greg said, stood up on tiptoes and started waiving madly at someone. "Hey! Hey, Ricky! This is *the new girl!*"

I looked over at Ricky, a short and stocky man making his way towards us. He grabbed my hand with both of his soft, pudgy ones, shaking it enthusiastically.

"Pleasure to meet you!" His eyes sparkled behind thick glasses. "I've heard so much about you!"

That was hard to believe, considering that I'd been at the company for all of fifteen minutes, but I took the compliment graciously. After all, a lot had happened in that short time.

"Very nice to meet you too!" I said as he was pushed aside by other people wanting to shake my hand. They were mostly men, although a couple of women came over as well. Suzie, in particular, seemed friendly.

"You are like Dorothy or something!" she laughed. "You show up out of nowhere and squash the Wicked Witch of the West!"

I tried not to worry about the fact that the Witch was not actually dead, and that she was most likely plotting her revenge. *I could always ask for a bodyguard or two,* I thought, since Mr. Hue seemed to have so many.

Somebody suggested that we take an early lunch to celebrate, and the crowd nearly carried me out the door. People were fighting over who would give me the ride to Applebee's, but I decided to take Beetle, just to keep it on an even keel.

It was a different Applebee's, not the one that abruptly ended my career in hospitality. Still, it looked practically the same, and I was overcome with feelings of dread and pride at the thought of just how far I'd come in such a short time. Once we'd found a big enough table, everyone ordered drinks. I was shocked for about a second, then asked for a margarita. What the hell, I had something to celebrate too. Everyone wanted to talk to me, and I basked in the attention. The personal questions I fenced off with witty jokes, which led to uproarious laughter and more questions. Cupid, whose real name was John, stayed close to me at all times. He turned out to be an Account Manager as well, and I made a note to ask him later about how one could balance a sheet.

The lunch went on for over two hours, and still nobody mentioned getting back to the office. I was a little surprised at such a waste of time, since time is supposedly money. Apparently, at Shizzle it wasn't.

"So," I asked the group after the third round of drinks. "How did you get to be so lucky? I mean, to work with Mr. Hue?"

Everyone stopped talking and looked at me.

"Yeah," said a pasty-faced girl from the finance department. "I'm so 'lucky' to have worked all of the last weekend because he's changed his mind on the numbers." She made flamboyantly sarcastic quotation marks with her fingers.

"Oh, I know," John sighed into his beer. "I'm so 'lucky' that he started showing a lot of interest in my reports lately. I'm dreading going back - they are probably back on my desk, covered in red."

"Isn't it good, though," I asked, "that he's showing interest in your work?"

"It would be good," Ricky said, "if he had a clue about the business. Instead, he just messes things up."

"I know," Greg said. "I've been programming for twenty years, but now he wants to check the source code himself. The other day he called me to his office to demand that we move our software platform with a data bus. He probably thinks a processor is for making smoothies!"

"It's not? I mean, he does seem to have a lot of ideas," I said. "He wrote three books!"

"Oh, please," Ricky grimaced. "He repeats the same things over and over. You may think they are clever when you hear them for the first or even second time, but after a while you realize he's just a parrot repeating someone else's words."

"Business is about getting things done!" Greg said in a parrot-like voice. "What I've learned, I've learned by doing stuff!"

"Shizzle spirit! Shizzle spirit!" Ricky joined him, flapping his elbows up and down like wings.

Everyone laughed, but the conversation sobered me up, and I didn't like the feeling. This job was supposed to be my lucky break and a path to fame and riches, not to middle-aged spread and bitterness. Luckily, my phone went off just as Greg tried to hoist one of the girls up for a photo. It was my Dad, which was highly unusual. Dad only called me on my birthdays. It was always my job to call with weekly reports on my endeavors so that he could question my every decision.

I answered the phone, but could not understand a thing Dad said. In the surrounding racket, his words sounded like sobs. I excused myself and went outside.

"What is it, Dad?" I asked.

Instead of answering, Dad actually sobbed. It was a shocking sound. Come to think of it, I'd never heard the Iron Man cry.

"Dad, what happened?" I panicked. "Did something happen to Mom?"

For the last year or so I'd had a nagging fear that Mom would one day overdose on her cocktail of pills. "Oh my God," I cried. "Is she dead?"

That paused Dad's hysterics.

"No, she is not dead!" he barked. "She is perfectly fine, it's me who is nearly dead with stress!"

"Oh!" I said, relieved. Dad had been stressed out for as long as I knew him and it wasn't going to kill him anytime soon.

"She left me!" Dad said and dissolved into another bout of wails. "Your mother left me!"

Everything is great at the Maxwells'.

"Your mother left me."

I understood the words, but could not comprehend what they meant. I tried to imagine my mother packing a suitcase and leaving. I simply couldn't. After nearly three decades together, my parents had grown into one being, like two old trees. Sure, some of the branches were strangling each other, but it seemed too late to separate them. I couldn't imagine either one of them existing on their own. Instead, I imagined my mother dragging a suitcase down some dark street, alone and confused, high on pills. In a homeless shelter, lining up for a free meal. Lying on a park bench, covered in newspapers, clutching an empty prescription bottle.

"Isa!" my Dad's voice pushed away the nightmarish visions. "You have to talk some sense into her!" He sounded pissed off and a lot more like his normal self. "She's just having one of those...what do you call them? Midlife crises!"

"Yeah, okay," I said. "I'll call you back."

I hung up. The shock wedged itself somewhere between my stomach and chest, making it hard to breathe. There was also something else down there. The familiar resentment at having to clean up another one of my Dad's "oopsies".

"I took a shower and oops, the bathroom is flooded, wipe it up for Daddy?"

"I tried to shake the ketchup out of a bottle and oops! Clean it up for Daddy?"

"The diesel pump looks just like the regular gas pump! Call AAA for Daddy?"

This time it was "I've ignored your mother for years and oops!"

How could he delegate something this enormous and personal to me? How could I convince her to come back, if I myself could not imagine living under one roof with him?

I dialed my mother's number, and thankfully she answered right away.

"Hello?" There was not even a hint of tears in her voice.

"Mom?" I said, flooded with relief. "Where are you?"

"Oh Isa, darling!" she trilled. "I'm so glad you called!"

"Are you okay? Dad said..."

"Isa, sweetheart," she interrupted me, "Mommy and Daddy love you very, very much..."

"Mom, I am not a child!" I said. "Please spare me the formalities, I just want to know that you are okay and not running away with the circus or sleeping on the street!"

Mom laughed. The laugh was joyful and genuine, not the fake "everything is great at the Maxwells'" she did when Dad got wasted at dinner parties and interrogated guests on their religious and political views.

"I'm fine, sweetheart," she said. "I'm staying at your Auntie Kelly's place for now, and we're about to go to dinner."

"Okay, that sounds nice..."

"She's going to introduce me to a couple of her single gentlemen friends!" Mom interjected.

"What?" Aunt Kelly was an old spinster who was almost famous for her carnal quests. Back in her heyday, she was connected to more scandals than Richard Nixon.

"We're going to the casino!" The excitement in Mom's voice was palpable. "I'm wearing one of her dresses. It's a little too short, I think, but it's sequined! I've never had a sequined dress!"

"Mom!"

"She took me to her beauty salon, and I had my hair and nails done, and they served champagne! I didn't know that you can get champagne in a beauty salon, can you believe it? Oh, and the music! It was like going to a club..."

"Mom! Mom!"

"Yes, sweetheart?"

"Don't you think it's a little too soon?"

"Oh, Isa," she sounded sad. "When it finally dawns on you that you've spent your entire life locked in a cage, the freedom can't come soon enough."

I didn't know what to say. Sure, I wasn't fond of our sprawling ranch-burger family home either, but it wasn't a cage. It had a really big backyard.

I heard voices in the background. "Gotta go, love you, kisses!" Mom volleyed into the phone, and the line went dead.

I was dumbfounded. I didn't expect Mom to be so...happy. She didn't sound like she was high on pills, either.

I dialed my sister's number. She was at work, so she seemed more relaxed than usual.

"Well, good for her!" she said when I finished reporting the news.

"But...isn't it, I don't know, bad? They will probably get a divorce!"

"About time, if you ask me," she said. "They should have done it a long time ago."

"You don't mean that!"

"I do," she said matter-of-factly. "If they divorced while we were still young, maybe we wouldn't have grown up to be so messed up."

"We're not messed up!"

"You know what I mean," she said amicably. "I'm married to a pathetic male nurse, and you have emotional issues..."

"I don't have emotional issues!" I shouted.

"Okay, okay, obviously not!"

"Are you being sarcastic?" I asked sarcastically. "Cause I think someone who doesn't care about her parents divorcing is the one with the emotional issues!"

Felicity laughed, and I hung up on her. I hated when she acted all cool, calm and collected. *Let's see how calm she is,* I thought, *when she goes home to her twin Chuckies.*

My chest was still tight, and my head felt like it was about to explode. I desperately needed a good cry to let out the pressure. Having a fit in Applebee's, in front of my new colleagues, was out of the question. I went back to the table and made a flimsy excuse about having to prepare for an important meeting. My new gang begged me to stay a bit longer, and John unnecessarily escorted me to my car, where he lingered and blushed until I got behind the wheel and sped off.

I would have wailed in the car, but the excuse reminded me that I indeed had a very important meeting tomorrow. I decided to swing by the office, grab the Yomama files and go home to work. In other words, cry it out.

Suzie did not question my motives when I explained why I was going home early and even offered to forward my calls to her number. Despite feeling distraught over my parents' breakup, I reflected with pleasure on this additional perk of my new promotion. It almost required me to boss people around.

Just as I was about to leave, Mr. Hue walked in with a Santa Claus-like portly old gentleman and a beautiful young woman, who I presumed to be the old gentleman's granddaughter. She was all cheekbones, tall and lean, kind of like Lucy Liu, except very pregnant. I observed her sparkling wedding ring set and swollen midriff with barely contained jealousy. She was dressed in a simple white shift dress, yet everything about her appearance screamed money, from the stylish handbag to the hoity-toity attitude.

The portly gentleman and Mr. Hue were laughing about something, obviously just returning from a lunch themselves. I was not sure if my promotion entitled me to leave work without asking Mr. Hue, so I decided to tell him about the working from home plan.

I walked a bit closer to the group and lingered, waiting for them to finish the conversation. The Grandpa Claus noticed me first.

"Hi there!" he said jovially. Mr. Hue turned around, saw me and nodded, still chuckling.

Encouraged, I stepped in closer and offered my hand. "Hi, I'm Isabella."

"Andrew." Grandpa shook my hand and smiled kindly. He had a very nice handshake, firm but warm, and his eyes were friendly amongst the deeply grooved wrinkles. I smiled back at him.

"Hi," I said to Lucy Liu, but she didn't seem to notice me. I've heard that pregnancy hormones play havoc with a woman's body, so I said "hi" louder and stuck out my hand further.

Lucy Liu didn't move. "I look forward to the Gala," she said to Mr. Hue in an overdone blue-blooded drone.

I should've pretended that I was trying to shake something off my fingers, or at least take my hand back. Instead I froze, holding my hand out like an idiot. Lucy Liu still did not notice, but thankfully Mr. Hue did.

"Isabella just won the national assistant search, and she's already in charge of the Yomama merger. I can see her taking over the entire business strategy division one day!" he said, putting his hand around my shoulders.

That seemed to awaken Lucy Liu to my presence. "Charming," she said, awkwardly touching my hand with her cool fingertips.

"Nice to meet you too," I said automatically, then realized that she didn't even tell me her name.

"Andrew is on our board of directors," Mr. Hue said. "You will no doubt get to know him once we start working through the fine details of the merger arrangement."

"Looking forward to it!" Andrew said and winked at me. Lucy Liu scoffed. He put his arm around her waist and added, "But right now I need to take the old ball and chain here to a meeting with the feng shui decorator. Nothing but the best for my baby!"

With that, he used his other hand to affectionately pat Lucy's pregnant stomach. I realized with growing horror that he was not the woman's grandpa, after all, that he was the one responsible for her growing baby bump, and that it had probably happened in the old-fashioned way, with a lot of Viagra. I gagged.

As the couple walked away, Andrew still patting his wife's stomach, I blurted, "How could she snub me like that?"

"Don't let it bother you," Mr. Hue said. "She married into the money and probably thinks that's how rich people are supposed to act. Trouble is, Andrew is sort of business royalty, so nobody would dare tell her she's acting like a cow. Even I don't want to do it."

"Somebody has to!" I said, close to tears. "She really hurt my feelings!"

It also hurt that, as usual, I couldn't think of a good comeback on the spot. It would probably occur to me later, in the middle of the night.

"It could make you feel better," Mr. Hue said contemplatively, "to know that her royal days are almost over. They've been married for five years, and she just turned thirty, so it wouldn't surprise me if Andy found himself a new wife next year. It could even be you!"

I gagged again. "No, thanks. I want to earn my millions, not marry them. Anyway, if they divorce, she would get half of all he owns. Why would that make me feel any better?"

Mr. Hue laughed. "Unlikely. He's been married a few times, and I guarantee that the prenup clauses are tighter than his wife's ass. She will get a few million, of course, but she'll spend it all on booze and plastic surgery. Just wait."

I didn't know that billionaires' wives had it so tough. It did make me feel a lot better. Making millions is probably easier than trying to hold onto them in a divorce battle. With that in mind, I asked Mr. Hue if I could go home to concentrate on the Yomama file.

"Of course!" he said. "That's the spirit!"

The files took up most of Beetle's backseat. As I pulled out of the parking lot, I noticed a man in a yellow banana suit hanging out near the entry. It seemed a bit odd, considering that the sidewalk was deserted. Also, he did not have any bananas or pamphlets to give away. Something about him just wasn't right.

I looked closer and noticed that the banana man was wearing a familiar pair of aviators. I honked and waved at him, but he pretended not to notice. A large SUV entered the parking lot and blocked him from my view. When the car passed, the banana man was nowhere to be seen.

Oddly enough, seeing Hot Cop again failed to lift my mood. Most likely it was because I desperately needed someone to talk to, a soft shoulder to cry on, and not necessarily a muscular chest. I thought about Harden, but I was still too pissed off at him. We would get over the fight, of course, but not until he admitted that he was wrong.

Brad was next to come to my mind. He was always there when I needed emotional support, telling me to toughen up or shut up. Maybe that's what I needed - someone to yell at me until I forgot all about my parents divorcing or the stress of the upcoming presentation to Yomama.

I swiped through my iPod until I found just the right song to lift my mood. I turned the volume up to the max and reclined in my seat, listening to Eazy-E muse about being the neighborhood sniper. I drove like a thug, with my arm out of the open window, tapping the beat on the car door. My other hand remained on the steering wheel, at the defiant 12 o'clock.

"Bam! Bam!" I yelled along with Eazy and the gang, feeling a lot less helpless and a lot more gangsta by the minute. The chorus lyrics sounded like gibberish, but cool gibberish, kind of like having a secret language with the baddest dude on the planet. I put the song on repeat.

By the time I got home I felt a lot better, pumped and ready to bitch-slap the Yomama case. I carried my pile of files inside, like a circus acrobat balancing a tower of spinning plates.

"Hi, Isa!"

I lost my balance with a surprised yelp, wholly unbecoming a gangsta. The carefully arranged file tower collapsed, sending paper flying everywhere.

"Oh shit! Sorry!" Tara said, but she was laughing.

"Damn it, Tara! Now I will never be able to piece it back together! It's a killer deal that I have to execute by tomorrow, and it's a mutha-fuckin' pain as it is!" I started picking papers off the floor. Tara tried to help, but I waved her off. She was still laughing, unaware just how pissed off I was with her, which was pissing me off even worse.

"What kind of a deal?" asked a smooth male voice from the couch.

I whipped around, startled. Hot Neighbor was sitting on our couch, as relaxed and casual as if he owned this place, too. He was wearing jeans and a white t-shirt, which contrasted beautifully with his smooth dark skin.

"This is David," Tara said. "He's our new neighbor. David, this is Isa, my roommate."

"We've met," I replied curtly. "He didn't tell you that we've met?" I tried to sound cool and not at all jealous.

"No." Tara went back to the couch and sat down next to David. She looked like a tramp in her tiny beach shorts and a skimpy tank top. I took a mental note for the follow-up fight.

"I didn't know you lived here," David volunteered without changing his relaxed posture. "You left so suddenly that I didn't get a chance to ask which one is your house."

"So what, you've been knocking on doors trying to find me?"

"No," he said. "I'm not into girls who play hard to get."

"David is here to borrow a screwdriver," Tara said.

"Really? Just a screwdriver?" I seethed sarcastically. I didn't like where the conversation was going, but it seemed that my mind was off like a spooked horse. I pulled on the reins as hard as I could, but it bucked and shouted, "Are you sure you're not looking for a screw as well?"

"Isa!" Tara said reproachfully, but David just threw his head back and laughed.

"Well, now that you mention it, I think I do need a couple of screws," he looked suggestively from me to Tara and back.

"Yes, you do," I said, "cause you obviously got a couple of screws loose!" I twisted a finger into my temple to make sure he got my point.

"Isa!" Tara scolded. I could not believe that she was on David's side. Suddenly, I remembered her nincompoop comment and it burned me all over again.

"Shut up, Tara," I said. "Why don't you go make some candles or something!"

That wiped the smile off her face. "*You* shut up!" she said, and suddenly her voice carried a real threat.

"No, you shut up," I said defiantly. "And put some decent clothes on. I don't know what you are trying to accomplish, running around half-naked!"

"What are you, my mother?" Tara jumped up from the couch. "I'll go get that screwdriver, David." She sauntered off to the basement, wiggling her butt suggestively all the way.

David kept on laughing. He had a beautiful laugh, hearty and full. It was the kind of laugh that puts people at ease and makes them want to join in, even if they don't get the joke. For some reason, probably because my nerves were already shattered by the day's events, it had the opposite effect on me. I wanted to say something really smart and venomous to stop him, but couldn't come up with anything half-decent. Instead, I got down on my knees and started grabbing at papers.

David shifted on the couch to get a better look at me crawling around on the floor.

"Can I help you?" he asked. "You seem frustrated..."

"No, thank you, I'm fine," I said, feeling very frustrated indeed. "I can get it done myself!"

"Are you sure you have a firm grasp of the subject?" asked David. "I'm very experienced, you know. You'd be satisfied with my performance, I can guarantee it."

"It's a merger offer," I said with contempt. "Like you have any experience with mergers?"

"I can't let a day pass without merging."

"Oh, yeah? How would you balance a sheet, then?"

"The same way I would balance anything else," he replied. "Slowly."

Tara reappeared from the basement, twirling the screwdriver in her fingers.

"I've had enough of this," I said. "I'm going to my room. You two can continue doing whatever it was you were doing."

I marched to my room, half hoping that one of them would follow me and try to kiss and make up. Neither one of them did. *So much the better,* I thought, slamming the door behind me. I would just have to concentrate on my work, get discovered, get rich, and get famous. Then we'd see who's laughing.

No daughter of mine shall plagiarize from Google!

After an hour of Google and Yahoo! Answers, I finally dissolved into tears.

Trying to come up with anything resembling a merger analysis was even harder than I thought. I started down my usual path of thesaurus-izing the bejesus out of Wikipedia, but I could tell that the end product didn't have any juice. Hell, it didn't even make sense. How could I ask Yomama to increase its offer if I could not figure out what the offer was in the first place?

My eyes swam with tears, but I kept trying to read the meaningless numbers, quietly impressed with my perseverance. *I'm just a little girl*, I thought, *caught in the cogs of a heartless business machine.* The first huge sob came up from deep within my chest and popped with a wretched wet sound. All I wanted was a little house on a beach, and maybe a pair of Manolos, just to see what all the fuss was about. I didn't know you were expected to pay for the dollars with such despair.

With that I let go of the papers, fell onto the bed and buried my face in the pillows. I gulped air in rapid short snorts, then let it out in long sensuous streams of "Aaaah!" and "Eeeeh!", secretly hoping that Tara would hear me. It had to be one of the better cries I'd had of late. I could feel the pressure on my chest and temples letting go with each heartbreaking wail. Finally, I rolled onto my back, spent but restored, wondering if I should have a cigarette. I didn't smoke, but it seemed like the perfect time to start.

My phone rang. I anxiously fished for it in my purse, hoping it was Mr. Hue calling the whole thing off. It was Dad. Common sense told me to let it go to voicemail, but I rarely listened to common sense.

I pressed the green button.

"Is she coming back?" Dad barked.

"Hi Dad," I said, trying to sound strong. It was so thoughtful of me to put on a brave face for him. I once again dissolved into tears of pity for myself.

"You...you were right," I sobbed. "I...I can't..."

"Of course I'm right," he dismissed me. "Have you talked some sense into her?"

"Who-what? Oh, Mom...no, but she's okay. She is staying with Auntie Kelly and they..."

"I knew it!" Dad was livid. "That woman is the devil! I always thought she was a bad influence. Did I tell you the story about how we almost bought that heritage house and she brainwashed your mother into going against my advice? You need to know these things! It was in October of 1991. No, wait, it was after your grandma died, so it must have been 1993. Yes, it was definitely in October of 1993 and your mother had just received the inheritance, so of course I had to think of how best to invest it..."

"Dad!" I interjected, "You've already told me that story, like a hundred times!" In fact, I knew that story by heart: all about how Dad wanted to buy a decrepit southern mansion in the boonies and how Mom put the money into the stock market instead.

"No, no, this is very interesting!" Dad insisted. "It's part of the family history. The house had seven bedrooms. Seven! And the ceilings were twelve feet high!"

"I thought it didn't even have a roof? Wasn't the whole thing rotten?"

"It was heritage!" Dad's voice boomed through the phone. "You know how much it would be worth now? Millions!"

"It would have probably cost a million to repair it. Mom said there wasn't enough money to keep it up."

"We could have borrowed!" Dad's voice rose another octave. "Only a blind and stupid person could not see an opportunity in such a deal!"

"Are you calling Mom stupid?"

"Not at all, she was just a pawn in the hands of your Auntie Kelly."

"That's basically calling her stupid!"

"How do you figure that?" Dad sounded genuinely surprised. "The pawn is a noble chess piece, often sacrificed to win the game. I don't see how it can be called stupid."

I gave up. "Okay, fine. But please, don't tell me the story again. I don't have the time right now."

"If she followed my advice, we would be millionaires now."

"She tripled the money in the stock market, didn't she?"

"Yes, at first, but then the stock market crashed!" Dad said with glee. "Do you know how much it's worth now?"

"I don't care!" I yelled. "The housing market crashed too, in case you haven't noticed!"

"The housing market is bouncing back," Dad asserted. "You can't go wrong with bricks and mortar. They are real, unlike the stock certificates, which are printed on paper. Paper! She says she owns a bit of Google. Ha! Just wait till Google has a merger with…I don't know…Boogle! The whole thing will go up in smoke!"

"Merger?" That reminded me. "Dad, do you know anything about mergers?"

"Do I know anything about mergers?" Dad was offended. "When I was working at Toys-R-Us, I drafted a ground-breaking business proposal for a merger with Koch Industries. Do you know anything about Koch Industries?"

He paused until I was forced to admit, "No, I don't."

"Ooh, then listen to this. This is very interesting!" Dad's excitement was palpable. "Koch Industries are in everything! You probably think that they just make paper towels, but they are behind half of the country's consumables, and most significantly, petroleum production!"

"What does that have to do with kids' toys?"

"That's what my manager said! He was a blind and stupid man," Dad said. I let that go. For once, I was actually interested in his story. It had to be a first for both of us.

"Kids toys are made from plastic, which is made from petroleum by-products," Dad said. "I proposed the construction of the largest-ever petroleum processing plant. Petroleum would go in, gas and children's toys would come out. The savings in double processing and freight would have made the company billions!"

I suddenly remembered the giant petroleum plant idea. "Dad, I remember now, you've told this story a million times..."

He didn't listen. "The management killed the idea!" I could almost see him spattering saliva at the other end of the line. "All I got was excuses! 'The name sounds inappropriate' and 'We already have billions' and 'Who are you?'. If only they listened to me, Kochs-R-Us would have been worth billions! My ideas are gold! Did you know that I came up with the idea for the Internet back in 1973? I had just graduated from high school. Wait, no, it had to be 1972..."

I half-listened to his rant, feeling marginally more optimistic. Sure, experience proved that Dad's ideas could be crazy, but the story about Kochs-R-Us had juice. It was fresh and visionary and had the kind of balls Mr. Hue would definitely grab onto.

"Dad!" I said.

He continued with another spat, this time something about the President.

"Dad! Dad!"

"What?"

"Dad," I said, paused, and then forced myself to say, "I need your help."

He was quiet for a moment. "You do?" he asked, almost tenderly. I've been fencing off his attempts at "helping" me for years, so the surprise was genuine.

"Yes," I said, "I do. I have a merger to analyze, and I've tried Google, but I just can't understand..."

"Google?" Dad was incredulous. "No daughter of mine shall plagiarize from Google! I can see that I'm going to have to do the analysis myself!"

The line went dead. I went to the kitchen to make a pot of coffee for the long night ahead. I was a little annoyed at myself. Asking my father for help constituted a major loss in my ongoing battle for independence. Still, nothing compared to the relief I felt in knowing that someone was coming to my rescue.

When Dad burst in half an hour later, I was checking my Facebook for Brad-related updates.

"Are you still wasting your time on this nonsense?" he asked. "Don't you know this fad will pass?"

"How can you say Facebook is a fad?" I said, kissing him on the cheek.

"Not Facebook," he said. "Computers. Just remember that I predicted the downfall of this digital disease. The world will eventually have enough of it and will revert to the old paper days. When people used fountain pens everybody had such beautiful handwriting!" he said wistfully.

"Dad," I said as calmly as I could. "The world can't function without computers. If we didn't have computers, planes would run into each other mid-flight."

"Planes!" Dad snorted. "Now there's another fad! I've never been on a plane and what am I missing? Nothing!"

"Well, you've never seen the Eiffel Tower!" I said. "You also haven't seen the Great Wall of China, or the pyramids, or that really big ancient stadium in Rome...what's it called?"

"The Colosseum," Dad said. "Why would I care to see a ruined stadium half way across the world, when I can see the Bryant-Denny one in Tuscaloosa any time I want? Did you know that it has a seating capacity of one hundred and one thousand, eight hundred and twenty-one? The last time I was there, Crimson Tide were playing..."

"Research!" I yelled, fearful that another story would eat away at the precious little time we had left. "We need to get started on the research."

"Yes, of course," Dad said.

Like an idiot, I couldn't help but try to have the last word.

"We certainly couldn't do the research without computers," I said smugly.

"That's where you are wrong!" Dad's eyes sparkled. He ran back to his car and returned momentarily with two huge gym bags. They hit the floor with muffled thuds. "We are going to use books!"

"Books?" I looked on in disbelief, as he unzipped the bags and started handing me volume after volume of dusty tomes.

"Yes, books! The original chronicles of human knowledge!"

I looked at a particularly worn-out volume in my hands. It did look like one of the first books ever printed, with a hand-drawn picture of barefoot men hunched over pottery wheels on the cover. In a bubble over the illustration floated a picture of the author, a bespectacled man with pomaded hair parted straight down the middle.

"*The Principles of Scientific Management*" I read the title and opened the book. "Dad, it was published in 1911! They didn't even have science in 1911, let alone mergers!"

"Boloney!" Dad declared, still rummaging through his bags. "Some things never change, such as the basic principles of business. Do you know who first defined the economic model of supply and demand? You probably think it's James Denham Steuart, and you are partially right. He coined the term in his *Inquiry into the Principles of Political Oeconomy*, first published in 1767."

"Dad!"

"However," he said dramatically and raised a finger for further effect, "the power of supply and demand was described by early scholars many years before him, one of them a *Muslim*." Dad raised his eyebrows to emphasize how multicultural he was to credit a Muslim with the discovery of economic principles.

"I don't see how…"

"Still, the earliest references to supply and demand can be traced all the way back to the Bible…"

I had a bad dream that night. In it, Dad was talking non-stop as I drank cup after cup of coffee and typed madly, pausing only to drink more coffee. The dream was like a fuzzy old movie, and I could remember only the most vivid images. Dad dropping stacks of books on my desk already covered in books. Dad making a raw egg milkshake. Me trying to drink the milkshake. More books. More eggs. More coffee.

Thankfully, the angry shrieks of the alarm clock shocked me awake. I punched blindly, and my fist collided with something that thundered down. I unglued my eyes and looked around. I was still at my desk. A puddle of coffee from a knocked-over cup was slowly spreading and dripping down onto the pile of books on the floor.

I wobbled over the books, cups, and crumpled up bits of paper toward the bathroom. My head pounded as if I had just finished spring break in Florida or maybe twelve rounds against Mike Tyson. I hardly recognized myself in the mirror. Smudged mascara framed my eyes, there was an imprint of a book cover on my cheek, and a yellow crust covered my chin. I mindlessly splashed water onto my face, which made me feel marginally more human. It also woke me up to the fact that my attempt at the merger analysis failed spectacularly.

I heard plates banging in the kitchen. At least I could ask Tara for a joint before going to work - it would take the edge off the embarrassment of getting fired. I shuffled to the kitchen, thinking that if I drove through the projects on the way to work there was still a good chance that I could be in hospital, prison, or witness protection by nine am.

Instead of Tara it was Dad, looking fresh and energetic as usual. The man was sixty, and he could still run circles around me.

"Good morning!" he said brightly and turned back to whatever was sizzling on the stove.

"Hi, Dad." I climbed onto a bar stool. "Thank you," I added as he slid two eggs over easy and a strip of bacon on my plate. My stomach churned.

Eating breakfast was the last thing on my mind. First on my to-do list was another cathartic cry, but I wasn't going to do it in front of Dad. He already had too much of an upper hand.

"Thank you for trying to help," I said, surprised that I actually meant it. "It's too bad that we didn't have enough time…"

"Oh, I almost forgot," he said and pushed a large package towards me.

"What's this?" I asked, poking at the package. It was in an oversized manila envelope.

"The presentation," Dad said, piling up his own plate. "I ducked out to Kinko's this morning to make twenty bound copies. Twenty is enough, isn't it?"

In an instant, I was on the other side of the bar with my arms around his neck. "Thank you, thank you, thank you!" I muttered as sweet tears of relief rolled down my cheeks, washing off yesterday's mascara and the unidentifiable crud.

"Don't mention it," Dad said casually, although his voice was full of emotion. "Go get 'em, kid."

When I pulled into the parking lot of the Shizzle, Inc headquarters an hour later, I was a different woman. I was bright and full of life, my hair washed and straightened, and a new coat of makeup hiding the dark circles under my eyes. My skirt suit looked smart, and my high heels clicked merrily as I ran up the endless front steps of the building. At the top, I couldn't resist turning around, throwing up my arms and giving the world one heartfelt "Woo-hoo!"

A tired-looking woman, who was walking up behind me, bumped me aside. She paused to catch her breath and added, as she dragged herself through the entry doors, "I give you six months."

Yomama is fat.

I wanted to tell Mr. Hue about my unexpected success at analyzing the merger, but he was not there. Suzie informed me that he was over at "the big house". I didn't know if "the big house" meant his house, or some government office, or even the toilet, but nodded in understanding. The merger meeting was scheduled later in the afternoon, so I had nothing to do until then.

I went to my office and dialed Mom. That was the least I could do to pay back Dad for his efforts. She didn't answer for a long time, and I was about to hang up when I finally heard her weak "Hello?"

"Mom! Where are you?"

She moaned. "Sweetie, please don't yell like that. My head…"

"What's wrong?"

"Nothing, I just had a little too much to drink, and now I'm having a little sleep…I'll be fine…" she trailed off.

She didn't sound fine. "Where are you?" I demanded.

"What's your obsession with knowing my whereabouts?" she asked defensively. "I'm not a child, I can take care of myself." She paused. "Where am I?"

"What do you mean? Aren't you at Auntie Kelly's?"

She sounded a lot more awake as she whispered hurriedly into the phone, "It looks like I'm in a hotel. Oh my God, I think there's someone in the shower!" I heard muffled noises, then she hissed into the phone "I'll have to call you back!" and hung up.

I called back immediately, but she did not pick up. I tried a couple more times and then called Felicity.

"Good on her!" she said.

"She might be in danger!" I said. "Maybe I should call the police?"

"And tell them what? That your mother is sowing the wild oats she's had since the eighties?"

"You don't think...she had *sex* with somebody?" I asked in horror.

Felicity laughed a full, throaty laugh. "I certainly hope so! Think about it. She married so young, Dad could be the only man she's ever had sex with!"

"Eew, I don't want to think about Mom having sex with Dad! Or anybody, for that matter!" I said.

"Okay, what about you? Have you had sex with anyone since Brad dumped you? It's been months!"

"I can't!" I said. "What would I tell Brad when we get back together? I can't believe you even..."

"Wait, don't hang up," she interjected.

"I wasn't going to!" I lied.

"Really?" she sounded genuinely surprised. Hanging up on family members was my "thing", just like hers was arriving late to every gathering.

"No," I said. "I can talk about sex. I am not a child anymore!"

I waited for her to laugh, so I'd have a better excuse to hang up.

"No, you are not," she agreed without a note of sarcasm. "You grew up so fast. Sometimes I forget. You were still a kid when I got married. Sorry."

That was so sweet and unexpected coming from her. I remembered with a painful longing how much fun we used to have together until she got knocked up in the last year of high school and checked out of my life. I choked up a little.

"Anyway, don't worry about Mom," Felicity said, all business-like. I stifled a tear and the impulse to tell her "I love you."

"Okay," I managed instead. I heard a booming voice in the hallway. "I gotta go!" I whispered hurriedly into the phone. "I can hear my boss coming!"

"Okay," she said.

"Honestly, he is, I'm not trying to..." I started, but she'd already hung up on me. God, that was really annoying.

I frantically moved the mouse and randomly hit on the keyboard keys, pretending not to notice Mr. Hue in the doorway.

"Ready for the presentation?" I looked up from the still-blank monitor. Mr. Hue was wearing a sleek black suit and an understated platinum silk tie. The blue eyes studied me from under the perfectly arched eyebrows.

"Oh, hi!" I said, trying to sound relaxed and casual.

I was actually tense as hell. It was half due to nearly getting caught making personal calls, and half from the shock of how stunning he looked, at least for a middle-aged man. Yet another half of the reason had to be the stress of my new working life. Maybe, I reasoned, looking at his self-assured pose and strong jaw, I *could* just marry him. Damn Harden and other nay-sayers, the man was not just rich, he also had a commanding and strangely attractive presence. Marrying him would mean the end of the constant anxiety over the credit cards, aging Beetle, and looming eviction. Sure, I could earn the money myself, since he promoted me faster than a new Hollywood darling, but working was exhausting. I could happily settle for being a billionaire's wife. Every now and then I could even do some charity work, maybe throw a party or take pictures with orphans, that kind of thing.

"Ms. Maxwell?" Mr. Hue interrupted my thoughts. "The presentation?"

"Oh yeah, of course, "I said and waved a hand dismissively. "Ready-Freddy. Sure thing. No probs. Got it covered."

"That's what I like to hear," Mr. Hue said and smiled. I beamed back.

"As you have no doubt heard, Eleanor chose to resign yesterday," he continued. "Unfortunately, it was before she was able to find a suitable evening dress for you."

I rolled my eyes and shook my head in my best "you just can't find good help these days" expression.

He shook his head in exactly the same way. We had such perfect rapport. That's what long-lasting marriages are built on, rapport and understanding, not youthful looks and passionate lust. Those fade.

He reached his hand back. A bodyguard materialized behind him and placed something in his palm. Without checking, Mr. Hue offered me the object, which looked like a black credit card.

"Use the rest of the morning to choose the dress yourself," he said.

I got up, walked around the desk and took the card gingerly by the corner. It was indeed a credit card, an American Express, although I'd never seen a black one before.

Mr. Hue kept a firm hold on the card. "I would have asked Suzie, but I can't trust her sense of style. It's very important that the dress matches the occasion," he said gravely, "so stick with tried and true, like Gucci or Versace."

I nodded and pulled on the card. "Maybe Armani or Givenchy," he continued without letting go, "but don't take risks with the new names, like Stella McCartney."

I nodded again and pulled a little harder. "And stay away from Dolce & Gabbana," he added. "We don't want to be linked to tax evasion or all that blackamoor business. There is no place for racism at Shizzle, Inc!"

With that, he finally let go of the piece of plastic. My hand jerked hard, and I tried to cover it up by pretending to examine the card closely. It looked very simple, without any diamonds or anything.

"Ahm...does it have a credit limit?"

"No, there is no limit," Mr. Hue said. "Within a limit, of course!" he added and left, laughing.

I laughed too, mainly to cover my embarrassment. It worried me that I still did not understand what he meant. Was there a limit or not? How much was a Gucci dress, anyway?

On the way out I remembered Mom and redialed her number.

"Hi, sweetie!" she sang into the phone.

"Mom, where are you?" I said and thought that I really should stop being obsessed with her whereabouts. Or maybe slip a GPS tracker into her purse instead. I could probably find one on the Internet. *That* would have been a good comeback to Dad's anti-computer rant the night before.

"I'm in a taxi!" she said excitedly. My parents never took taxis because Mom was always willing to chauffeur drunk Dad back home from their rare evenings out. Lately, of course, she was always on Vicodin or Percocet, but, unfortunately, the slogan only said "don't *drink* and drive."

"That's great," I said, relieved. "Can you meet me for a coffee be-

128

fore going home? I need to talk to you."

"Coffee?" Mom said, delighted. "Just you and me?"

"Yes, in the mall food court. I'll meet you at the Starbucks."

"Oh my God!" Mom squealed with joy. "This is so exciting! Catching up over a coffee! It's like we're in *Sex and the City*! You're the clever Carrie, and I'm the mature and sexually confident Samantha!"

"You are not Samantha! We are not in *Sex and the City*!" I yelled, although I couldn't help but be pleased about being compared to Carrie Bradshaw. "Please, don't do anything else rash, just meet me at the Starbucks in fifteen minutes!"

When I finally got to the Starbucks half an hour later, I could not see her at first. An irrational fear crept over me. It painted a picture of my middle-aged mother running off again, this time with the taxi driver, or maybe an underage Starbucks barista. Then I saw her, or rather I saw an unfamiliar woman waving madly at me.

I sat down across from her. "What did you do? I mean, to your hair?"

Mom's usual mousy-brown ponytail had transformed itself into a fashionable chin-length bob, shimmering with every shade of blond.

"Oh, this," she giggled and smoothed a lock behind her ear. "I just wanted a change, I guess. What do you think?" she added anxiously.

She was also wearing mascara and lipstick, and a ridiculously low-cut gold sequined dress.

"You look…good," I said. It was only half-true. She actually looked hot for a middle-aged woman. It made me uneasy. Middle-aged mothers are not supposed to look hot. They are supposed to stay home with their husbands and bake or clean, or whatever.

"Thanks, sweetie!" She beamed. "I feel great!"

"Yeah? What about Dad?"

Her face darkened, and she busied herself with the straw of her Frappuccino.

"How is he doing?" she asked finally.

"As good as can be expected under the circumstances," I shrugged. "I think he is living off frozen leftovers and canned goods. He keeps asking when you are coming back. By my estimates, he probably has another four days of supplies left."

"That's just like him!" Mom cried out. "That's all I ever was in that marriage, a cook, a maid and a nanny for his children. Why is he so shocked that I finally left? I could do those jobs elsewhere and at least get paid for them! He never appreciated anything I did, just took it for granted that I would always be there to clean up his oopsies."

I could certainly sympathize with that. "Well, then, why now?" I asked. "Was it because of..." I almost said "Mr. Hue".

"It was because of many things!" she said, and her chin trembled. "Ever since your father retired last year, he practically hasn't left the house, and he constantly demands that I 'spend time' with him." She made sarcastic quotation marks with her fingers. "It's just that 'spending time' means watching the news for hours on end and then listening to his commentary on current events. We never do anything I want to do!"

I could sympathize with that, too. When I was little, I knew all political figures, past and present, by name. That was about the only way I could have a conversation with Dad.

"And then there was my birthday!" Mom cried. "I turned fifty, and I was feeling...emotional. I expected something romantic from him. I'm not sure what. It certainly wasn't a KitchenAid! He didn't even give me any flowers or anything!"

"But...but I thought you wanted a KitchenAid?" I asked, feeling a cold wave wash over me. I myself gave her a bathrobe and slippers. And at the birthday party Felicity and I got into a screaming fight with Dad over the correct way of cutting a cake. Was I partly responsible for my parents' split?

"Of course I did," she carefully dabbed at her eyes with a napkin. "Just not as a birthday gift. He couldn't even manage a few words on a card! I bet he forgot that it's our silver wedding anniversary next Monday. If not, he was probably planning to give me a lawn mower!" She laughed bitterly.

I laughed along, trying to cover up the panic of completely forgetting about their wedding anniversary.

"I'm sure he has something special planned," I said lightly, though I didn't really believe it.

"No wonder I've been feeling so depressed lately," she said. "I've even been…taking some pills to make me feel better."

I feigned surprise.

"Don't worry, I don't need them anymore," Mom said and sucked on the straw again. "These Frappuccinos are amazing! Do you want one?"

"No, sorry, I actually have to go. I have too much to do," I said. It was true, for once.

"Okay," she said, disappointed. Then she brightened up again. "Maybe we can do one of those brunch things next time, with Felicity?"

"I'm sure she'd love that," I said. Then I imagined the three of us together in the city, Felicity giving Mom tips on dating and Mom sharing the intimate details of her latest conquests.

"Please take it slow for a little while," I said and squeezed her hand. "You never know, this separation may just remind Dad how much he loves and appreciates you. He will probably try really hard to win you back!"

She smiled coyly. "He should hurry up then. With this new hair-do, I won't stay single for very long!"

I dialed Dad as soon as I was out of Starbucks.

"When is she coming back?" he barked into the phone.

"Hi, Dad," I said.

"Did you talk to her?"

"Yes, I just did. Say, are you aware that your wedding anniversary is coming up on Monday?"

I could tell by the long pause that no, he was not.

"Is this what it's all about?" he finally said. "The anniversary?"

"No, Dad," I said in the same patient voice I used to explain to Tommy and Jimmy that kicking people is not nice. "It's not all about the anniversary. It's all about the fact that you've been taking her for granted, and the romance is gone from your marriage."

"How can she say that?" Dad was incredulous. "I just cleaned the gutters! And for her birthday I got her a KitchenAid! Do you know how much one of those damn things costs, even on eBay?"

"Well, that's the thing, Dad. A KitchenAid is not romantic, it's a kitchen *tool*."

"I think tools *are* romantic!" Dad countered. "I hope she got me a new drill for the anniversary!"

"If you keep thinking like that, you'll get brand-new divorce papers instead!"

Unfortunately, that had a little more effect than I expected. The Iron Man crumpled on the other end of the line.

"She can't...," he sobbed. "She can't just..."

"Listen to me," I said as confidently as I could. "It's not over yet." I thought back to Mom's hair, lipstick, and the low-cut dress, and winced.

"It's not?" he said in an almost child-like voice and sniffed. It broke my heart.

"Not yet," I continued. "But you have to act quickly. You have to woo her, sweep her off her feet, charm her like you did when you first met. Tell her how you feel."

He thought for a second. "When we first met, I told her that I will marry her one day. But we are already married, so what do I tell her now?"

"Tell her that you love her!"

"She already knows that," Dad dismissed me.

It dawned on me that my father, who could recite the entire human history complete with dates and names, had no idea what to say to a woman. It also dawned that there was no time to coach him, so it was time to start throwing money at the problem.

"Okay," I said. "Meet me at the mall food court, under the clock, in half an hour. Bring your checkbook."

He tried to protest, but I hung up. If he truly wanted to save his marriage, he would come. Plus, I needed time to think of a cunning plan.

By the time he showed up, flushed and cross, I had a plan ready.

"What's this all about?" he demanded.

"What do women want most of all?" I retorted as we walked down the wide mall promenade.

That took him by surprise. "I don't know," he finally admitted. "I thought they wanted security, house, and children, but I guess I was wrong!"

He directed the last bit at a young mother with two little kids in a double stroller. Poor thing hovered protectively over her progeny and made a sharp turn to avoid us.

"They want to feel *special*," I said patiently. "Every woman wants to feel like she's the one and only. She wants her man to go to the end of the Earth for her."

"I would go to the end of the Earth for your mother!" Dad puffed out his chest. "You know once, just after we got married, she had to go to Phoenix on some kind of a training course. No, wait, it was Albuquerque. Anyway, it was the pits…"

"That's great!" I said brightly and pulled him into a travel agency.

Dad was still in the middle of the story of how he surprised Mom by showing up unannounced and "having a chat" with her lecturer, so he offered little resistance until I sat him down in front of a desk equipped with a travel agent.

"What are we doing here?" he demanded.

"How y'all doin'?" asked the agent, a woman in her late fifties, with a halo of teased henna hair and bright red nails.

"We need some help booking a honeymoon trip," I said to them both.

"Y'all married?" the agent asked with obvious disgust.

"Are you getting married?" Dad asked. "I hope not to that buffoon Brad!"

"Brad is not a buffoon! And we are not married, this is my Dad, and it will be my parents' second honeymoon," I explained to the agent.

"Thank God," she said and started clicking her shiny nails on the keyboard. I was about to tell her that I was, in fact, considering marrying someone almost my Dad's age and that he was so cool she would nearly die if she only knew who he was, but thought better of it. There would be no discounts for the future Mrs. Hue.

"What honeymoon?" Dad asked. "We didn't even have the first one, so I don't see why…"

"Do you want to get Mom back?"

"Yes," he said, "but don't you think a honeymoon is a bit much? I thought that maybe I can get her a really big bunch of flowers, and maybe one of those damn Hallmark cards, even though you know how I feel about the exploitation of the public by the marketing..."

"Desperate times call for desperate measures," I interrupted him, "and I think the times are pretty desperate for your marriage, don't you agree? I think you are way past grocery store roses."

Dad sulked silently.

"Y'all getting divorced, huh?" the agent butted in. "I'm divorced too. Name's Sharon. Pleasure to meet you." She extended her hand across the desk to Dad.

"My parents are getting back together!" I snapped. Dad didn't react, seemingly preoccupied with his misery.

"Fine," Sharon said and took her hand back. "In that case I know just what you need. We have a special on honeymoon packages in Kauai."

"Ka-what?" Dad came out of his stupor. "I'm not going to some third-world country full of terrorists!"

"It's in Hawaii," Sharon said. I was quietly impressed with her unflappable manner. "Y'all don't even need visas. It's goorgeous!" she drooled and turned the monitor to show us the photos.

It really was "goorgeous". I made a mental note to book my own honeymoon there one day. The most amazing photo was of the pool - the elegant lounges seemed to be floating on top of the azure water, which disappeared into the ocean, which itself blended into the blue sky.

"Infinity pool," Sharon said in response to our astonishment. "Pretty sweet, huh?"

"Yes," I managed to pull myself together and speak. "That's exactly what we need. A week there, for two people, flying out on Monday."

"Sure thing, hon!" Sharon started clickety-clacking away.

"How much is *that* going to cost?" Dad said in a pained whisper.

"Just seven thousand, nine hundred and ninety-nine dollars!" Sharon said brightly. Dad wheezed and grabbed at his left chest.

"That includes airfare, accommodation and breakfast for two," Sharon said as if it made things any better.

Dad continued groping at his chest and gasping for air.

"Okay, suit yourselves," Sharon said, disappointed. "We do have a motel on the main island..."

"No!" I interjected. "They need this one!"

"Let the lady speak," Dad said. "Let's see what other options are available..."

"Don't you understand?" I said, feeling like Joan of Arc calling soldiers into battle. "There are no options! Either you win her back now, or forever regret being a tight-ass!"

"What if she doesn't even want to come to Hawaii?" Dad whined and pouted like a child. That was even more annoying than his usual self-assured and overbearing manner. I made a mental note to tell Felicity all about it.

"I'll come!" Sharon said. I shot her a look. She grimaced and busied herself with the keyboard.

I took Dad's hand. "At least you'll know that you've tried everything possible," I said gently. "At least you've tried."

He nodded. "I don't have that much in my checking account," he said finally.

"How much do you have?"

"I can't take a check for this, y'all," Sharon said.

Dad consulted his checkbook register. "Seven hundred and change," he said gloomily.

"I'm gonna need a credit card, y'all," Sharon persisted.

"What about your savings?" I asked.

"It will take a few days..." Dad started, and then Sharon finally lost it.

"Y'all are wasting my time," she threw her hands into the air and waved them like she no longer cared about the sale. "Coming here and talking about honeymoons in Hawaii like y'all got mad money, but I bet y'all never even seen more than fifty..."

I stuck Mr. Hue's black American Express in her face.

"What's this?" she asked.

"A corporate American Express," I said smugly. "Bet you've never seen one of these before?"

"Plenty of times," she said arrogantly, but her demeanor changed. She took the card and looked it over, even holding it against the light, as if it was a counterfeit bill.

"I can't let you pay for it!" Dad protested.

"You can pay me back," I said calmly, although my hands started shaking. Desperate times, I kept thinking, desperate times. Plus, Mr. Hue may not even notice anything if I paid it all back before the next statement. "Oops," I would say. "It looked just like my own black American Express!" How we would laugh at that...

I continued breathing in and out until the sale was finalized. Dad seemed to be as overwhelmed as I was. We said awkward goodbyes outside the agency and he hobbled off towards the parking lot with the travel vouchers. I checked my watch. I had only an hour left to nail the perfect dress, but lucky for me, the mall had a Gucci store. *I don't have enough time to shop elsewhere*, I thought, *so Gucci would have to do.*

*

I walked up to the marble and glass shopfront bathed in strategically positioned spotlights. In its display windows, the emaciated faceless mannequins contorted in physically impossible poses. I took a deep breath and walked in.

The store seemed deserted. It was a large room, with a plush white carpet floor and metallic gold walls. In the center were a coffee table, chairs, and even a lounge. It could be mistaken for a luxury apartment, if not for the long shimmery dresses hanging from nearly invisible cables along the walls. I remembered the scene from *Pretty Woman*, the one where the prostitute got turned away from a fancy shop by nasty shop attendants. I wasn't a prostitute, but I was poor, and I was definitely out of my depth.

I lost my cool, turned, and would have bolted, if not for a shop attendant who materialized quietly behind me. She looked like a Victoria's Secret angel - tall and slim, tastefully draped in a bit of silk and jewels.

"May I help you?" Angel asked in a musical voice.

I was so ready for her to kick me out, the question took me by surprise.

"Ahm...yes, actually," I said. "I need an evening dress."

"Certainly, Madame," she said. "You've come to the right place. We have dresses suitable for any occasion."

Nobody had ever called me "Madame" before. I felt a bit more confident.

"It's quite a conservative affair," I remembered Mr. Hue's words. "A Gala."

Angel smiled pleasantly. "Yes, of course. I can help you find just the right gown."

I sighed with relief. It was good to have a professional on the job.

"Please, have a seat," she gestured to the chairs. "May I offer you a Perrier?"

"No, thank you," I said. "I'm pretty sure it has to be a dress."

"Very well." Angel floated to the nearest wall. The plush carpet muffled her footsteps, which explained how she was able to sneak up on me like a ninja.

She picked a dress, seemingly from thin air. It was peachy-gold, long and drapey. "This would look stunning on you," she murmured. "Would you like to try it on?"

It looks pretty stunning on the hanger, I thought and stifled the impulse of saying "I'll take it!". I was pressed for time, but the thought of trying on a Gucci dress was too exciting. Once behind the heavy velvet curtain, I tore off my bargain suit and slipped into the silky luxury. The dress was very long, and I had to tiptoe outside to keep from tripping on the hem.

"You look beautiful!" Angel purred.

I studied myself in the mirror. I turned sideways, then again to the front. Then to the other side.

"Don't you love it?" she asked.

"Is it supposed to look like this?" I said.

The dress was shimmery and luxurious to the touch. It was everything I expected from Gucci, except it looked like...well, like a robe.

"It looks stunning on you!" Angel said. "Let me just adjust the sash...here!" She turned to the mirror with a triumphant smile. The dress, however, looked the same.

I stared at the mirror.

"This is the very latest fashion," Angel said. "The return of the kimono. Everyone in Paris will be wearing kimonos this season."

"Ahm, okay," I said. "It's beautiful, of course, but maybe I can look at something else? You know, just to compare to this...kimono?"

"Certainly," Angel said in a slightly frostier tone. She picked off a black dress from a rack. "This is a more conservative piece, but still very beautiful."

The second choice was marginally better. I've always been a bit curvy, but the thin, unforgiving fabric clung to me in all the wrong places. At least it was shaped a bit more like a dress. It had a deep front slit; I tried cocking my hip and showing a bit of a leg.

"Very sexy, isn't it?" Angel gushed. "Yet conservative, very conservative!" she added quickly.

"Yeah, okay," I said. It certainly looked expensive, and Mr. Hue would be happy that it was Gucci. Plus, I was running out of time. "I'll take it." I sighed.

"Marvelous!"

I put my suit back on, feeling slightly depressed. They say money can't buy happiness, but I was sure it could buy stunning dresses. I just wasn't sure where to find them.

"That'll be just two thousand and five hundred dollars," Angel sang and began fiddling with effervescent layers of delicate tissue paper. "How would you like to pay for this beautiful dress?"

I handed her the American Express. She smiled appreciatively and swiped it. It looked like black American Express cards visited this place regularly.

"There seems to be a tiny problem," Angel said, knitting her satiny-smooth brow. "The card has been declined. Do you have another card you may want to use?"

"What?" I felt a cold chill.

"Looks like maybe you are over the limit."

"Shit!" I slapped a hand on my forehead. "I just spent almost eight grand on it! Idiot!"

"Do you know how much credit you have left?"

"No," I said. "I thought it didn't have a limit."

We stared at each other for a moment.

"Well," she said. "Maybe we can try a cheaper dress?"

"You are an angel!" I said, instantly forgiving her previous hoity-toity attitude. "Let's try a cheaper dress!"

Twenty minutes later, sweaty and exhausted, we were out of options.

"Are you sure you don't have anything cheaper?" I asked again in desperation.

"Not a fucking thing," Angel said. "Unless you're willing to wear underwear to the Gala."

"As long as it's Gucci!" I laughed hysterically.

"Wait," she said. "I have an idea." She disappeared into the storeroom and returned with a wisp of silky black fabric.

"It's a slip," she said, "but with the right accessories..."

*

I made it back to the office just in time. The Yomama delegation was already waiting in the lobby. The businessmen looked nearly identical with their black suits and matching haircuts. At first glance, the only distinguishable feature was the degree of plumpness. I assumed that the chubbiest members of the group had to be the most senior.

Suzie rushed towards me. "Mr. Hue is stuck in traffic," she whispered. "He asked that you make some small talk until he gets here."

"No problem," I said breezily, inwardly terrified at the prospect of being alone with the delegation. They were just so...Japanese. I tried to smooth down my hair and skirt and approached the group with exaggerated confidence.

"Hi," I said and stuck my hand out to the most distinguished-looking representative. "I'm Isabella Maxwell, nice to meet you."

My sudden appearance caused a pronounced confusion among the men. They consulted with each other in Japanese, which sounded as if they were all trying to clear their throats at once. After a moment of this exchange, the apparent head honcho finally shook my hand. His handshake was tentative and limp, and would have caused my Dad to immediately label him a wuss.

"Herro," the old guy said. "How you do."

I almost blurted "What?" before understanding what he meant. I smiled broadly to cover up my near slip-up and to put the lovely old man at ease. He was adorably short, and I towered over him in my stilettos. I could barely resist the urge to pet him on the shoulder.

"How do you do?" I said instead.

We stood there for a bit, looking at each other while I tried to come up with what to say next.

The head honcho said something to his companion, who produced a beautiful small silver box from his business case. He opened the box and held it out to the old guy, who in turn took out a card and offered it to me with a funny stiff bow. He held out the card with both hands, and I noticed his well-manicured nails. Dad would definitely disapprove of that, too.

I took the card. The head honcho bowed again, and I did a little curtsy. The men again mumbled amongst themselves. Others also took out their cards and offered them to me, one by one. They all bowed to me, and I curtsied back, which made them grunt with what I hoped was approval.

Just when it seemed that I was getting on top of the situation, they stopped bowing and stared at me in expectation.

"Oh," I said, suddenly understanding. "I'm new here, so I don't have a business card yet!"

That produced more mumbling and confusion.

"That's okay!" I said brightly. "I can give you my phone number for now."

I scribbled my name and number on the back of one of the cards and offered it back to the head honcho. He recoiled from the card as if it was a venomous snake.

"Okay, maybe not," I said and stuffed the cards into my pocket. The delegation continued to stare at me.

"Let's go into the boardroom, shall we?" I made a grand gesture with my hand.

The head honcho nodded, and I led the way. I took a seat near the head of the table, closest to the presentation screen. There was more confusion as the delegation members chose their seats. That gave me a bit more time to think.

"So," I said. "Is this your first time visiting the US?"

The head honcho looked at me for a moment.

"We have many location in USA," he said sharply. "Many, many location. We make much business in USA."

"Great," I said brightly. "That's just great!"

Everyone was silent for a bit. My throat was painfully dry. The only drinks available were Shizzle Colas nestled in large bowls of ice. I opened one and sipped it slowly, desperately trying to think of something to say, but the only thing coming to mind was that the cola truly was an acquired taste.

The men had another brief consultation amongst themselves and the younger minion reached into his business case again, this time producing a beautifully wrapped small package. He offered it to the head honcho, who in turn ceremoniously offered it to me.

"Wow," I said. "Thank you so much!"

I tore open the pretty wrapping paper. Inside was a small lacquered box with a silver pen.

"Wow!" I said. "It's a pen!"

I smiled in appreciation while trying to think of what to do next. I opened my folio, took out the plastic Bic pen and offered it to the head honcho with much ceremony and bowing.

"American pen!" I exclaimed, pointing at the Bic. "A souvenir!"

"Arigato," the head honcho said politely and passed the Bic to his colleagues, who all took turns admiring it and nodding.

I was feeling a lot better and was about to ask them how come the company was called Yomama, and maybe make a joke about how in the US "yo mama" is always fat, when Mr. Hue finally arrived. He came in flanked by a couple of worried-looking execs and the usual bodyguards. One of the execs was Old Man, the one who wanted so desperately to talk to Mr. Hue about the share prices. I waved at him, but he didn't respond.

Mr. Hue apologized for being late, shook hands with everyone and slapped the head honcho on the back. I instantly felt better now that someone with international business experience was here to help.

The Japanese started another bout of rapid stiff bows and offers of business cards and gifts, but Mr. Hue waved them away.

"I dislike formalities," he said passionately, sitting down and putting his feet on the table. "They gum things up. Let's just get down to business."

I thought the head honcho was going to have a heart attack right then, by the way his face and neck lit up with fiery color, but he just sat back down.

After some small talk about the weather and the current state of the economy, Mr. Hue handed the presentation over to me as his "right hand" and someone who "cracks the whip around here". One of his execs, an aging woman, looked at me with open contempt. I decided that I didn't like her either.

I was almost bursting with pride and excitement as I opened my presentation folder.

"We are here today to reach an agreement on the proposed merger of Shizzle Cola and Yomama Kabushiki Gaisha," I said. "As you all know, the offer includes the exclusive distribution rights for Shizzle Cola throughout Japan."

Everyone was listening to me intently. It was pretty amazing, to have a room full of executives hanging on my every word, as if I really was someone who could crack a whip.

"I've read your proposal with great interest," I read from my printout. "The history of mergers and acquisition of American companies by Japanese investors and counterparts is truly intriguing..."

"Indeed," Mr. Hue interrupted. "I am truly intrigued by this merger proposal. I do have a gut feeling about it!" He waved for me to continue.

"You are probably not old enough," I continued reading, "to remember the 1980s Japanese buying spree of American assets. The Japanese acquisitions of American real estate included the Rockefeller Centre in New York, major companies such as Firestone Tires, and media and entertainment icons, such as Columbia Pictures."

The Japanese mumbled to each other, and the head honcho looked unsettled. The execs shifted uncomfortably in their seats and exchanged furtive glances, but remained silent.

"I remember when Sony bought Columbia Pictures!" Mr. Hue exclaimed. "It was in all the papers, and I was already the CEO of Shizzle, Inc. I guess I'm giving away my age! How old do you think I am?" he asked the delegation. When nobody volunteered, he said, "That's right! A lot older than I act!" and waved for me to continue.

"What circumstances allowed such an orgy?" I looked up dramatically. "America was weak, and an up-and-coming financial enemy swooped in like a kamikaze."

Several of the delegation members were scratching their heads. Funny, I didn't actually remember writing anything about kamikazes. It sounded like a cool name for a band.

"Today, over thirty years later, we find ourselves in a similar situation. We have been hit by the GFC - some may go so far as to say we have started the GFC - and what are we witnessing? Yet another spending binge by the Japanese. A small-minded person, a fool so to speak, may even see this renewed trend as a positive one, sort of a financial boost to the struggling American economy."

That particular statement had a strong Dad flavor to it. I was suddenly worried, not only because I no longer had any idea of what I was reading, but also because all color had drained from the head honcho's face. Several other members of the delegation were hissing and fidgeting in their seats. Mr. Hue's execs engaged in a conversation of raised eyebrows and silently mouthed words.

Desperate, I tried to think of something more appropriate to say, but nothing came to mind. I took a big gulp of my Shizzle Cola to buy another few moments to think. It indeed had too much caffeine. My mind was racing. I couldn't hold onto a single thought for more than a second. In any case, none of those thoughts were helpful - they were mostly about invading Japanese. I willed my mind away from an army made up of identical businessmen and back to what was in front of me.

"The Japanese government is all but pushing their venture capitalists to purchase foreign assets," I read on autopilot. "The Japanese businesses seek to capitalize on mergers and acquisitions to grow their market share by acquiring well-established brands. It's not surprising, since American brands have a proven reputation for being the best and biggest around the world. And it's not just Japanese - other assorted Asians are doing the same, with the Industrial and Commercial Bank of China buying an 80% stake in an American bank last…"

"I just had an idea!" Mr. Hue exclaimed suddenly. "A bank with nude tellers and free massages for the waiting customers. The Shizzle

Bank! Wait till Alan hears about this!" He began to thumb away on his phone.

I took that as my cue to continue. "If not stopped, this unrelenting Asian invasion will create a virtual economic Pearl Harbor, until the day we will wake up to find that the whole country is speaking Japanese," I said before realizing what it actually meant. My armpits were swimming with fear, and I wanted to punch myself in the ovaries for letting Dad get me into this.

I looked at the delegation. They were talking louder now and obviously upset. Mr. Hue did not seem to notice, still typing away under the edge of the table. The woman exec smirked at me while Old Man just looked dejectedly at his hands.

"And so now the Japanese want to take over the Shizzle brand. All we can do is take solace in another history lesson, in which we learn that most of the 1980s acquisitions turned out to be pathetic losers. Rockefeller Centre was forced to file for bankruptcy by its Tokyo owner on May 11, 1995. Firestone Tires has recalled millions of defective tires, and we can thank Columbia Pictures for such gems as *Blankman, Superbabies,* and *Gigli.*

"That was a great film," Mr. Hue said. I wasn't sure which one he meant, but it no longer mattered, as suddenly the Japanese all stood up at once.

"Sank you for presentation," the head honcho said. "You count-aoffa under consideration!"

He looked mad as hell, but took several bows before leaving, followed closely by his equally polite minions.

Mr. Hue got up and looked keen on doing more handshaking and backslapping, but the delegation cleared out faster than the after-Christmas sales. He turned to me instead.

"Great work!" he said. "I've never seen them this worried. I'm sure they will be back with a much better offer! Am I right?" he asked Old Man.

"I think it's us who should be worried," Old Man started to say, but the woman exec interrupted him.

"I don't think they will be back," she said.

"What makes you think so?" Mr. Hue asked.

"Well," the woman said sarcastically, "for starters, I'm not sure how much they appreciated the references to Pearl Harbor."

Mr. Hue turned to me for an answer, and I had to think quickly.

"Yes, they did," I said. "They were very impressed with my knowledge of history."

"Really?" she grimaced. It made the small wrinkles around her bright red mouth that much more apparent.

"Yes, really," I said. "I could tell!"

"That's true," said Mr. Hue. "Ms. Maxwell speaks Japanese."

I almost said that I didn't, before remembering that I'd put it on my résumé. I never thought that it would come up. I mean, what were my chances of meeting real Japanese people?

"You do?" the woman exec challenged. "Then say something in Japanese." She was unbearable.

"Do you speak Japanese?" I asked.

"No," she admitted.

"Okay then. Hakuraki karuto rigato," I said confidently, trying to imitate the delegation's throaty grunts. "That means 'a remarkable young lady.'"

"A remarkable young lady indeed," Mr. Hue said. "I hope they don't think they can steal you away from Shizzle!"

The woman exec pursed her lips but didn't say anything else. She shook hands with Mr. Hue, mentioned something about settling and executing, and left with the dejected Old Man in tow.

"What was that thing you mentioned about Yomama taking over the Shizzle brand?" Mr. Hue asked as we walked towards his office.

I tried, but could not recall saying anything about the brand take-over. The relief of the torture being over practically wiped my mind clean.

"Ah," I said and waved my hand dismissively. "That was just a shock-and-awe ploy to shake them up. I wanted to show them that we were onto whatever they might have masterminded."

"Great tactic," Mr. Hue approved. "I am myself a big fan of shock-and-awe ploys. I'll share an important tip with you - any ploy is instantly better if performed in the nude."

"What?" I asked, shocked.

"Naked. Show them that you've got the balls to go all the way. Well, in your case it may be the boobs. Or the ass. It doesn't matter, as long as it gets them confused and embarrassed. The key is never to be embarrassed yourself."

I stared at him in disbelief, as he continued. "I've told you that you seem like a Shizzle type. I have a strong gut feeling that you may be on your way to becoming the Vice President of Shizzle, Inc sometime very soon."

I nodded, worried about where he was going with that.

"But," he paused and looked straight into my eyes. "I need to know that I can count on you being there for the company, nude when the situation calls for it. It may be riding a tandem bike across the US to raise money for Shizzle Kids or parachuting into a new venture launch. I don't know. But I do know that your heart and your unmentionables must be in it. Are they?"

I had to think about it for a moment. I didn't expect the request, and I wasn't sure it was legal, but Mr. Hue spoke so passionately and sincerely. Anyway, it had to be okay to get naked for the kids - celebrities did it for the animals all the time.

"Will I have to...sleep with anyone?" I asked.

"God, no!" Mr. Hue said, appalled. "What kind of a joint do you think I'm running here?"

"Then I'm in!" I said, and we shook hands. I felt great, and not just because of the Vice President job promise. It meant that my obvious bomb of a presentation did not matter or, inadvertently, was just the right thing to do at Shizzle, Inc.

We walked back to his office, and he sat in his throne chair. I sat in one of the other chairs, but without the usual fidgeting. Mr. Hue held out a cigar box, and I took one, although I didn't know how to hold it, let alone smoke it. I clenched it between my teeth like Schwarzenegger and listened intently as Mr. Hue continued to divulge his plans for my bright future.

"After this," he said, circumcising his cigar with a tiny guillotine, "I might need your help with Shizzle Time, our time-machine project."

"But...I don't know anything about time machines!" I said, reaching for the guillotine thingy.

"It doesn't matter," he said. "You can learn the skills. It's the attitude that's hardest to change, and you've got one of the best attitudes I've ever seen!"

As usual, he made it hard to argue. I wondered if one day I might, in fact, become Vice President of Shizzle, Inc.

"They desperately need someone like you at Shizzle Time," he said. "So far, they have not come up with anything even remotely resembling a working prototype. They desperately need an infusion of Shizzle spirit!"

"Isn't time travel impossible?" I asked, trying to light my cigar.

"Nonsense," Mr. Hue said and took a puff. "Don't let anyone tell you something is impossible. I will share another business tip with you, Ms. Maxwell. The vast majority of people are stupid. Once you understand and accept this fact, innovation just happens naturally."

I nodded, secretly relieved that he considered the majority of others to be less intelligent than me. Dad often talked about people being idiots, but I never paid him the same rapt attention.

"However," he continued, "some people are very smart. You should learn from those people, because you could take their ideas and turn them into profit. For example, I got my idea of commercial time travel from this one scientist, Einstein something or other. He claimed that time is relative to how fast you move. It doesn't take a genius to figure out that the faster you go, the slower you'll age."

He got animated, the way Dad does when he recites obscure historic facts.

"Imagine if you could invest a measly million dollars today in a safe and secure bank, say Shizzle Bank, and then take a ride into the future aboard a superfast Shizzle Time craft. Sure, when you arrive, everyone you know will be dead, but in less than fifty years your bank account would have grown to something like fifteen million dollars. In a hundred years, it could be close to a quarter of a billion! You could be almost as rich as me. Can you imagine?"

I couldn't. For starters, I couldn't imagine scraping together a measly million-dollar initial investment. Plus, time travel didn't seem possible, no matter how many millions you threw at research and development.

"How much would you charge for a ticket to the future?" I asked, giving up on the cigar.

"That's the best part!" Mr. Hue beamed. "We can charge whatever we want. I mean, is there another time-travel agency offering better rates?"

I looked at him expectantly, and he said, "No! There isn't!"

"Oh," I said. "I see!"

"It's only natural to be reluctant when you are first faced with something as bold as commercial time travel," Mr. Hue said. "You have no idea how long it took me to convince my board of directors to invest in Shizzle Time. But," he added proudly, "I can be quite persuasive in getting people to accept my point of view."

The "Eye of the Tiger" rang in his pocket. He reached in and produced a black, shiny ball covered in a shimmering pattern.

"Shizzle Ping," Mr. Hue said with pride. "Shizzle's answer to iPhone. It's critically acclaimed in Bangladesh."

He held the ball to his ear and listened, then shoved it hastily back into his pocket.

"Damn it!" he exclaimed. "Ever since Eleanor left, I just can't keep up with my appointments. I am late for the aperitifs with Lady Gaga!"

"Wow!" I said and wondered if I could tag along. I would kill to have aperitifs with Lady Gaga, no matter what that meant.

"Indeed," Mr. Hue said. "I must go, but I will be back in time to pick you up for the Gala. Be ready at seven and looking sharp!"

I nodded, disappointed, and he disappeared along with the bodyguards.

I dragged myself to the lunchroom to make a cup of coffee. I was so tired that even the drive home seemed impossible, let alone getting ready and looking sharp. A group of people crowded together around the TV, one of them baby-faced John.

"Hi, John," I said, considering if I should ask him for a lift home.

John turned around, blushed, and elbowed the man next to him.

"What are you guys watching?" I asked.

Everyone turned, but instead of answering, they just parted in silence. I could see the TV screen and an attractive news anchorwoman with sleek blond hair and ample cheekbones.

"It has been described as a 'milestone merger' and 'the deal of deals,'" she said. "However, not everyone was as optimistic about this 'marriage made in cola heaven.' One of these nay-sayers, Chief Executive Mark Rosensomething, joins us now from his New York office. Thanks for being with us, Mr. Rosensomething." The screen split in two, revealing a gloomy guy with long dark hair.

"Great to be here, Samantha," he muffled. He looked kind of like Severus Snape, a little sexy in an odd way. "My name is actually pronounced..."

"You've been critical of this merger from the beginning, Mr. Rosensomething. What exactly was your problem?" the anchorwoman interrupted him.

"I didn't have a problem with the merger idea per se," Snape said. "It's just that there was so much hype about it that nobody noticed the panic and greed on which it was based. The merger was fundamentally a 'misery loves company' attempt at throwing money at the problem."

"Wow," the anchorwoman said. "That's not very nice of you to say! So you disagree with all those other accomplished businesspeople, who mourn the breakdown of this merger as the 'most significant loss in cola wars' and 'the one that could have really stuck it to Coke'?"

She assumed a probing pose, leaning in and attempting to furrow her botoxed brow. I wondered what it took to get her job.

"Well," Snape said. "I agree that it is a significant loss, but we need to, ahm, think about what that means. It would have resulted in a brutal price war between Shizzle Cola and Coca-Cola, and yes, that would have meant cheaper drinks in the short run, but, ahm, it would have resulted in huge losses for Coca-Cola and falling share prices."

Shizzle Cola, my brain noted but went straight back to watching anchorwoman's attempts at interrupting Snape.

Snape ignored her, "...and since most of our nation's retirement funds are invested up to the ears in Coca-Cola, it would have resulted in huge 401k losses for our pensioners. Despite the short-term losses, the outcome is better for the economy in the long run."

His whining was starting to annoy me. On second thought, he looked more like Daniel Radcliffe with long hair. Not sexy at all.

"So there you go," the anchorwoman finally forced her way into

Snape's monolog. "Soft drinks will stay expensive, a powerful billionaire has his nose out of joint, and nobody cares about pensioners."

Soft drinks and powerful billionaire, my brain registered. Did she say something about a merger and cola wars?

"Mark Rosensomething," the anchorwoman said, "thanks for being with us."

The guy started to protest, but his side of the screen disappeared.

"And we'll be back," said the anchorwoman in a sexy purr, "with further reports on the unexpected collapse of the merger between Shizzle Cola and Yomama Kabushiki Gaisha."

The unexpected collapse of the merger. Suddenly it was hard to breathe, as if the walls were moving in on me. I stared at the CNN logo until it changed to a commercial and finally dared to look around.

Everyone was staring at me in silence.

"But they said it's 'under consideration.' Honestly, they did," I said.

There was more uncomfortable silence.

"He couldn't be *that* mad," I said. "Could he? John?"

I tried to touch John's arm, but he jumped away from me as if I was a leper. "Look," he said, "I'm sorry, but I don't want to be anywhere near here when he goes off. And in any case, I think I feel a cold coming on." He rubbed his throat.

"Good idea," said his companion. "I mean, I think I got the same thing."

The group dispersed, clearing throats and talking in hushed tones. I started walking towards my office, my mind a complete blank, when my phone rang. It was Dad.

"Hi, Dad," I said, feeling close to tears.

"Have you talked to your mother yet?" he commanded. There was no trace of the tenderness I'd glimpsed a few hours ago.

"No," I said. "I haven't had a chance, what with the presentation and the resulting collapse of the merger negotiations!"

"You think the presentation did it? That's great!"

"Great?" I yelled into the phone, feeling the hot angry tears rolling down my face. "Are you insane? Have you seen the news? I'm gonna get fired!" I got to my office, grabbed my purse and almost ran towards the exit.

"Why would he fire you?" Dad asked. "The deal would have been a disaster for Shizzle, and that's what you told them. No wonder they are backing out, you called their bluff."

"I didn't know I was calling their bluff!" I cried, charging across the parking lot. "I didn't know what I was doing! Why did you make me write all that stuff about Asian invasion?"

"You thought it was clever!" Dad said.

"I was obviously high on caffeine!" I cried, digging in my purse for the car keys.

"Pull yourself together!" Dad said. "How can you be so selfish, when your parents are on the verge of a divorce?"

"Selfish? How can you call me selfish? I just maxed out Mr. Hue's credit card for you! Oh my God, I am so gonna get fa-ah-ah-ired!" I practically fell behind the wheel.

"Well, ahm, I gotta go," Dad said. "I got something on the stove." With that, he hung up. Dad feared nothing in life, except for crying females.

I dropped the phone on the passenger seat and let go with a liberating, bawling, snorting wail. It took a few minutes, but when the last of the shuddering sobs died down, I felt better. My head cleared up, and a plan began to form somewhere in there.

It's, like,
we're kidnapping you and stuff.

If life really were like a box of chocolates, then every now and then, when you bit into one, there'd be a turd inside.

I couldn't stop thinking about the shit I got myself into. On the ride home, I turned on the radio and searched obsessively for more reports on the collapsed merger. Things were going from bad to worse. Shizzle, Inc's stock price plummeted in the wake of the news that Yomama backed away from the merger, with millions of shares being sold in a matter of minutes. One of the reporters called it 'the kind of punishment only acceptable at fraternity hazings.'

I called my sister.

"You were right," I said.

"I know," she said. "About what?" She could be irritatingly Dad-like.

"About Mr. Hue. I need to snatch him up, and the quicker, the better."

"Why the change?" she asked. "What about the poor and ridiculously handsome option?"

I thought about Hot Cop and sighed.

"I can date him later when I separate from Mr. Hue due to irreconcilable differences," I said. "I don't even need to get married, or anything. I just need him to be smitten with me when he finds out about the merger. Then maybe I won't get sued for bringing down the Yomama deal and the entire company with it."

"Wow, you did that? I'm just watching it on the news!" There was unmistakable pride in her voice.

"Not by myself," I said. "Dad certainly helped!"

"Don't touch that!" she screamed. "Why did you get Dad involved?"

"What?"

"I thought we'd agreed never to ask Dad for advice?" she asked in a more normal voice. "Remember that time he talked you into buying that ancient Lincoln Continental?"

"I know, but I was desperate! You have no idea how hard this job is!"

"Put it down!" Felicity screamed. "Why didn't you ask me for help?"

"I wanted to," I said, "but you always seem so…"

"I am counting to three! One! Two! Two and a half! Two and three-quarters…"

I hung up. Talking to her was pointless when the twins were around. Plus, I was finally home, ready to execute my contingency plan with a vengeance.

Tara was out, which was for the better. She'd probably try to help by rolling a joint. In my current state of mind, I would have accepted it, with extremely counterproductive consequences. My eyes were already red, and I needed all of my wits to get through the rest of the day.

I had just over two hours to get ready. Hardly enough, when you consider all the exfoliating, waxing, trimming, washing, drying, rolling, painting, applying, spraying and polishing I had to do. I was starving, but as usual there was no food in the house, except for a few Red Bulls. I popped one open and drank it, thinking how I could not afford to eat, both literally and figuratively. I'd maxed out all my credit cards, and I was paranoid about looking fat at the Gala.

When I finally finished the prep work it was about a quarter to seven. I slithered into the silky Gucci slip and studied myself in the mirror. I turned sideways, then again to the front. Then to the other side.

I looked good. The slip, oddly enough, looked better than any of the dresses I'd tried on. It complemented my curves, and the Gucci logo on the left strap confirmed my abundance of class, despite the fact that I didn't have a bra to fit the low-cut back. A loose French twist and vampy red lips completed the look, and the fake diamonds in my ears added much-needed wattage. *Good enough to pose for photos with Mr. Hue*, I thought, *and hopefully good enough to win his heart.* Seal at least one deal today, dammit.

I had just a few minutes left to call Mom. I couldn't take a risk that Dad would call me all night demanding that I fix things up for him.

The phone rang forever, and I was ready to hang up when she answered.

"Hello?"

"Hey Mom, it's me," I said. "Where...I mean, how are you?"

"Oh, hey sweetie," she said without her new-found exuberance. "I'm okay, I guess."

"Just okay? Hungover from another wild night?"

"No," she said. "I didn't drink."

"Are you taking any new...supplements?"

"No," she said gloomily. "Don't worry, I haven't taken any meds. I'm just feeling a bit down, I guess. Divorce is just not what it's cracked up to be."

"Oh," I said, my go-to response when trying to stifle a completely inappropriate knee-jerk reaction.

"No, and dating at my age is not fun either."

"But I thought you had fun last night?" *Like, way too much fun*, I thought.

"Not really, to be honest," she said. "I think my expectations were too high. Men my age are just so...old!"

"Oh," I said.

"Yeah, and they're bitter, too!" she said bitterly. "Your Auntie Kelly set me up with this one gentleman, a millionaire no less." *For once*, I thought, *Dad was right. Auntie Kelly really should keep her nose and contacts out of my parents' business.*

"His name is Victor," Mom said. "He actually looked pretty good for his age. He's even got a good head of hair, although he could benefit from a bit of Just For Men, if you ask me. Anyway, we had a good time while he was telling me about his Porsches and his beach house, but then he got onto the subject of everything he lost in the divorce, and it just went downhill from there. Kelly's date joined in the conversation, it turned out that he'd been divorced twice, so they spent most of the night getting smashed and bitching about 'the bitches'. I could hardly take it."

"Oh," I said. What I meant was, "Aren't you used to Dad doing the same?"

"And the worst part was," Mom continued, "that they had nothing else to talk about! I tried to change the subject by asking Victor if he'd read any good books lately, and you know what he said?"

"What?"

"That he hadn't read a book since college! He said that once that 'torture' was over, he never opened a book again! Can you believe it?"

I couldn't. Dad spent all of his free time reading books unless, of course, the news was on.

"He sounds like a prick. Why on Earth did you sleep with him, then?"

"I didn't," Mom said in a tired voice. "Apparently I got so drunk that I refused to get into the taxi, so Kelly got a hotel room for us. That was her in the shower. And anyway, Victor is not interested in seeing me again. He told Kelly that I am 'hard to handle' and 'judgmental'. How could he say that?"

"Hmm," I said, another good way to avoid saying out loud things like, "Did you by any chance call him illiterate?"

"So, tonight I'm staying home and watching TV," she said. "Kelly is going out alone. I can't face another one of her gentleman friends."

"Do you miss Dad?" I asked.

"Of course I do!" she said indignantly. "We've been together for most of our adult lives. We were so in love once! You know what he told me when we first met?"

"That he would marry you one day."

"Yes, he did," she said with a bittersweet sigh. "I was dating this college student, Alex, but your father told him to stay away from me, and that I was his woman. He never let me out of his sight from that day on."

These days Dad's 'courting' would more likely result in a restraining order than a marriage, but Mom was from the generation that considered jealousy a good way to show someone you cared.

"Do you still love him?" I asked.

"Of course I do! But I can't spend the rest of my life being taken for granted by a self-absorbed man. I just can't!"

"Maybe he's changed," I said. "What if this separation taught him something?"

"You think so?" Mom asked hopefully.

"Well, he actually made me breakfast yesterday."

"Really?" The shock in her voice made me smile.

"Really. And he barely burned the bacon."

She was quiet for a moment. "It will take more than one breakfast to prove that he's changed."

"Give him a chance. You may be surprised." I sure hoped that eight grand worth of surprise would make a difference. It looked like I was going to pay more than that in return.

A horn beeped outside.

"Gotta go, love you!" I said into the phone on the way out. "I'm late for a Gala with Mr. Hue!"

"Be careful," Mom said. "He probably doesn't read books."

I stuffed the phone into my tiny evening bag. I tried to stuff one of the handguns into it as well, but neither one fit. Well, I thought, there will be plenty of bodyguards around. I shoved both guns under a pile of junk in the hallway.

I hurried to the door, then paused and collected myself for a grand entrance. I put one hand on a cocked hip, pursed my lips, and pushed the front door open.

What I saw made my jaw drop, which ruined the first part of the plan, in which I was going to sashay over to the limo like a Bond girl. What I saw looked like a spacecraft, all silver and sleek, covered in holographic patterns. The car, if it could be called that, seemed to hover over the ground and sported some sort of alien-looking antennae.

One of the bodyguards, the slightly more handsome one, stepped out and held the door open for me. I stumbled in and lost what little was left of my cool. Inside, the limo looked like a blend of the Starship Enterprise control deck and an exclusive nightclub. A continuous line of black leather seating flowed along the walls, as if sculpted by a lava flow. There was not a single seam or a straight line in sight. Hidden shimmering lights cast an eerie glow onto metallic walls and plush black carpet. One side of the limo housed a bar, sparkling with bottles, glasses, and more lights. Smokey windows wrapped around the perimeter, ending in a huge TV at the back.

I landed on a plush leather seat next to Mr. Hue.

"Hi!" I said. "Wow! This is the best limo I've ever seen!" That was true, although my entire previous experience was limited to the one that took us to and from the French lunch.

"Indeed, this is the largest Shizzle limo in the world," Mr. Hue said, but his eyebrows were knotted in deep thought as he looked me up and down.

"It's a Gucci!" I exclaimed in defense of my almost-dress and pointed out the logo on the strap.

"Excellent," he said, "although completely unexpected. I remember specifically saying that this was a conservative affair?"

Before I could answer, he continued, "However, I am thrilled that you've immersed yourself in my shock-and-awe entrepreneurship philosophy. This dress is perfectly positioned somewhere between butt-naked and appropriate attire."

He smiled earnestly, and I started to relax.

"Sex sells," Mr. Hue continued. "I've launched Shizzlex wrist-watches with nothing but a gold timepiece covering my privates!"

"Oh," I said, wondering if he had a small penis. "By the way, how was the Shizzler?"

"Eh," Mr. Hue said. "We had sandwiches. I must have a chat with the marketing director. I don't find sandwiches very shizzling, no matter how full of Russian caviar they may be. Do you?"

I'd never tried Russian caviar, but I shook my head and asked, "Was Gaga there?"

"Yes, of course," Mr. Hue said. "We discussed Global Youth Elders Council, my new idea of bringing together the most respected youth leaders of today. Imagine young leaders meeting somewhere, like my Paradise Island, a couple of times a year to discuss how they can help solve youth issues. Lady Gaga agreed to become the founding member of the Council and to pick the rest of the members. She's already nominated Fozzi, her gorgeous dog, and will have a think about the others."

"Wow," I said. "Global Youth Elders, who would've thought!" I wouldn't have, but it had to be a great idea if a billionaire was willing to back it up.

"I know," Mr. Hue said. "Gaga was also impressed. She's very passionate about empowering young people. She even said something about cherishing their psychotic parts. Such an inspirational lady!"

"That's inspirational!" I agreed, feeling pretty psychotic myself.

There was a pause. "Let's have a look at the news," Mr. Hue picked up the remote, and I almost lost it.

"Ahm, did you talk about anything else?" I asked, trying to control my breathing. "You had so much to discuss! It would probably take the rest of the ride to tell me."

"Well," Mr. Hue wrinkled his forehead. "We did talk a lot, but I can't remember about what. Funny, how you can spend two hours in deep conversation and not remember anything."

He reached again for the control. "Did you take any notes?" I said with feverish enthusiasm.

"Aha! You are learning quickly," he pulled out his notebook. "I must have jotted something down...let's see...here we go!"

He poked the page repeatedly with his finger. "Here it is, a completely genius idea, and I would have forgotten it, if not for this notebook. Honestly, I don't know how other people manage their business without writing things down."

"Shizzle Royale Club," he read. "A million-dollar donation to Shizzle Kids gets you a royal title and access to the most exclusive club in town. Rub shoulders with other princes and duchesses, that kind of thing. Lady Gaga to officiate."

"That's so clever!" I said passionately.

"It is," he agreed. "We already have King of Pop, King of Rock, and Hollywood royalty, but all those celebrities claimed their titles without permission. All we have to do is buy exclusive US territory knighting rights from the Queen and then sue anyone who refuses to pay."

"Wow!" I said, leaning over as if to look at his notes while attempting to knock the remote off the seat.

"And here's another idea," he continued, completely oblivious to my fidgeting. "Launch Church of Shizzle to spread the spirit around the globe. Like Scientology, but with a twist of cool. Convert Tom Cruise. Isn't it great?"

His enthusiasm was contagious, in the sense that I was sure it would eventually kill me. I mumbled my agreement and finally succeeded in knocking down the remote, only to have it picked up by the handsome bodyguard. He put it back in the console without so much as a look in my direction. Mr. Hue did not notice a thing.

"You see," he beamed at me, "I would have forgotten all about the Church of Shizzle, if not for the notes. I'll call Tom later tonight. For now I just need a break."

He nodded to the bodyguard, who opened a bottle of Veuve Clicquot with an elegantly understated pop. Mr. Hue reclined back in his seat and accepted a bubbling flute.

"It's exhausting at times, but I plan to work till I drop," he said.

I too want to work till I drop, I thought, taking my own flute. I sighed into the bubbles, realizing that there was a major risk that I would never work in this hemisphere again.

Mr. Hue took a sip of champagne and looked around for something. Before I could react, the dastardly bodyguard reached into the console and handed him the remote. As if in slow motion, I watched Mr. Hue point the remote at the TV, biting his lower lip as he tried to figure out which one of the myriad buttons actually turned the thing on.

Just as everything seemed lost, the limo jerked violently. The remote flew out of Mr. Hue's hand, and I flew into his lap, screaming. Champagne splashed everywhere. There was a screech of tires as the driver tried to regain control.

"What the hell was that?" Mr. Hue demanded as I detached myself from his crotch.

"Looks like somebody bumped us," said the bodyguard. That was the first time I'd ever heard him speak, and I squeaked again in surprise. His voice was too high, completely unbefitting his muscular physique.

Just as I was about to suggest that we pull over and get the driver's details, the car in question bumped us again. It was impossible to see who it was because of the huge TV. I could only assume it was a case of evening commute road rage.

"What the fuck?" I cried. "Did we cut them off or something?"

"I know what this is all about," Mr. Hue said with a dismissive wave. "It's paparazzi. You get used to paparazzi following you everywhere when you're famous. It's part of the job. They'll leave when they get their money shot."

A huge black SUV came into the left side view and bumped us yet again.

"Leave this to me," Mr. Hue smiled enigmatically and started to unzip his pants.

"What are you doing?" I scooted away from him. I expected a few candlelight dinners before it ever got to that.

"Just giving the public what it wants," Mr. Hue said and pressed the window button. "Once they get a good shot of this they'll speed off to sell it to tabloids."

As the tinted glass lowered, he pulled down his pants and stuck his rear end out the window. "They're gonna love this," he said, bent over with his face uncomfortably close to mine, "I just had the Shizzle logo tattooed on my left butt cheek."

"Oh," I said.

The driver of the SUV lowered his own darkened window, but instead of camera flashes, bullets whizzed through the air and ricocheted off the limo's body and bulletproof windows.

"What the hell!" Mr. Hue dove down onto the floor and hastily pulled up his pants. I screamed and pushed the window button as hard as I could.

"I don't think these are paparazzi!" Mr. Hue said, observant as ever. "Who are these people, Serge?" he asked the bodyguard.

"I dunno, but we could pull over and see what they want," Serge said. I was about to say that we should call the cops instead, or at the very least return fire, but Mr. Hue brazenly nodded approval. With his pants and windows up, he had returned to his usual unflappable self.

Serge pressed the intercom button, mumbled something, and the limo coasted to a stop on the shoulder. It was still light out, and the highway was full of evening traffic, although I doubted anyone would try to help us or even report suspicious activity. I desperately wished I'd managed to fit a gun into my purse, or maybe slip one into a garter, like a spy. That would've been so cool.

The SUV pulled over in front of us. We all watched as the driver's door opened and a black stiletto leather boot appeared. It was joined by another boot, followed by a pair of long slender legs clad in tight black leather pants. A woman in a sort of a sexy ninja outfit emerged. A black mask covered her hair and face, only revealing her eyes, which burned into us like laser beams.

Without warning, the woman swung a stubby looking rifle from behind her back and opened fire on the limo. Bullets bounced off the windows. I screamed like a girl, but Mr. Hue remained as composed as ever.

"She can do this all day," he said proudly. "This is the very latest prototype of Shizzmo, the ultimate in transportation safety and luxury for the discerning tycoon." He turned to Serge, "What are you waiting for? Shoot her in the kneecaps or something!"

Serge took out his Smith & Wesson Bodyguard and pointed it at Mr. Hue's head. I giggled at the irony of his weapon choice and also because I no longer had any idea what the hell was going on. Serge suddenly looked nervous, and a lot less handsome.

"Not me, you idiot!" Mr. Hue screamed at him. "Her!"

He pointed at the sexy ninja, who was reloading her Ruger Mini.

Serge swallowed hard. "It's, like, we are kidnapping you and stuff," he said.

"Kidnapping?" asked Mr. Hue. "Are you kidding me? Wait, am I being punked? Who put you up to this? Was it Donald? I'm onto you Donald!" he laughed and waved around at hidden cameras.

I laughed too, but Serge didn't. "I'm, like, totally serious," he said. "This is a kidnapping, and you're gonna pay us tons of cash."

"Ransom!" Mr. Hue laughed hysterically. "That's rich!"

Serge scratched the back of his head, then pressed the intercom button and whined, "He's, like, not buying it!"

"Rough him up a bit!" said a voice over the intercom. "No, wait, put the partition down. I wanna watch!"

"Ah, okay," Serge said and pressed a button. The screen separating us from the driver lowered soundlessly, and I saw Serge's smiling almost-twin.

"What up, motherfucker!" he greeted Mr. Hue.

Mr. Hue stopped laughing. "That's enough," he said in a steely voice. "It's been fun, but we're late for the Gala and I am not..."

"Shut up and listen, dumbass," said Serge's accomplice. "We. Are. Kidnapping. You."

I felt a cold chill creep up my back. I was utterly unprepared for any of what was happening. Should've at least brought along a pashmina or something.

"You? Kidnapping me? Then who's that?" Mr. Hue gestured towards the sexy ninja.

"The mastermind," said a woman's voice, and the ninja gracefully slipped inside.

Are you going to kill me too?

"Let's go, Kurt," Ninja said to the driver, and he obligingly started the engine.

She ordered Serge to check us for weapons. He didn't find any, but he took my purse and Mr. Hue's weird ball-phone. Ninja settled into her seat and studied us from behind her mask. "Do you know why this is happening to you?" she asked.

"Because I'm rich and you want my money?" Mr. Hue said.

"Well, yes," she said with a touch of irritation. "But do you understand why this is happening to *you* and not to Bill Gates or Donald Trump?"

"Because I have such shitty protection services?"

"Well, that will teach you to offer your staff competitive salaries and benefits!" Kurt burst out from the driver's seat.

"Okay, fine, that's also part of it," Ninja rolled her eyes. "But can you think of something else? Maybe there was something you did, say about thirty years ago, something that deserved sweet cold revenge?"

I was completely lost, and so, it seemed, was Mr. Hue.

"No," he said after a pause. "I can honestly say that I've never done anything that warrants a kidnapping and pummeling my car with bullets."

"Really?" the woman seethed. "What about a betrayal?"

"No," Mr. Hue said. "I've never betrayed anyone."

"Oh, that's rich! What about your first partner?"

"No, of course not! Old Bill and I were friends." Mr. Hue said good-naturedly.

"Friends?" Ninja exclaimed. "Friends? What kind of a friend buys out his partner before revealing that he'd negotiated a ludicrous military contract?"

"Oh," Mr. Hue said. "Now I remember. I bought Bill's share in Wellbred Chips, then rebranded the company as Shizzle Wieners to supply the US Army with high-quality sausages. That's how the Shizzle empire started," he added with a sentimental sigh.

"That's right!" Ninja exclaimed. "William Wellbred would have made a fortune from his share of that contract! He never got over the loss and tortured his family with stories of what could have been, even on his deathbed!"

"Did he die from grief?" I asked.

"No," she said. "It was years later, from pneumonia. But that's not the point!"

She shook an accusing finger at Mr. Hue. "On his deathbed, he made his only daughter promise that one day she would avenge him and recover the fortune that was rightfully his!"

"Okay, okay," Mr. Hue put his hands up. "But how is that any of your business?"

The woman stared back at him for what seemed like an eternity, then closed her eyes in exasperation. "*I am* his daughter, you moron!" she said finally and tore off her mask.

"Eleanor?" Mr. Hue exclaimed in disbelief.

Indeed it was Eleanor, elegant and pissed off, as usual. I almost peed myself and scooted away, as if she was the Terminator coming back from the future to kill me. Luckily, all her attention was on Mr. Hue.

"He said that if I didn't avenge him, he would haunt me till the end of my days and then in the afterlife," she said gravely.

"Wow, that's some fucked-up shit!" Serge said.

"There are no ghosts, you know," Mr. Hue declared. "Those TV shows are all hoaxes; they proved it on Sixty Minutes."

"I know," Eleanor snapped, "but I was eight, and it just stuck with me, okay? I still sleep with a nightlight and a cross, you bastard."

"Okay, fine, how much do you want?" Mr. Hue asked.

Eleanor's eyes sparkled dangerously. "The ransom shall be equal to my father's rightful share, plus interest and CPI," she said dramatically. "Four hundred and twenty-seven thousand, eight hundred and sixty-three dollars, and eleven cents!"

"Ok," Mr. Hue said. "Will you take a check?"

Kurt hit the brakes. The tires screeched, and we veered madly side to side, before coming to a halt on the shoulder. Guns and glasses went flying everywhere, as we once again slammed into each other. The air was thick with profanities. Serge came up with the most creative ones, featuring unexpected combinations of female body parts and breakfast items.

"What the hell, Kurt?" Eleanor demanded when everybody got themselves sorted out and back in their seats. I realized, too late as usual, that I should have taken the opportunity to grab one of the guns.

Kurt killed the engine and turned to us. "What was that amount again?" he asked Eleanor with eerie calm.

Eleanor stuck her chin out defiantly. "Four hundred and twenty-seven thousand, eight hundred and sixty-three dollars, and eleven cents!"

"Thousands?" Kurt asked. "You mean to tell me that we are all going to be thousandaires?"

"This is a matter of principle!" Eleanor said. "I'm not doing this to get rich."

"I am," Serge said.

"That's right," Kurt echoed. "We got into this thinking that the ransom would be more like a hundred million. He's a billionaire, for Christ's sake!"

"I can't ask for a hundred, or even one million," Eleanor said. "That would make me a common criminal. I am not stealing, only taking back what had been stolen from Wellbreds. It's a matter of family honor!"

"I don't care," Kurt said. "We are in this together, and I'm revising the ransom to a hundred million dollars!"

"I don't have that much in my checking account," Mr. Hue said.

"I'm gonna need a hundred million dollars in small, non-sequential bills," Kurt said slowly. "And I don't wanna hear another word about family honor or daddy issues."

"I'm gonna need you to start driving and keeping your mouth

shut!" Eleanor said and pointed her rifle at Kurt.

In a well-practiced, almost elegant move, Serge pushed the barrel of her gun down with one hand and slammed her in the throat with the other. The gun let off an erratic stream of bullets that ripped through the plush carpet and leather upholstery. Before I knew what was happening, Serge had Eleanor's arms twisted into a pretzel behind her back.

"Well, well, well," Kurt said. "Look who's in charge now?"

Eleanor wheezed like a retired Marlboro man.

"What do I do now?" Serge asked in his annoying voice. "Do we, like, kill her?"

"No," Kurt said. "The more hostages, the better. Check to make sure she has no other weapons."

Serge patted down wriggling and protesting Eleanor. He found a handgun inside her right boot and a switchblade strapped to her forearm. I couldn't help but be impressed. Sure, the bitch was crazy, but she was certainly well prepared. If anything, the whole ordeal was proof that situations demanding firearm protection apparently do happen outside the movies.

"Okay," Kurt said. "You can let her go now."

Serge let go of Eleanor, who pushed away from him and scooted into a corner, rubbing her arms. Her formerly perfect hair got messed up in the struggle, and she looked to be close to tears.

"Do you know how many years I've spent working for this monster?" she asked nobody in particular. When nobody answered, she said, "Seventeen. Seventeen years of getting closer and closer, plotting, calculating, and waiting patiently for just the right moment. Seventeen years of planning the perfect revenge, all ruined by greed!"

"Greed is the root of all evil," Mr. Hue agreed. "I've always said that you can't be in it for the money."

"Yeah, that's how you got so much of it!" Eleanor said. For once, I had to agree with her.

"I'm quite serious," Mr. Hue folded his arms. "My motto has always been 'do it for fun and the money will come!'"

"Was it fun cheating my father out of his fair share?" Eleanor asked. The deranged look was back on her face, and she seemed to coil up in her corner, like a snake ready to strike.

Mr. Hue didn't notice it. "I didn't cheat your father out of any-thing," he assured Eleanor. "In fact, your father chose to leave the company, because he didn't like the name Shizzle Weiners. He just didn't get my business philosophy. Did you know that he laughed at me after I bought his shares? He said I would go under in less than a year."

"That's not the story he told me!" Eleanor said.

"My Dad tells me lots of stories," I offered from my corner, "but I don't believe half of them. For example, he always told us that he got accepted to Harvard, except that..."

Just at that moment, Eleanor launched at Mr. Hue with a scream of "I'm gonna get you, bastard!". Lucky for Mr. Hue, Serge stopped her mid-flight with another elegant karate chop. He wasn't a quick think-er, but he had the reflexes of a cat.

Eleanor landed in a heap at our feet, moaning.

"Look," Serge said serenely. "Just take it easy, okay? We gonna kill him, so you'll have your revenge in the end."

"Kill me?" Mr. Hue asked dubiously. I searched Serge's face for any sign of a joke, but there was nothing there. My pulse quickened.

"Shut up, you moron!" Kurt yelled from the driver's seat and slammed on the brakes, swerving to a halt on the shoulder. He turned back to us and gave Serge a menacing look.

"Are you going to kill me?" Mr. Hue asked indignantly.

"No," Kurt said evenly. "We are not going to kill anybody."

"But I thought you said..." Serge whined. My pulse went through the roof.

"Zip it, Serge!" Kurt commanded. "Leave them alone and get in the front with me."

"Cool!" Serge said and jumped out, slamming the door shut be-hind him, which gave me the first good idea of the day. With shaking hands, I jerked my door handle as hard as I could, but the door didn't budge.

"It's no use," Mr. Hue said. "Childproof locks."

"What? Why the hell are there childproof locks in the limo?"

"Why not?" Mr. Hue said. "It's not too late for me to have a family!"

Serge got into the front passenger seat, and Kurt started the engine. "Are you going to kill me too?" I asked him, but he just raised the partition, and we drove off. What a couple of bastards. I couldn't believe that I was once hot for either one of them.

"Of course they will," Eleanor said calmly. "You know their names and faces."

I almost fainted. This wasn't happening. I tried to calm myself down by thinking that kidnappings are simply business transactions in which large sums of money are exchanged for freedom. Except, of course, in *Pain & Gain*. Or in *Fargo*. In fact, I could not think of a single story in which the victim returned home safe and sound. Then I remembered something else.

"Wait," I asked Eleanor. "We know you, too. Were *you* going to kill us?"

"Well, it wasn't in the original plan," she said, "but then this idiot practically forced me to reveal my identity!" She nodded at Mr. Hue.

"Oh, please!" Mr. Hue said. "Just admit that you crave the limelight! Always bitching about how you don't get any recognition for your work!"

"What's wrong with that? You know, it's a travesty that a corporation like Shizzle doesn't even have a reward and recognition policy!"

"Again with your policy and procedures! How can you be such a bore?" Mr. Hue bellowed. "You know how much I hate rules! No wonder you never advanced beyond your secretary position!"

"Executive assistant!" Eleanor screamed in his face.

I turned away from them, pressed my forehead against the window, and let the tears flow. Other cars were driving alongside us on the highway, but there was no use in crying for help. The bulletproof windows were so thick and heavily tinted that nobody would hear or see me getting shot down in the prime of my life. I poked mindlessly at the childproof locks, thinking about how close I came to being a billionaire's family matriarch. That got the tears switched into the second gear.

Just as I was imagining visiting my little darlings in a magnificent nursery full of nannies and nearly drowning in tears and snot, there was another bump. It wasn't very hard, and at first I thought we just hit a pothole, but then there was another one. I looked out the window and saw that somebody else was trying to force us off the road. That alone was surprising enough, but it was their car that gave me the real shock.

It was a dinged-up yellow Beetle.

The environment must be, like, so important!

I stared at my car in astonishment. In the glare of the setting sun, it was hard to tell who was driving it, or even if it was a man or a woman.

Only Tara knew that I kept a spare key in a magnetic box stuck to Beetle's belly. She'd used it without permission before despite my repeated threats, but why was she driving it now? And how did she find me? Slowly, and with delicious glee, I realized that Tara was trying to save me. We were best friends, of course, but she has never done anything like that before. Her most heroic achievement to date was yelling at Brad once when he got a little too verbally abusive with me. Yet there she was, ready to risk her life to save mine. What can I say, she had to be in love with me.

"Isn't that your derby car, Ms. Maxwell?" I heard Mr. Hue exclaim.

"What? Oh yeah, it kind of looks like it," I said. "But the dents are different. Mine has a big scratch on the passenger side, where I did some body work with a bollard."

"We can't see the passenger side from here," Eleanor pointed out.

"I guess not," I said and scratched my nose with a fully extended middle finger. "Oh well, there could be millions of yellow Beetles in the city."

"No," Mr. Hue said. "I think this is indeed your car. It's very striking. I don't think I could confuse it with any other. Why, I even recall the bumper being a different shade of yellow, look!"

He pointed.

"Oh yeah," I said. "Now that you mention it, I also recall the bumper being a different color. But how often do you look at the bumper of your own car, right?"

Beetle bumped us again. The partition lowered.

"Friends of yours?" Kurt asked.

"Not mine," Mr. Hue said indignantly. "It appears that the car currently pursuing us belongs to Ms. Maxwell." He pointed to me, and I squirmed.

"It's a piece of shit," Kurt said. "What do they want?"

"I don't know," I said earnestly. "I have no idea who's driving it."

Beetle bumped us again.

"This is getting on my nerves," Kurt said and veered to the right. As if in a recurring nightmare, we were once again on the shoulder, watching the driver climb out from behind the wheel.

To my delight, it was Tara, although I only recognized her face. Her body looked strange, bloated like Violet's from *Charlie and the Chocolate Factory*. She was wearing combat boots and a large house robe. We looked on as she shuffled closer until she was standing next to the driver's window.

Kurt lowered it.

"What do you want, fatty?" he laughed in her face. "Want some fries and a diet Coke? This ain't no drive-through."

"Drive-through!" laughed Serge. "That's funny because she's fat!"

Tara looked serious and composed. "Hand over Mr. Hue!" she said, pointing at the back of the limo.

Kurt and Serge laughed uproariously.

"I think she means hand me over," I said, but everyone ignored me.

"And what if we don't?" Kurt asked. "What will you do then? Fart us to death?"

"Haha, fart to death!" Serge said. "Can she?"

"Hand him over," Tara said, "or we all die!"

With that, she threw open her robe and let it fall to the ground. Underneath, she was dressed in a simple tank top and shorts. Well, that, and a vest with stitched-on pockets stuffed full of uniform round objects. Kurt stopped laughing and reached for the ignition.

"Stay still!" Tara screamed. "One move and I push the button!"

She held up a small square pad with a red button in the middle.

Kurt froze. I pinched myself, really hard.

"What's that?" Serge asked.

"It's a bomb!" Eleanor screamed, and then, as if on her command, everyone was screaming. Only Kurt stayed silent, frozen and pale as snow.

There was nowhere to go, so after a while the screams died down, and we huddled together in a corner, whimpering and staring at Tara. Kurt, on other hand, seemed to get a bit of color and attitude back.

"You know what I think?" he said to Tara. "I think you're bluffing! You look like a college kid and this suicide bomb of yours looks like a fake."

"No, it's not!" Tara said and I, for one, believed her. Standing there, in her worn out shorts, with her greasy black hair and tightly pressed lips, she looked like a guerrilla fighter. Crazy cool.

"Yes, it is," Kurt said. "I was in the FBI, so I know for a fact that it's impossible for civilians to get explosives. Every bit of C-4 and Semtex in this country is traced and accounted for. Where did you get this, Wal-Mart?"

"Good one!" Serge snorted. "Wal-Mart is funny."

"I made it myself!" Tara said, still holding up her trigger box, like some kind of a revolutionary flag. "In the basement, from the stuff I bought at Wal-Mart!"

"That's not true," I said, relieved. "She makes candles. Candles don't explode!"

"Are you sure?" Serge asked, concerned.

"Shut up, Serge," Kurt snapped at him, then turned back to Tara. "Go home, little girl."

He was about to start the limo's engine when Tara pressed her lips even tighter and pushed the button.

The explosion was spectacular, like a fourth of July gone wrong. Bits of metal and clogs of dirt pummeled the limo's roof like a drum set. An off-yellow bumper landed on the gravel outside of my window. I screamed from fear and from the realization that I would never again hear Beetle's erratic heartbeat. Everyone else was screaming too, and Serge was crying like a little girl.

The force of the explosion knocked Tara down, but now she

scrambled back up again.

"That was nothing!" she shouted victoriously, her face covered with dirt smudges. "One wrong move and they will have to identify you by your dental records!"

"Okay!" Kurt yelled and unlocked the doors with an audible pop. "You win! You can have him! Get out!" he screamed at Mr. Hue.

"No, thanks," Mr. Hue said. "I'm not going anywhere with that psycho!"

"Not so fast," Tara said with the cool arrogance of Dirty Harry. "As you can see, I now lack in the transportation department." She motioned to late Beetle's remains.

"What is she talking about?" Serge whined, and Kurt slapped him. I wished I could slap someone too, preferably Tara.

"So," she continued, "why don't we start by having the two of you idiots come out with your paws up?"

Kurt obeyed wordlessly, and Serge followed his lead. They emerged from the two sides of the limo and started backing away, hands in the air, not taking their eyes off Tara.

When they were a few yards away, Tara started moving around to the driver's door, also not taking her eyes off them. Just as she was about to get in, I heard a door open, and Eleanor jumped out with a hysterical scream. She ran along the shoulder, waving madly at the passing cars. Mr. Hue and I looked at each other. We were about to jump out ourselves, when Tara screamed "No!" and dashed inside.

The next few seconds played out in slow motion. Tara's vest catching on the edge of the door. A loud ripping sound. A clatter of bouncing dings. Screams. Kurt's distant and distorted voice: "What's that?" Serge, happy and confused: "Ping-pong balls!"

As reality sped up back to normal, I watched Kurt pounce on Tara like a tiger.

"Unhand me, oppressor!" Tara wheezed, trying to wiggle out of his choke hold.

Her vest ripped even further, and I saw that Serge was right - the objects sewn into its pockets were ping-pong balls, not plastic explosives as we all thought.

"Go get the other bitch!" Kurt yelled. Serge sprang into action, running after Eleanor in huge bounding leaps. He caught up with her quickly, as the stiletto boots turned out to be a poor, albeit very hot, choice for this kind of action. He carried her back, slumped over his shoulder like a caveman's trophy wife. Eleanor pounded her fists on his back, to no avail.

Serge and Kurt shoved both women into the limo, locked the doors and drove off.

"Hi, Isa," Tara said, still huffing and puffing.

"Do you know her?" Mr. Hue and Eleanor asked in unison.

"Hi there yourself," I fumed. "What the hell was all that about?"

"I'm just trying to protect the environment," Tara said, defensive and apologetic at the same time. "This asshole here," she pointed at Mr. Hue, "is about to destroy one of the last habitats of the foothill yellow-legged frog!"

"Who...what?" Mr. Hue asked.

Eleanor started looking through the bar bottles.

"The environment?" I exclaimed. "Wow, the environment must be, like, so important if you are willing to blow up your best friend for it!"

"Who is this girl, and why are you keeping such bad company?" Mr. Hue demanded.

Tara rolled her eyes. "You were never in any danger. You saw that my vest was full of ping-pong balls."

"You know what I saw?" I said, bracing against the seat and getting ready to unleash the world's greatest bitch-slap. "I saw my car blown to bits. Without my permission!"

"I did you a favor!" Tara said. "Didn't you say the transmission had to be replaced, and it would've cost more than the car was worth?"

"Yeah," I said, unsure of where she was going with that.

"Well, it's gonna get written off now and you can get a new one."

"Oh," I said. "Still, you could've told me! I seriously thought I was gonna die!"

"So did I," Mr. Hue said. "Frankly, Ms. Maxwell, I'm disappointed in you!"

I suddenly remembered that while being car-less was equivalent to a social death, I had a much bigger problem at hand. Something that could result in a professional or even real death. In some ways, Mr. Hue scared me even more than the homicidal bodyguards. At least I knew exactly what Kurt wanted. I decided to forget about Tara for the moment and concentrate on my original plan of seducing Mr. Hue.

"I'm disappointed that you're disappointed," I said, leaning towards him with what I hoped was a sexy and playful pout. Mr. Hue looked confused. He was about to say something when a loud pop rang through the interior, making me scream and jump back in my seat.

Eleanor held up an overflowing bottle of champagne.

"Might as well," she shrugged.

The others took turns filling their flutes and, grudgingly, I followed suit. I drank my champagne, determined not to enjoy it, while Tara explained the foothill yellow-legged frog dilemma. Apparently, this particularly ugly creature was fast disappearing from California landscapes, and Mr. Hue's latest hydroelectric power plant construction was threatening to flood the last of the frog's habitat.

"This shameless exploitation of natural resources has to stop!" Tara declared. "Our environment is changing!"

"For better or worse?" Mr. Hue asked.

She ignored him. "Someone has to do something, but nobody is doing nothing."

"Yeah, okay," I said, feeling a little tipsy. "So how is blowing up my car going to save the environment?"

"That wasn't the original plan," Tara said. "I was getting ready to blow up the dam when you got the job working for him," she jerked her chin towards Mr. Hue. "I thought it would be easier and safer for the frogs just to kidnap him and demand that he abandon construction."

"Kidnapping is much harder than you think," Eleanor said. "I have been planning this one for years and look how well it turned out!" She laughed bitterly into her flute.

"Why are you, like, so interested in this frog?" I said. The words didn't come out quite right, and I regretted not eating anything earlier. "Who would even care if they were gone? They're so ugly!"

"That's the point!" Tara exclaimed. "It's all too easy to protect koalas, cause they are so cute. The poor ugly frog is not getting any media coverage or respect from the authorities. The Fish and Wildlife Department listed it as a 'species of special concern'. That's a joke! It should be listed as a threatened species."

"That's appalling," Mr. Hue said and took a swig of champagne. "If we get out of this alive, I pledge to support this frog in any way I can!"

"So you'll stop the dam?" Tara asked.

"I didn't say that," Mr. Hue raised a finger. "I'm sure we can find a way the frog and the dam can coexist in harmony."

"They can't," Tara said slowly. "It's like saying water and fire can coexist, or Paris Hilton and Nicole Richie."

"They used to be best friends," I said.

Tara ignored me. "You are a capitalist bully," she said, "and you will answer to God for your crimes against this frog!"

"I think God has bigger fish to fry!" Mr. Hue said.

Tara started screaming about how in Hell, where Mr. Hue was obviously going, fish and frogs would get to shit in his water supply. Eleanor pointed out that the fish and the frogs were already shitting in our rivers, and then Tara pretty much lost it. She went on and on about the environmental crisis and saving the threatened species, and I went on drinking and thinking about how to save myself.

You stole my gum!

It would've been quite a road trip, if not for the looming threat of digging our own shallow graves. There was plenty of champagne on hand, fueling the arguments about which charitable causes were more important. Mr. Hue was hell-bent on saving starving children, and Tara was hoarse from screaming about overpopulation and its impact on the environment. I brooded quietly over my inability to direct Mr. Hue's attention away from the argument and towards my cleavage. He was the first middle-aged man ever to resist my charms.

"Earth's last hope is in capitalism," Mr. Hue said.

"Really?" Tara said with a lethal smile. "Do tell how capitalism, with its never-ending quest for economic growth and hunger for non-renewable resources, is going to save us from global warming?"

"It's quite simple," Mr. Hue said. "Capitalism is the driver of innovation, which will eventually figure out how we can continue living without worrying ourselves sick over the carbon footprint of a Kobe steak or a private jet. As we speak, entrepreneurs around the world are busy figuring out how to turn used Pampers into an environmentally-friendly fuel, cool down the warming oceans, and so on and so forth. You get the idea?"

I didn't get the idea, but nodded anyway and leaned towards him, propping up my breasts with my elbows. Any more squeezing and I risked a wardrobe malfunction, but my efforts were wasted on Mr. Hue. His full attention was on Tara, who looked hot, her cheeks flushed with righteous anger and alcohol.

"How are they going to cool down the oceans?" she raged. "Tow the icebergs to the Atlantic?"

"That's not a bad idea!" Mr. Hue said. "They can do that using the

Pampers biofuel, of course. There is also the option of pumping the deep ocean water up to the surface, to mix things up, so to speak."

Tara squealed something about pipe dreams, Eleanor said something about smoking crack, and soon they were all shouting. Just when I felt like my head was about to explode, colorful lights began dancing in the cabin, bouncing off the polished chrome fixtures.

"What's that?" I heard Eleanor ask.

"Thank God!" Mr. Hue said, and I suddenly understood what was creating the light play - the flashing lights of a police cruiser in hot pursuit. Everyone quieted down, and I could hear the faint sound of a siren through the thick windows.

Kurt lowered the partition. "Who called the cops?" He was clearly freaking out.

"It wasn't us," I said. "You took our phones, remember?"

"I did," Serge confirmed.

"Then how did they find us?" Kurt demanded.

"Probably the same way I did," Tara said. "Traced one of the phones."

"You traced my phone?" Mr. Hue asked incredulously.

"No," Tara said. "I traced Isa's."

"How?" I couldn't believe it.

"Hacked into your Find My iPhone app. You should think about changing your password. It's not smart to use the same one for your Facebook, email, and even bank accounts."

"You hacked into my *Facebook*?" I jumped up in my seat. She was going to get bitch-slapped after all.

"I had to!" Tara said. "I had to block that idiot Brad. It was the only way to stop you from constantly whining about his updates!"

"So Brad didn't block me?" I asked, dumbfounded and happy. "Then there's still a chance!"

"No, there isn't," Tara said. "I blocked him because he updated his status to 'In a relationship with Tiffany.' I'm sorry, Isa, I really am."

That knocked the fight right out of me. "Tiffany? Which Tiffany, the queen bitch or the one who was homeschooled?"

"Which do you think?" Tara stared at me for what seemed like forever. "The queen bitch."

I nearly fainted. Tiffany went to the same community college as Brad and me. She could afford to go to a proper university, but she was still puzzled by the multiplication tables, so her parents got her into "something". Tiffany was the ultimate rich kid and a poster girl for anti-feminism. She and I had a brutal war going for at least two years, and this latest defeat made me want to surrender. It was possible that Tiffany had no idea there was a war to begin with, and why would she - she had her cars, her hair, and her cool friends to worry about. I had to carry that flag alone, burning with outrage every time I overheard her talking about how it was "time to trade in the Beemer" or that yellow gold was "sooo kitsch". I tried shooting back by writing lengthy articles in the school paper on topics such as "Material Girl: Alive and Well" and "Sluts: Have They Ruined the Feminist Movement?" but she probably never even read them. She was too busy juggling at least three boyfriends at once - the not-quite-ex, the current squeeze, and the next victim.

And now Brad had fallen victim to her! I was so devastated, that I was only marginally aware of Kurt yelling at Serge, something about how he had told him to get rid of the phones.

"You didn't tell me *why*!" Serge cried. "I didn't know they could be traced! I was just going to sell them on eBay…"

"For the love of God, why? You were going to be a millionaire after this!" Kurt bellowed.

"Millionaire with a few extra hundred in the bank!" Serge held his ground.

I snapped all the way back to reality when the cops turned on the speakers and ordered the "driver of the weird-looking limo" to pull over.

"It's not weird, it's innovative and visionary!" Mr. Hue huffed.

Serge tried to throw a cell phone out the window, but Kurt slapped him on the back of the head and pulled over. He pressed his forehead to the steering wheel and moaned quietly while we watched the cruiser pull over next to us. The driver got out and boldly approached the limo, holding a gun that I couldn't identify.

"Hey," Serge said. "Looks like there's only one of them."

Kurt moaned something.

The police officer came closer, and suddenly I recognized him. He wasn't wearing the aviators this time, but there was no mistaking the toned V of his body, the hollow cheeks, and the badass attitude.

"Hey," Serge said. "That's not even a gun!"

Kurt raised his head to look, and then he was out the door, rushing at Hot Cop. Serge, the ever-obedient dog, followed his lead.

Hot Cop seemed to change his mind. He ran back to the cruiser, but the two bodyguards caught up with him just as he was reaching for the door handle. There was a brief struggle, punctuated by hollow thuds and shrieks of pain, after which they dragged him back to the limo and unceremoniously threw him in with the rest of us. Laughing and high-fiving each other, they got back into the front seats and drove off.

Hot Cop scrambled up on the seat next to Tara and looked around wildly. He looked hot as hell even without the aviators. His dark brown eyes were huge with surprise, and his hair was disheveled in a very appealing way. I couldn't help but be turned on by his brave, if failed, attempt to rescue me. I cried inwardly for what could have been.

"And who the hell are you?" Eleanor asked him. "Another kidnapper? Take a number."

"I'm not a kidnapper, I'm a police officer," Hot Cop said smugly. "I'm here to *stop* a kidnapping."

"You are doing one hell of a job, then," Eleanor toasted him with her flute. "Why didn't you shoot them or something?"

Hot Cop blushed. "I only have a radar gun...I'm still in the patrol division."

"Oh my God, a rookie!" Eleanor rolled her eyes. "What are you doing chasing criminals, baby doll, unarmed and alone? Where's your partner?"

"We don't have partners anymore, that's only in the movies," Hot Cop said moodily. "Budget cuts and all that."

"I'll tell you how capitalism could help," Mr. Hue chimed in. "Imagine privatizing the police force, where employees are incentivized by getting a cut of whatever crime they helped to stop! Drug cartels and jewelry heists would be a thing of the past!"

"Did you call for backup?" Tara asked.

"Yep," Hot Cop said. "But I'm not sure if dispatch took it seriously, though. I sorta been trying to solve me a major crime for a while, you know, to get promoted to detective. So far all my leads turned out to be duds. The boys at the station have been calling me 'the prick who cried wolf.' Sucks, you know?"

"Well, this will show them!" Tara said encouragingly and patted his arm. "What's your name?"

"Wait," Mr. Hue said. "How did you know I was getting kidnapped?"

"I didn't, until the last moment. I've had a hunch that Tara here was going to blow somethin' up, ever since I saw her buying bags of fertilizer at Wal-Mart. Been watching her a while and today just happened to follow her here."

"So you were stalking me?" Tara said and gave me a smug smile.

"Sure was," said Hot Cop. "Name's Chad, by the way."

"Wait a second," I said, confused. "Then who was stalking me these last few days? Do you have a twin or something?"

Chad laughed. "Nah, that was me. I was following you to get closer to Tara. You know, looking for evidence for an arrest." Tara gave me another triumphant smile.

"Did you trace my phone?" she asked, touching his forearm.

"No, couldn't hack your password," he admitted. "Traced Isa's. Only an idiot would use their birthday as a password."

"But it's okay if you type it in backwards, right?" Mr. Hue asked.

Chad gave him a puzzled look, and Mr. Hue scribbled something down in his notebook.

"You're the one who's an idiot!" I snapped at Chad. "What kind of a cop are you? You stole my gum! And you were drunk on the job!"

He winced. "Yes, it's true," he said and buried his face in his hands. "I'm an alcoholic and a kleptomaniac. I guess that's why I've always wanted to be a cop. Should've been a psychologist, I guess, with all my problems." He moaned into his hands.

Tara pulled him in closer and cooed like a mother hen. At least for the moment, saving the ugly frog seemed to have been replaced by soothing a hot, damaged man.

Chad responded quite well to the treatment. Within minutes, he took his hands off his face and planted them on Tara's flat chest. I waited for Tara to flip out, but she just slid her own hands all over Chad's body.

"What's going on here?" I finally asked when they started kissing. Somebody had to. Mr. Hue was still scribbling in his notebook and Eleanor was busy trying to open another champagne bottle.

"What?" Tara countered. "We're just trying to comfort each other in the face of imminent death." Chad nuzzled her neck in agreement.

"What about me?" I asked. "Why aren't you comforting *me*? What happened to 'I love you, kid'? Maybe the face of imminent death made me reconsider that first lesbian experience offer?"

"What are you talking about?" Tara asked. Chad broke the suction hold on her neck and looked back and forth between us with great interest.

"You know!" I said, no longer sure myself. "All that 'I love you like a girlfriend' and the hugging? And looking at the stars? And that time in the hallway?"

"Thank you, God!" Chad moaned and looked around. "We can go over there," he pointed to where a leather seat peninsula jutted out and made a semi-enclosure.

"What are you talking about?" Tara asked again, slowly.

"I don't know!" I said. "I mean, aren't you a lesbian, or at least bi-sexual?" Chad looked at her, the same question clearly written on his face.

Tara's eyes bulged.

"Lesbian?" she said dangerously. I pulled my head into my shoulders, but she just busted out laughing.

"Lesbian?" she snorted. "Jesus, Isa, where did you get *that* idea?"

"I don't know," I said. "Maybe it's your hair, and the fact that you never date, and that you said you love me?"

"I do love you, you bonehead!" she laughed. "Seriously, only Isa can come up with something that dumb," she said to Chad. "Lesbian!"

Chad smiled, but the smile seemed sad. Tara grabbed his neck and whispered something in his ear. Whatever she said seemed to make him forget all about Tara's disappointing sexual orientation and inspire another bout of dry humping.

Nobody bothered to ask me how I was feeling about it. I was so upset that it physically hurt somewhere down in my stomach or spleen, or maybe some other organ I didn't know I had. I'd lost count of how many times life had sucker punched me that day. I was busy massaging my stomach and wondering if I'd finally hit rock bottom when Mr. Hue let out an unholy wail. I looked up and saw that someone had turned on the TV. Mr. Hue was pointing a shaky finger at the same damn blond anchorwoman I'd seen earlier. At first I thought that he was appalled at her low-cut turquoise blouse, but then I saw the tagline.

Under the anchorwoman's cleavage, in bold white letters, it said, "BREAKING NEWS: SHIZZLE EMPIRE LOST IN HOSTILE TAKEOVER."

God's gift to His prodigal daughter.

Mr. Hue's scream fizzled out like a teakettle taken off the stove. We all watched the news in dead silence. Even Tara and Chad opened their eyes for a moment, although they remained tightly woven around each other.

"Following earlier news of the sudden Shizzle, Inc share-price plunge, we bring you further dramatic developments," the anchorwoman said.

"What plunge?" I heard Mr. Hue whisper. His finger was still pointing at the screen. He seemed dazed, as if caught in a dream.

"The selling panic was first attributed to the breakdown of the merger deal between Shizzle Cola and Yomama Kabushiki Gaisha."

"What breakdown?" Mr. Hue said and turned to look at me. He was still pointing his finger, but I could tell he was waking up to the reality and that he didn't like it. I moaned and curled into a ball, trying to hold my aching guts in place.

"The latest reports show that Yomama is still interested in the Shizzle brand," said the anchorwoman, and I breathed a sigh of relief.

"In a plot twist worthy of *The Sixth Sense*, although with much less adorable actors, Yomama is now showing interest in the whole kit and caboodle. We have just learned that Yomama is behind the astonishing buying spree that saw over two hundred million shares change hands in a matter of hours. Our sources indicate that Yomama has already acquired forty-nine percent of the outstanding share stock and is fast on track to secure the needed majority."

"Hey!" Eleanor pounded on the partition until Kurt lowered it. "Hey! Listen to this, morons! You are not going to get your millions, after all!" She turned up the volume.

"What?" Kurt yelled and pulled over for the umpteenth time that day.

The anchorwoman put a hand to her earpiece. "We are now going live to our field correspondent Adam Baskin, reporting from Shizzle, Inc headquarters."

The screen split in two and showed the excited correspondent Baskin in front of the now-familiar marble steps. "Thank you, Samantha," he said, fidgeting and smiling nervously. "It seems that the Hue camp has thrown in a white flag, with many of the Shizzle executives seen visiting the Yomama headquarters, presumably to declare allegiance and beg to keep their jobs."

"What's going on?" Mr. Hue demanded. "Eleanor, do something!" His normally impassive face was contorting itself into an unfamiliar expression of terror.

"I don't work for you anymore, asshole!" she replied. "Sort it out yourself!"

"The annual Shizzle Gala event has been canceled," continued the correspondent. "The CEO of Shizzle Corporation could not be reached for comment."

"Aargh!" Mr. Hue roared. I shrank further into my corner, afraid to breathe. Eleanor laughed with delight and clapped her hands.

"This is NOT the American way!" Mr. Hue repeatedly punched the limo wall, although I noticed he was targeting the padded upholstered part, and not the hard trim. His face got dangerously red as he roared, "It's against the constitution! Stay away from my company!"

"It's not yours anymore!" Eleanor said with glee.

That was a major mistake on her part. Mr. Hue abandoned his wall demolition efforts and lunged for her throat with a hearty "Traitor!" scream. Eleanor and everyone else screamed too. Chad and Tara tried to pull Mr. Hue off, but it was no use, the man was powered by a full bucket of crazy. Eleanor would have been a goner if Kurt hadn't intervened.

We were all trying to peel Mr. Hue's fingers from Eleanor's esophagus when Kurt stuck a rifle out the window and shot a volley of bullets into the darkening sky.

The inside of the limo got instantly quiet, with only the TV still babbling away. Nobody else on the road paid much attention to that display - it was the evening commute and the prime time for road rage. We all stared at Kurt. He didn't look so pretty anymore. His hair looked like he'd been trying to pull it out, and his face was covered in angry red blotches.

Kurt pointed the rifle at Mr. Hue. "What's all this? Who's going to pay the ransom? Are you really broke?"

"Looks like it," Mr. Hue said haughtily. "I guess there's a silver lining in every cloud!"

"Well, that's bad news," Kurt said. "Really, really bad news."

"Indeed," Mr. Hue said. "I guess I'll be leaving now. I can hitchhike back, it's really no trouble..." he reached for the door handle.

"Not so fast!" Kurt interrupted him. With his messed up hair and bulging eyes, he looked like Jack Nicholson from *The Shining*. I half-expected him to bust out in "Here's Johnny!"

"You know what," he said instead. "Now that there are no millions, or yachts, or expensive hookers in my future, I think I will just keep on truckin' until I find me a nice secluded place in the country."

"That sounds nice!" I said, relieved. My stomach cramps let go a little.

"And once I'm there," Kurt continued cheerfully, without taking his eyes off Mr. Hue, "I'll take my time cutting y'all into a thousand pieces, slowly, one by one, while the others are watching!"

My stomach lurched. I heard a collective sharp intake of breath and a weak whimper from either Tara or Chad.

"Do I have to watch?" Serge asked. "Cause that would definitely make me barf!"

Kurt ignored him. "And I will leave *you*," he pointed the gun barrel at Mr. Hue, "for dessert!"

There was another whimper, and this time I was sure it was Chad. Mr. Hue, visibly deflated, tried to hold on to some of his poise. "You can't do that! I'm a celebrity!"

"Well," Kurt said, "celebrity or not, that's what's gonna happen. Unless, of course, you have an idea where I can get me a hundred million dollars?"

"I have an idea," Eleanor said.

"Shut up, Eleanor!" Mr. Hue whispered through a fake smile and tried to kick her.

"You shut up!" she said. "Would you rather die?"

"It's a bluff!" Mr. Hue continued like a ventriloquist. "They're not going to kill the seventh-richest man in the Southeast, it's just not possible!"

"You idiot!" Eleanor hissed. "In case you didn't notice, your ranking just took a nose dive!"

"You know, we can hear you!" Kurt said. Serge nodded.

Mr. Hue gave up and deflated all the way into an average, gray-haired, middle-aged man. Eleanor spilled the details of his "rainy day" stash, distributed among a dozen Swiss bank accounts. All in all, Mr. Hue had stashed away close to a billion dollars. The rainy days must be a lot harder on the rich folk.

After Kurt pinkie-promised to let everyone live and take only a hundred million dollars, Mr. Hue brightened up a bit, even offering to pilot his private jet to "Swissland". I poured myself another glass of champagne. It seemed that, one way or another, I was going to die that day.

After we'd driven off, and the partition screen went up again, Mr. Hue turned to Eleanor.

"I curse you, woman!" he said with an occultist's flair. "I condemn thee to suffer my pain thousand-fold!"

"Oh, fuck off, will you?" Eleanor replied. In her cool accent, even common cuss words sounded somehow superior. My gratitude to her for averting slow death at the hands of Jack Nicholson was so overwhelming that I was ready to kiss her.

"She's the one who started it!" she added, pointing at me. Suddenly I didn't mind Kurt killing her slowly while others watched.

Mr. Hue halted his voodoo rituals and turned his attention to me.

"No, I didn't," I said quickly. "I didn't do anything!"

"Wait," he said. "You did do something. You did the last presentation to Yomama."

"What? Ah, that was nothing," I said, waving my hand dismissively.

"They left," Mr. Hue said, furrowing his brow. "But you told me they were impressed!"

"They were!" I nodded enthusiastically and slid further away from him.

"You speak Japanese, so surely you would have overheard them talking about the plot?" he said. "Are you part of the plot?"

I tried pointing out that I was not qualified to take part in any sort of a decent plot, but he started a new tantrum, this time something about industrial espionage.

"Leave her alone," Tara said. "She doesn't speak Japanese!"

"Shut up, Tara!" I snapped.

"I'm just trying to help!" Tara said and turned her attention back to Chad. She was as shit at helping me as she was at terrorism. There was no hope for that frog.

Mr. Hue leaned in, burning me with his eyes and flaring his nostrils like a prize bull.

"Do you or do you not speak Japanese, Ms. Maxwell?" he asked.

"Ahm…" I said.

"I want an answer, Ms. Maxwell!" He looked like he was ready to punch something else, maybe even me.

I looked around for support. Eleanor was watching us with feverish anticipation. Chad was doing something with Tara's ear, and Tara was giggling like an idiot. Kurt and Serge were once again behind the divider.

I decided to throw myself at the mercy of the court. "I'm sorry!" I cried. Tears were my last line of defense against a billionaire scorned. "I don't speak Japanese! I don't know anything about marketing strategies or mergers! I tried so hard, but I was in over my head! It's not my fault! I just graduated from a community college, what do you expect from me?"

"Community college?" Mr. Hue was visibly confused. "I thought you graduated from Harvard?"

My tears dried instantly. "I thought you didn't care about credentials?" I mumbled.

"This is better than soaps!" Eleanor said.

"You know what I care about?" Mr. Hue said. "I care about a person's character! And you know what makes up character?"

I shook my head.

"Loyalty!" Mr. Hue shoved a fist in front of my face and theatrically unfolded his thumb. "Attitude! Credit history! Balls!" he kept on unfolding fingers, "And finally," he held out his pinkie, "Honesty!"

I felt the tears welling up again.

"I can get away with an occasional lie," he continued, seemingly unconcerned about my obvious distress, "but that's the benefit of being a celebrity CEO! You, however, don't have that luxury. You're fired!"

"What?" I knew it was coming, but it was still a shock.

"Fired! And you can expect a visit from my lawyers very shortly!" He moved back into his seat, spent.

The fear and anxiety practically shredded my guts. The pain was immense, like that last time I had a gas station sandwich. It had to stop before my insides spontaneously combusted.

"Honey," I tried one last card, my ace. "You don't mean that! I know you're upset, but don't forget that we love each other. We can weather this storm together."

That got his attention.

"Love?" he asked, turning to me. Behind him, Eleanor was openly laughing.

"So I said it first. Big deal!"

"Eew!" Tara tore herself away from Chad. "He's almost as old as your Dad! That's, like, so gross!"

"Don't judge our love!" I snapped at her.

"He doesn't love you," Eleanor said, wiping away tears.

"What would you know about love, old maid?" I said.

That must've hit a raw nerve. Eleanor started screaming about her *Kama Sutra* skills, and I hit back with "Karma Chameleon". I'd almost forgotten about Mr. Hue until he yelled "Enough!" at the top of his lungs.

That got everyone's attention. Tara even stopped sucking Chad's thumb.

"Honey," I said reproachfully. "You shouldn't get so worked up, it's not good for your…"

"Stop saying 'honey'!" Mr. Hue barked, his face the color of beet-root dip. "And for the love of God, stop saying I love you!"

"Why?" I demanded. "Are you ashamed of our love? I am not

afraid of saying it! I love you! I love you! I love you!"

"Stop it!" Mr. Hue yelled.

"Never!" I said, defiant. "Now you say it!"

"Fudgesucking Christ!" Mr. Hue screamed and tried to rip out handfuls of his hair. "For the last fudgesucking time, stop it! I don't love you, I never have, and I never will!"

"Told you," Eleanor said smugly.

"Why?" I persisted, even though the small voice of reason inside me said it was time to shut up. "Never mind, I know! It's cause you're a bitter old man incapable of love!"

"No!" Mr. Hue screamed, veins threatening to explode from his temples. "I am *so* capable!"

"Oh yeah?" I said, "Then how come you're single? How come you're so rich, but don't even have a girlfriend? Huh? Huh?"

Mr. Hue's face contorted, almost like that metal robot in the last scene of *Terminator II*. A strange emotion was trying to make its way to the surface of the usual mask.

"Because," he finally managed to say, "I'm gay."

The last words came out slow and deliberate, and even though he said them quietly, they hit me with hurricane force. I crumpled, not believing what I'd heard.

"What?"

"I'm gay," he said a bit louder, for everyone to hear.

"Told you," Eleanor said.

"Yeah, we know," Tara said, and Chad nodded.

"You do?" Mr. Hue and I asked in unison.

"Everyone does!" Eleanor said. "The only reason it's not in all the papers is because you own them!"

"Everyone?" Mr. Hue said, confused, but visibly relieved.

"I didn't know!" I said.

"It doesn't surprise me," Mr. Hue seethed, his face returning to its lethal expression. "Frankly, Ms. Maxwell, I've started having doubts about your supposedly superior cognitive abilities ever since Eleanor told me that you are an idiot."

"Told you," Eleanor slurred. I gave her a look which, while it could not kill, hopefully gave her cancer.

"But," continued Mr. Hue, "I persevered in believing that you were special, despite all the evidence to the contrary. I even chose to ignore your obvious fashion faux pas." He gestured at my dress.

"I thought you liked it! You said it was…"

"Never mind what I said! What matters is what I thought when I said it! And I thought you looked like a cheap hooker!"

Eleanor laughed like a drunk hyena and, to my horror, Chad and even Tara chuckled.

"And now," Mr. Hue continued, "I find out that all this time you were the only one dumb enough to believe my heterosexual facade? Just how blond are you, Ms. Maxwell?"

I looked from him to the others, speechless. They were all laughing. Even Tara, my supposedly best friend, was barely concealing her giggles.

"Well," I said, choking back tears. "Fine. I know when I'm not wanted!"

"Are you sure you do?" Eleanor asked with mock concern.

"Yes!" I said. "I do! I am outta here!"

"The doors are locked," said Eleanor, which set off another bout of hysteria.

She was right - I was trapped. The tears in my eyes distorted my companions into laughing monsters. It was hard to believe that not long ago I considered some of them my friends and even potential lovers. Except for Eleanor, of course, who was an enemy from the get-go. Desperate, I turned to the last resort, usually reserved for final exams and near-collisions.

Dear God, with art in heaven, I prayed to the omnipotent being in whose existence I usually did not believe. Father be thigh name, and kingdom come will be on earth.

Overcome with emotion and hope that the Almighty would consider getting me out of this mess, I raised my tearful eyes towards the heavens. And there it was, in all its glory - God's gift to His prodigal daughter.

The sunroof.

*

I jumped up and pushed the "open" button. The roof retracted in a smooth whoosh, and I felt a wave of unfamiliar rapture, which made me momentarily jealous of church devotees. I stuck my head outside. The night was advancing quickly, and the cool air rushed past me, drying my tears.

"Sometimes I feel like a superhero!" Eazy-E proclaimed in my head.

I looked down at the laughing fools below.

"I'm gonna jump!" I declared, my head swimming with new resolve and close to a full bottle of champagne.

"Don't be stupid," Tara said. "You'll die!"

"Don't call me stupid!" I yelled back at her. "And if I do die, then who's gonna look stupid at my funeral?"

For some reason, my declaration sent them into further hysteria. That did it. I grunted and hoisted myself up onto the roof. Luckily it was covered in alien-looking patterns that afforded a decent grip, otherwise the wind would have blown me off. I carefully twisted around and sat on the edge, my legs dangling inside the cabin.

"C'mon, Isa," Tara called from below. "Come down, we are all sorry."

"I'm not!" Eleanor snickered.

I ignored them. The fresh air cleared my head enough for me to realize that jumping off the limo would be definite suicide. Still, I couldn't just go back down and give Tara the satisfaction of being right. I decided to sit on the roof for a while, until it was clear to everyone that the decision to abandon the jump was my own and not Tara's.

In any case, it was super cool to sit up there. I suddenly got why all those teenagers died trying to surf buses and trains. Stupid or not, it was exhilarating. I was facing the back of the limo and had an awesome view of the clouds, painted all the different colors by the last rays of the dying sun. The wide highway looked like a shiny black river, carving its path through thickets of trees and subdivisions. I put my arms out and sang "Perched up high on a rooftop, like a bird, I'm havin' evil thoughts!" along with Eazy-E in my head.

Indeed, I was having all kinds of evil thoughts, from using my charm to disarm Serge, to kicking all of my former friends and colleagues in their various body parts, to later stealing Mr. Hue's millions myself. It was strangely satisfying.

Tara popped her head out just as I imagined walking into a Swiss bank, disguised as Eleanor.

"Isa, I'm serious," she said. "Come down at once!" She tried grabbing me, and I slapped her hands away.

She kept on grabbing, and I was about to smack her good and proper, like I should have done earlier, when I saw something on the horizon. At first it was a tiny shimmering speck, but it quickly grew larger, and then separated into a whole orchestra of flashing lights.

"It's the cops!" I yelled in excitement. "We are saved! Praise the Lord!" Religious beliefs aside, I believe in giving credit where credit's due.

Other heads popped out of the sunroof, "What? Where?"

I pointed at the fast-approaching police convoy and laughed with joy, completely forgetting just how much I hated everyone only a few minutes ago.

Just at that moment, the limo suddenly jerked. Either Kurt noticed the cops himself, or he lost control slapping Serge around - either way it was enough to knock me off my perch. I went tumbling down the side. Death seemed imminent until I managed to grasp the edge of the sunroof.

Everyone screamed, myself the loudest. I was hanging for dear life on the driver's side of the limo. My legs were dangling so low that I could run alongside if I was a superhero, except it was now painfully clear that I was not.

"Help!" I yelled the obvious.

"Give me your hand!" Tara screamed.

I tried to think what to do, but all I could think about was how everyone yells "help!" and "give me your hand!" in these situations.

"I can't!" I yelled back. "I'm using it to hold on!"

Tara and Chad held onto my wrists as I continued dangling, wishing desperately that I'd spent the last couple of years going to the gym and doing chin-ups. I thought about how all those stupid bodybuilders would have already pulled themselves back up, and how those people who thought that bodybuilders were stupid were themselves the real idiots.

I could hear Eleanor banging on the partition and yelling for Kurt to stop. Mr. Hue was also helping, directing Chad and Tara to continue holding me, and Eleanor to keep banging and yelling at Kurt.

Kurt didn't stop. He didn't even slow down. The limo was going faster and faster, as the police cars came closer and closer. Chad reached down and tried to get a better grip on me, but his hand slipped.

"Pull yourself up!" he yelled. For once I had a good comeback, something along the lines of "Shut up, Captain Obvious", but I was too busy screaming.

Eventually, with everyone's help and encouragement, I managed to pull myself up a little higher and was hanging on the edge by my armpits, trying to catch my breath.

Just as salvation seemed near, the cops opened fire on the limo. Bullets zipped through the air, bouncing off glass and metal.

"Stop!" I screamed. "Stop shooting!"

My helpers ducked down inside, thankfully still holding onto my hands. I slipped back and started thrashing about again, trying to get a foothold on the side.

Suddenly I felt an angry bee sting my butt. "Aargh!" I screamed, wondering if it could get any worse, now that bees were attacking me as well.

Just then another bee stung me in the arm, except it was not a bee after all. The familiar smell of spent gunpowder told me the impossible. I'd been shot.

Considering how many hours I'd spent at shooting ranges, it was actually surprising this was the first time I ever felt a bullet ripping through my flesh. Somehow, nobody had accidentally discharged a gun in my direction, at least not yet. It was probably only a matter of time before I myself forgot the safety switch and wrecked my foot. Regardless, until that moment I had no idea just how much it could hurt.

And oh my God, it hurt! My right hand, instantly rendered useless, slipped out of Tara's grip. I was hanging on only by my left, and I could feel it slipping, too.

"Help me!" I begged Chad. "I'm too young to die!"

"You're not going to…" Chad bellowed and let me slip out of his grip.

God, or whatever is up there, was once more on my side. One of my Gucci straps got caught on an alien antennae ornament and halted my fall. I watched Chad's mouth form a surprised "oops", just as a police cruiser attempted a fishtail maneuver. Kurt tried to avoid the impact by swerving to the left, and I swung around onto the front shield, facing him and Serge.

I screamed. They screamed back at me but did not stop, instead wrestling over the control of the steering wheel. I slid back and forth on the windshield of the runaway limo, feeling the strap giving way with every move. Still screaming, I did the only thing I could think of. I pulled down the other strap.

Serge pointed at my boob, his face a picture of childish delight. Not to brag, but Kurt also lost attention. That, and control of the limo.

The cops took advantage of the situation and tried fishtailing again. This time, they succeeded. The limo's rear tires lost traction, and it began to skid, spinning out of control. Finally, like a rag doll, I flew off into the summer dusk.

The afterlife is just like I imagined it, all white and empty.

That should've been the end of this story, but God bestowed me with a third miracle that day. This one came in the form of a huge trash pile.

That particular stretch of the highway shoulder happened to be the city's most popular illegal dumping spot. Over the years, it had become a landmark, with locals giving direction to their homes as "the first exit after The Tip". The Tip was enormous. Its humble beginnings were in just one man's refusal to pay for municipal services, but it grew quickly, as others used the excuse of "everyone's doing it".

At first, the city council kept trying to clean up the mess, but this only encouraged residents to dump again. Fines didn't work either, as the officers trying to issue them were regularly assaulted, pelleted by rotten tomatoes, or even thrown into the trash pile. The city tried to organize a volunteer clean-up program, but nobody volunteered. The problem was exacerbated by the homeless, who took up residence in the valleys of The Tip and adamantly protected their territory.

On the day when I flew head-first into the sprawling landscape of mattresses and garbage bags, the city was trying out a new "zero tolerance" policy. The idea was that after a few weeks of living with a stinking fly- and rat-infested pile, the locals would come to their senses and start using dedicated bins. The exercise proved yet again how out of touch the government was with their constituents. The locals objected, staged protests, signed petitions and condemned the council officers as 'dirty pigs', but did not stop dumping. In the end, I owed those council pigs and stubborn citizens my life. Thanks to the extra layer of freshly deposited garbage, I did not break my neck and got away with just a concussion and severe blood poisoning.

I still can't recall the actual flight over The Tip. According to the accounts of homeless inhabitants, I looked like Superman in a black negligee. What I do remember is waking up in a bright white place without walls, or a ceiling, or even a floor. It was like floating on a cloud. I thought that I've died and went to Heaven, except there were no other dead people around. A wave of dread came over me. It had to be Hell, my own personal version where I wouldn't get to talk to anyone or watch TV for all eternity. Just as fresh tears welled in my eyes, a black man dressed in all white appeared before me. He looked a lot like Morgan Freeman, although afterwards I couldn't be quite sure.

"Are you Morgan Freeman?" I asked.

"No, I am God," He said.

"Wow," I said, impressed. "God is a black man after all!"

"No," He corrected me. "I am an omnipotent and omnipresent being of pure energy. I only appear as a man to you, because that's all a human mind can comprehend. And *yours* can't even imagine a female deity. Do you understand just how self-limiting your beliefs are about women? You and only you stop yourself from becoming the President, or at least the CEO of a major company."

"That sucks," I said. "It's like the end of *Contact*, where the alien turns out to look like Jodie Foster's father. I always thought they must've run out of budget for proper computer graphics."

"Trust me," God said. "You can't handle my true form. It would blow your mind so hard that…"

"Funny," I said, looking around. "The afterlife is just like I imagined it, all white and empty."

"No," God said impatiently. "The afterlife can be anything your mind can imagine. Apparently, this is all yours is capable of, the scene from *Bruce Almighty*."

"That was a great film," I said defensively.

"It's goood!" God agreed.

"Hey!" I said. "That's straight from *Bruce Almighty*! You get on my case for borrowing the afterlife scene, and then go on and quote from it yourself!"

"So what?" He said. "I created it."

"No, you didn't. I am pretty sure it was that comedian, what's his name?"

"Jim Carrey," He said. "But no, it was in fact written by Steve Koren, Mark O'Keefe, and Steve Oedekerk."

"Who?"

"It doesn't matter. I created life on Earth, and therefore by definition I created everything, including Steve Koren and *Bruce Almighty*."

"You sound just like my Dad," I said.

"I know," He said smugly. "I created him, too."

"Well," I matched His tone, "you could have tried a bit harder there!"

"Look," He said, sounding strangely tired for an immortal. "Let's just get to business. I am here to help you learn a lesson in life, blah, blah, blah. Let's make it quick. I have other souls to attend to."

"Jeez, what's so good about being God if you have to work so much?"

God rolled his eyes, "I can see this is going to be one of those days. How about this, we'll make it a multiple choice."

"Jesus fu— I mean God. God, I just finished my exams. Do we really need this quiz? Is this Hell?"

"No." He closed His eyes and pinched the bridge of His nose. "Think of this as a waiting room. I need to know that you've learned your life's lesson. You can't proceed to the afterlife until you've answered correctly."

"Wait a sec," I said. "So you're telling me that if I answer *wrong*, I get to go home, but if I answer *right*, I stay dead?"

"Jesus Christ!" God exclaimed, throwing His hands up. "Enough of this! Here is your life lesson. I know you feel lost and alone, and you think that money and fame are the answer to your problems. They are not. Discover your true purpose. Love yourself. Cherish your family and friends - they are all you have. *That's* the meaning of life."

"You're doing it again!" I pointed at Him, excited. "That's basically what the father-alien told Jodie Foster on that fake beach! Did you create *Contact* as well? Cause that was a shit movie!"

"That's it, I give up!" God said and then, just like that, I woke up in a garbage pile, looking up at concerned dirty faces.

*

The homeless guys turned out to be very nice, except for a scrawny little man called Fat Joe. He tried to claim ownership over me because I landed in his patch, but he shut up quickly after Midget put a huge hairy fist in front of his face.

They helped me get out of the rubbish but refused to go anywhere near "the fuzz". Holding my bleeding butt cheek with one hand and the broken Gucci strap with the other, I hobbled over to the assembly of flashing lights and spectators. I managed to squeeze through the crowd in time to see Kurt regain consciousness with the help of smelling salts and a lot of yelling from paramedics. A police detective bent over him, demanding to know his name.

"Aargh!" Kurt yelled and spat in the detective's face. "Take that, you fucking pig!"

Serge, who until then was quietly sitting on the ground nearby with his hands cuffed behind his back, took Kurt's spitball as a call to battle. He jumped up and head-butted one of the paramedics. He got knocked back down, but wouldn't give up, biting ankles like a dog. The other cops started to push back on the crowd, asking everyone to "move along" because there was "nothing to see here". Behind them, the detective began to administer police brutality to Kurt and Serge with the help of the injured paramedic and a couple of beefy police officers.

At first I got pushed back with the others, probably because I looked like one of the homeless. I certainly smelled like one. After a lot of explaining and presentation of bullet wounds, I was taken to one of the ambulance vans. By then Mr. Hue had already left in a private helicopter and Eleanor had been taken into custody. Tara and Chad were still on the scene, making out in the back of another ambulance. Looking at their carnal display, I realized that I no longer cared about them, or Mr. Hue, or my failed career. In fact, I cared so little that I passed out again.

I didn't see God this time. Instead, I kept running through derelict backyards in some abandoned suburb, looking for something, although I didn't know what it was. It was probably water, because it was hot, and my lips were cracked. I pushed on through scraggly bushes and weeds, getting scratches on my butt and arm. There was no water anywhere, not a drop. It was like drowning in the dust. I would have given half a kingdom for a Red Bull, but nobody answered my cries for help.

When I eventually broke through the surface of that nightmare and cracked my eyes open, Harden was there. I was lying on a hard, narrow bed, and he was sitting on a chair next to me. My hand was lost somewhere between his face and huge paws. It was wet.

"Harden," I croaked.

His head shot up, and he looked at me in disbelief, his eyes swollen and red.

"Water," I managed.

"Nurse! Nurse!" Harden roared. I heard a stampede of feet and fell back into the dream.

I wasn't as thirsty after that, but the dreams got more intense. Everyone was angry with me, and I didn't know why. Every time I woke up shouting "No, you're a turd!" and "Yomama is fat!" I got pumped with sedatives. That went on for weeks. As the doctors explained later, I picked up a vicious bacteria in the sea of garbage, and it was a miracle that I survived. The bacteria strain was new and resistant to antibiotics, which created much hype in the scientific world, but went unnoticed by the general population. That was understandable, considering that all the newspaper print space was filled with images of Duchess Kate breastfeeding on a remote private island. You've got to give it to paparazzi - they work hard for their money.

Picking up that bacteria turned out to be a lucky break for me, because a research grant paid for all my medical expenses. Of course, the downside was that I almost died, but it was still better than getting forever trapped by a crippling medical debt. The research guys even named the bacteria in my honor, *Streptobella* or something like that.

I spent so long in the suspended state between life and death that when I finally woke up in an empty white room and saw my parents holding hands, I knew for sure that it was the afterlife.

"Mom...Dad..." I croaked. "Why are you dead?"

"We're not, honey," Mom said gently and wiped my forehead in the way a movie nurse would comfort a mortally wounded soldier.

"Am *I* dead?" I asked, confused.

"No," Dad said. "But you *almost* died! You made us look like idiots!"

I was trying to get enough air in my lungs to attempt a scream about his selfishness when I saw Mom put her hands up to Dad in a familiar pacifying gesture.

"Are you back together?" I asked instead.

"Yes," Mom beamed. "Your father apologized and took me on a most spectacular second honeymoon! Can you believe it?"

I could not believe the "Dad apologizing" part, but I remembered paying an exorbitant amount for their honeymoon on Mr. Hue's credit card. The memory brought tears to my eyes. Mom started crying too. Dad mumbled something about inspecting the facilities and left.

After we were done hugging and crying, Mom caught me up with the goss, the juiciest bit of which was that my sister and Mark had separated.

"But don't worry," Mom whispered conspiratorially. "They're both happy and dating new people."

I was about to ask how it could be possible that my older, divorced with children, sister was dating, and I was not when Felicity came in. I'd never seen her so relaxed and satisfied - she looked like the proverbial cat that ate the canary. The canary turned out to be David, my hot neighbor.

"I'm happy for you," I said. "I'm just so confused right now...I honestly thought David was coming onto me."

"Oh, he probably was," Felicity said. "The man's a horny dog. I have to keep him on a short leash and trust me, I do!" she added, raising her eyebrows. Mom and I exchanged a look of acceptance that neither one of us would ever understand Felicity. It felt good to find something in common with Mom.

Mom was doing much better, despite getting back together with Dad. The separation, followed by a romantic trip, had done wonders for their relationship and Mom's self-confidence. She'd even started working again, first volunteering to help in my ward and then getting a part-time nursing position, thankfully on another floor. Dad rumbled threats against the hospital's doctors and came every day to have lunch with her, to make sure some "hotshot" was not planning to steal his wife. In other words, they were in love again.

There was so much love around me, it was depressing. I was too weak to Google-stalk Brad, but not too weak to flirt with hospital staff. Unfortunately, none of my attempts to attract a doctor's interest in something other than my rare bacteria strain had any success. I even tried to hit on one of the students when he came around to rebandage my damaged butt cheek, but he just blushed and left.

The most embarrassing fiasco occurred when I tried to chat up a male nurse, who turned out to be none other than my sister's ex-husband Mark. In my defense, I did not recognize him. He not only got a new haircut and started working out, but slight changes, like the way he stood up straighter and laughed easily, added up to a completely new man.

Mark was the picture of professionalism and pretended not to get my lame come-on. We never talked about it again, but ended up having great conversations about everything else, sometimes in the middle of the night. It was too bad that we didn't get to know each other while he was married to Felicity, because he turned out to be very funny and a good listener. He always had something encouraging to say whenever I felt sad over my miserable job prospects, loneliness, or scarred body parts.

"One day," he'd say, "when you least expect it, a Prince Charming will find you." I didn't believe him, of course, but it always made me smile. I tried asking Mark about his Princess Charming, but he avoided the subject, so I assumed she was a stripper or something.

The cops came and questioned me. I told them everything the first time around, but the whole unit showed up again, because they had to "hear it for themselves". Thankfully, they returned my evening bag and my phone, so I was able to call Harden.

"Hey," he said. "You're awake!"

"Yeah," I said, "and look, I'm calling you, and I don't even need your help!"

"That's cause you already got my blood," he said.

"What?"

"You needed so many blood transfusions that the hospital asked friends and family to donate. Turned out you and I have the same blood type."

"Wow," I said, touched. "It's almost like we're relatives now!"

"I guess so."

"That's too bad," I laughed. "Now we definitely can't have sex!"

He didn't laugh.

"C'mon, Harden, I'm joking!"

"I know," he said.

We kept talking, and I told him all about the kidnapping ordeal, but something was wrong. There was a new awkwardness between us, and too much politeness. I didn't know what to say or do about it. Later, Harden came to visit me several times, but his visits were the same, awkward and polite, and too brief. There were hardly any jokes, and I couldn't bring myself to ask him about crying over my hand.

Except for the boredom, hospital life was great. Anytime I needed something, I just had to press a button. It was almost like being rich. According to Mom, it was even better in the mental health ward, where you could be called "Your Majesty" if you so desired. Strangely, I found I no longer wanted the riches or a celebrity status. So what if I didn't own a house or a car for that matter? At least I didn't have to worry about getting kidnapped or losing my fortune. *"Better to have loved and lost than never to have loved at all" doesn't seem to apply to the love of money*, I thought, recalling how Mr. Hue flipped out over the news about the hostile takeover. No wonder rich women were often too thin. It was probably from stressing so much about their cash.

Gradually, my preoccupation with fame and fortune was replaced with a new and a much nobler passion. It was a logical one, considering that I was never going to find another boyfriend. Instead, I was going to pick up where Mother Teresa left off.

I googled the woman obsessively. I didn't like the organized religion bit or the vows of obedience, but I admired her dedication to the poor. My brief experience with the truly destitute at The Tip proved to me that the homeless were nice and generous. One of them even offered to bandage my wounds with the hem of her dirty skirt. Of course, I wouldn't live with them like Mother Teresa did, but I could help by throwing fabulous fundraising parties. At least I would use something I'd learned during my short stint as Mr. Hue's protégé, since I was never going to see that first paycheck.

Thinking of Mr. Hue and Shizzle, Inc made me so anxious that I refused to watch the news. Dad tried to tell me something about how history will look back at the event, but I burst into such intense tears that he cleared out of the room and never brought the subject up again.

I was pretty good at ignoring Mr. Hue during the day, but he haunted me in my dreams. They all started innocently, with me at a picnic in the park, or naked at the final exams, but always ended with the same dreadful scene. Mr. Hue, grotesquely deformed after the limo accident and dressed in a horrific striped sweater, demanded that I pay back his billion-dollar losses.

"But I'm broke!" I would scream.

"Not quite yet," he'd say, stretching his bony fingers with long, blade-like nails to my throat, "Let me show you how it's done!"

I'd wake up screaming, covered in sweat. The nightmares continued, despite my attempts at self-medicating with Tara's contraband, until one morning I woke up to find Mr. Hue manifested in my visitor's chair.

Show us ya' tits!

Mr. Hue was wearing a terrible striped polo shirt, although not as bad as the one in my dream. He was eating the hospital version of Jell-O.

"Are you going to kill me?" I croaked, well aware that I would not be able to defend myself if he was.

"Goodness, no!" Mr. Hue daintily dabbed his mouth with a tissue. "I hope you get better very, very soon. As a matter of fact, I'm here to offer you a job."

"A job?"

"Yes," he said gravely. "That's the least I can do."

The rest of the conversation was not at all like the one in my dream. Mr. Hue was convinced that I not only saved his life and fortune from Kurt but also ran off Yomama on purpose, after expertly discovering a hidden clause in the merger contract. Had the contract been executed, the clause would have transferred the ownership of the Shizzle brand to Yomama.

"I can't believe nobody read the contract!" Mr. Hue fumed.

"Did you read it?"

"Don't be ridiculous," he said. "I *pay* people to do that. In that particular case, I paid Thomas, but it turned out that so did Yomama. Of course, it was a stroke of brilliance on my part to take the project away from Thomas and give it to you instead. I must have had a gut instinct!"

"So what about the hostile takeover?"

"It looked pretty bad there for a few days," Mr. Hue shook his head. "But as I always said, possessions don't matter as long as you have a billion stashed away in a Swiss bank. In the end, Yomama couldn't get the majority of votes, because one of our employees bought enough of the company shares when everyone else was selling. You may remember him, an annoying old guy in big glasses, constantly whining about the falling share prices?"

I nodded. "Are you going to promote him, now that he's shown how much he cares about Shizzle?"

"I would," Mr. Hue said, looking through an assortment of foodstuffs on my bedside table. "Unfortunately the old bastard threw a tantrum, sold his stake after the prices shot back up, took the millions and went to retire on an island somewhere." Mr. Hue sighed. "You know, he had the nerve to call me a 'rich jingoist' and a 'warmonger.' I don't even know what that means! What does it mean?"

I assured him that it probably meant a philanthropist or something like that. When he asked what *that* meant, I had to explain it as "someone who helps the poor". That seemed to settle his nerves.

"How about it, Ms. Maxwell?" he asked, opening another container of Jell-O. "Will you come back to Shizzle, Inc? I owe you a debt of gratitude."

"Are you apologizing for yelling and firing me? That's pretty big of you!"

"Oh, that's nothing," he said through a mouthful of Jell-O. "This one time, I accused an entire country of genocide, and then had to take it all back. Now, that was a doozy!"

He scooped the last bit of the Jell-O out of the cup with his finger. "So, what's your answer, Ms. Maxwell?"

I thought about his offer and what it would be like to work again with a bipolar idiot. "No," I said politely. "I just don't think I'm cut out for the corporate mosh pit. Too much drama, too much stress." The memory of him hulking up in the limo was still too fresh to let me say what I really thought.

"Suit yourself," he said, licking the Jell-O cup. "What is this magical dessert? It's delightful!"

I explained what Jell-O was and where one could get it.

"Grocery store?" he asked in disbelief. "I must dispatch Jean Baptiste to that place at once! I'm starting to question the point of importing Parisian chefs."

He got up to leave, I presume to get some more Jell-O, when Mark came into the room carrying a lunch tray.

"Hi!" Mark squeaked and dropped the tray. The gooey gray hospital porridge went flying everywhere, but Mark just stared stupidly at Mr. Hue.

"Hi, Mark!" I said, sympathetic to how intimidated he must feel in the presence of the famous billionaire. "This is Mr. Hue. I used to work with him before the..."

"I've never met him!" Mark exclaimed. From my newfound pedestal of Mother Teresa-like piety, I couldn't help but feel superior to Mark's celebrity worship.

"This is Mark, my ex-brother-in-law," I said to Mr. Hue.

Mr. Hue started to say something, but Mark jumped in with "What a pleasure to meet you!" and a violent handshake.

"Honey," Mr. Hue said. "We have nothing to hide."

Honey. That one word sent me straight back to the limo, to the feeling of being cornered by laughing hyenas. Blood rushed to my face.

"What?" I couldn't believe my ears. "Did you just call me honey?"

"Yes, we do," Mark said to Mr. Hue. "I have the boys to think about."

"They will love you just the way you are," Mr. Hue said.

"Who is 'they'?" I said. "What the hell? You know, I said I forgave you for yelling and embarrassing me, but really, this is off-pissing! Remember how you humiliated me for calling you 'honey' and saying 'I love you'?"

"And what about you and your reputation?" Mark asked. "It will be in all the papers!"

"Good point!" I said. "My reputation is already ruined, thank you very much!"

Mr. Hue shrugged. "Any publicity is good publicity, right? I'll probably end up making even more money."

"Money?" I yelled. "Unbelievable! All you think about is money! What am I, just a pawn in your game?"

"I'm just worried that you..." Mark kept trying to butt in.

"Don't worry about me," Mr. Hue smiled gently.

That hit a nerve. "Worry about you? You know who should

worry about you? You! You should worry about how I'm finally going to lose it and smack you upside the head! And I would get away with it, too. I've got a concussion!"

I was waving my arms about, demonstrating how close I was to losing it when they kissed. I froze with my arms still in the air. They ignored me, kissing passionately, their hands caressing each other's cheeks. I'd never seen two men kiss in real life, and the show had me mesmerized for a few moments.

"Hey!" I finally managed, feeling more confused than ever. "Hey, what the hell is going on here?"

They tore away from each other and turned to me, looking like two teenagers on a prom date.

"We're in love!" Mr. Hue announced.

"What?" I said. "But I thought you said that you're gay!"

"Yes," Mr. Hue said slowly, as if to a child. "That's why I'm in love with a man." He nodded to Mark, who was looking down and blushing like a new bride.

"But, but," I stuttered. "Mark is not…"

"Yes, I am," Mark said, looking up at me. "I've always been. I was just too afraid to admit it to myself."

He told me the story, still holding onto Mr. Hue, as if afraid. It turned out that he was always afraid, first of what his old-fashioned parents would say, then of what his high-school football teammates would do. Then he met Felicity and liked her, probably because she acts like such a dude. Before he knew, they tried sex, and she was pregnant.

"And just like that," he told me, "I was locked in the closet forever."

When Felicity got drunk on the night of my near-fatal accident and announced that life was too short and that she wanted a divorce, he broke down and cried with happiness. They hugged like old friends who'd found each other again. Mark said that Felicity tried pulling down his pants "for old times' sake", but he was not going to fall for that again.

I asked if anyone else knew about their relationship. Mr. Hue got all misty-eyed, squeezed Mark's hand, and said something about how he was tired of pretending and that they may even get married, once his lawyers prepared a watertight prenup agreement. He'd already met the twins and couldn't stop gushing about the "little darlings". I almost asked if they were the same twins I knew, but Mark made a pleading face, and I shut up.

I thought Mark was crazy for picking a self-indulgent old weirdo as his first boyfriend, but he seemed happy, and so I was happy for them. Seemed that everyone was loved up, including Tara, who was the last one to visit me in the hospital. Not because she didn't care, but because she got into a bit of trouble for blowing up cars, attempted kidnapping, and whatnot. Lucky for her, Chad got promoted to detective for his heroics and used his newfound authority to mess up the evidence. The case against Tara was dismissed, the judge calling it "the worst case of police corruption since I was accused of DUI." As a punishment for his incompetence, Chad was suspended, which basically meant he got three months' leave with full pay. He and Tara were going to celebrate in Italy and invited me to come along with them, but I politely declined. I'd seen enough of their face-sucking already. Plus, staying in the hospital was already the best vacation I'd ever had.

Unfortunately, I was eventually asked to leave. The rare bacteria were gone, and the researchers were no longer interested in me or in paying my medical bills.

"But I still *feel* sick!" I pleaded with the head researcher, an emaciated bald man who looked like he was full of deadly bacteria himself. "Something is definitely wrong with me! Every time I think about going outside, my stomach hurts. Honest!"

"A psychosomatic response to trauma," he said, pushing his bony fingers into my neck. "It's interesting, of course, but not covered under our research grant. You have to go home. It's time for you to rejoin society."

If it were up to me, I would prefer to go live on an island somewhere and never see society again.

"Society and I grew apart," I told my parents and Harden when they came to pick me up. "I'm done waiting by the phone while it's out on the town, hanging out with its cool friends."

I was in the middle of explaining just how much I didn't care what anyone thought about me when I noticed a crowd of people near the entrance. At first I thought that there had been another accident, but then someone shouted "There she is!" and everyone snapped their necks to look at me. For one eerie moment, they looked like a mob of zombies sensing a fresh meal. I looked at Harden for an explanation. Then the mob surged towards me.

"Isabella! Ms. Maxwell!" Men and women I'd never seen before were shouting my name and shoving microphones into my face. Some were yelling out names of TV and radio channels while others were peppering me with questions.

"Ms. Maxwell, are you pregnant with the heir to the Shizzle fortune?"

"Isabella, can you comment on the rumors that you and Mr. Hue are engaged?"

"Where you part of the kidnapping plot?"

The paparazzi assault was petrifying and not at all exciting and glamorous, like it looks on TV. I shrunk back into the safety of Harden's bulk. He put one protective trunk-like arm around my shoulders and used the other to carve a path through the crowd towards his car. I looked back and saw that Mom and Dad were falling behind. Mom seemed to be enjoying the attention, striking poses for the cameras, as if she was on her way to the Oscars. Dad grabbed hold of one reporter's mike and was talking passionately. The reporter tried desperately to get the mike back, but it was no use.

"Who is Isabella Maxwell?" a frenzied woman shrieked in my face. "And how was she able to stop the runaway limo?"

Another reporter, an aging man with a full head of silver hair, shoved her aside. "Ms. Maxwell, everyone knows you did it by flashing the kidnappers. The public wants to know, it *deserves* to know, the power of your weapon of choice. Show us ya' tits!"

Harden roared and shoved him aside, instantly gaining another dozen brownie points in my book. The reporter, helpless against the force of mass-times-anger-squared, lost his footing and brought down a half-dozen other people. Harden took advantage of the opening in the crowd and dragged me towards the car. I wondered if the scene looked anything like the one from *The Bodyguard*. Probably not, considering that Harden had a hard time carrying his own weight, but it was still kind of romantic.

We made it into Harden's massive old Ford Bronco and locked the doors. The reporters surrounded the car, knocking and yelling. The silver-haired pervert was at the front, still demanding I take off my shirt. Others joined him, and soon everyone was chanting "Show us ya' tits!" and pounding on the car windows. I looked at Harden in horror, wondering if I should just do it and get it over with.

Harden looked ahead, determined. His set jaw and squinted eyes made him look like a Viking saving his mate from a pack of wolves. He revved the engine several times and made a small lurch forward. It was enough to get the people in the front out of the way, and the Bronco slowly rolled out of the parking lot.

"What about my parents?" I asked.

"They'll be fine," Harden said. "I'm sure they're loving it."

I nodded, and we drove in silence to my parents' house. My old place had been reclaimed by the rightful owners, who managed to sell it for a profit in the middle of the scandal. I was afraid there would be more reporters waiting for me, but there were none there. Yet.

Harden brought in my bag. "See you around," he said and made to leave.

"Wait!" I said. "Don't you want to stay for a coffee or something?"

He smirked, "Will ya show us ya' tits?"

I laughed and slapped his sleeve.

"Didn't think so," Harden sighed and lumbered away, leaving me standing in the hallway, speechless. This was the first time he'd said no to me.

I closed the door and went inside. My head was heavy, and I felt like a good cry. At first I thought it was because of the paparazzi, then maybe because I was back living with my parents, but neither were quite right. I took my bag to my old bedroom and rifled through it until I dug out my journal. I found a pen and wrote.

The heat.
The blinding sun.
They scream at me.
We run.

You protected me.

You've always protected me.

I took it for granted.

Forgive me.

I stared at the words, thinking about Harden. I hoped that there was still time. He always forgave me, no matter how emotional or crazy I got. I pushed the journal away and bawled into the pillow, overcome by a feeling that something, possibly everything, was wrong with me.

Say you want a guy to marry you...

I didn't see Harden again. I waited for a couple of days, but he didn't call. When I tried to call him, an automated voice informed me that the service had been disconnected. I called his mother.

"Didn't he tell you, hon?" she asked. "He's joined the Peace Corps. My baby lost his mind, is what he did."

She went on talking about how she begged him not to, and how "that boy never listens", but I wasn't listening either. Harden had left me.

To make matters worse, the paparazzi discovered my parents' house. My parents didn't seem to mind the obsessive attention, often stopping to chat with the army of reporters camped on the front lawn. I, on other hand, avoided going outside altogether. There was no need, really. Mom overfed me as usual, and there was plenty of money, at least for the moment. Mr. Hue sent over a lawyer with a fat check, and all I had to do was sign some paperwork. I did. I wanted the whole thing to be over so I could go back to my normal life, whatever that meant. Deep down, though, I knew that nothing would ever be "normal" again.

I spent most of my days writing in my journal. It was a cathartic experience to put all my jumbled thoughts down on paper. I also wrote long emails to Harden, but he never replied. He was probably on a tiny boat somewhere, throwing himself against Japanese whaling ships or protesting oil rig construction. I missed him like I would miss my arm or leg if it were cut off in some horrible accident, even though I never said so in the emails.

Somehow my cell number got "out there" and the phone never stopped ringing. Just about every morning news show asked to interview me, but I declined. I also declined offers of starring in bra commercials, being a spokesperson for a self-defence school, and even a weight-loss clinic. That last one really pissed me off. There were so many calls and offers that I forgot most of them.

Except for one. I remember that phone call as if it happened yesterday. It was almost lunchtime, but I was still in bed, sulking. The cell vibrated, and I saw "private" displayed along with the generic gray silhouette. *I should just change my number*, I thought, pressing the green button.

"I don't want to show my boobs on TV," I said angrily into the phone.

The woman on the other end chuckled. "I will keep that in mind. Still, I thought you might want to tell *your* side of the story." I was about to hang up when she added, "In a memoir, perhaps?"

The woman introduced herself as Sandra Torrent, a literary agent. She assured me that if I wanted to write a tell-all book, she could get me an advance from a major publisher.

"What's an advance?" I asked.

"It's a sum of money the publisher gives you in exchange for a promise that you will publish your story exclusively with them," she said. "How does a hundred thousand sound?"

I said that a hundred thousand in exchange for a promise sounded good indeed, and the rest was history, as Dad would say.

Sandra took over my life from there, pushing and prodding until I turned my journal entries into a somewhat coherent manuscript. Maybe it wasn't a product of a literary genius, but it was pretty good for a first book, and I wrote it all myself. My dream was coming true. Any normal person should've been happy, but I felt like something was missing. I didn't even have anyone to talk to, since Harden was gone, Tara moved in with Chad, and my sister was constantly in bed with David. That just left my parents who, to their credit, tried everything to cheer me up.

"One day," Dad would say, "you will look back at this time as a formative period in your writing career. This Shizzle story is nice, but you need to think about writing some serious fiction with a strong voice. Nobody's going to hand you a Pulitzer or a Nobel prize for this fluff."

I would scream at him, to prove that I did have a strong voice, but Dad would continue to motivate me against my will.

"You simply can't write anything meaningful without first experiencing the pain of living in this thankless world," he said to me one night, at the end of an hour-long lecture. "You must suffer first!"

"I *am* suffering!" I said, exasperated. "Right now, right this minute!"

"It's amateur suffering," Dad assured me. "Just imagine how much pain Emily Dickinson had to feel in order to write 'Heavenly hurt it gives us, we can find no scar...'"

"Dad!"

He ignored me. "...but internal difference, where the meanings are.' Did you know she had seasonal depression? Well, that, and all her loved ones kept dying. How's that for a heavenly hurt?"

Mom's advice was even worse. Pretty much all of it centered on some fairytale-perfect Prince Charming, who was going to run into me one day when I least expected it and fix everything. For some reason, the exact same well-meaning bullshit that I welcomed from Mark was pissing me off when she served it up.

"Enough with the Prince Charming!" I told her. "Why does everybody insist on that stupid story? I stopped expecting him a long time ago, so where is he? And I don't want him anyway! Life is not all about sex and babies. I'm going to stay single and help the poor!"

Mom and Dad usually supported all of my questionable initiatives, but they drew the line at my Mother Teresa plans and utterly forbid me from going to India.

"I'm going!" I screamed, even though the thought of getting on a plane made my stomach churn with fear. "Just as soon as my book is launched, and I finish the tour, I am *so* going there!"

Dad put together lengthy lectures of all the unsanitary horrors I was going to encounter, complete with photos and testimonies. He compiled death statistics on foreigners, categorized by diseases, traffic accidents, and armed robberies. Mom just cried and cried.

Thankfully, they got distracted a bit when Mark moved in with Mr. Hue, and they had to redirect all their energy to giving Felicity unsolicited advice on how to explain the situation to the twins. The boys continued acting like little monsters, so it was hard to say if the divorce had a negative impact on their already bad behavior. At least they each got a nanny, so the number of accidents and anti-social events reduced dramatically. I haven't visited them in a while but, judging from Mom's stories, they didn't miss me.

"They each got a pony," Mom said excitedly. "I don't approve, of course, that's just dangerous, but a *pony*! Can you believe that?"

Very soon after moving in together, Mr. Hue proposed to Mark with a diamond-encrusted Rolex. I got invited to the wedding as the one directly responsible for their off-chance meeting and also as a celebrity of sorts, which proved that Mr. Hue did welcome even bad publicity. I should've been happy about going to a party with a host of celebrities and watertight security, but instead kept freaking out over what to wear. The wound in my butt left a depression about the size of a devilled egg, and it showed through every dress I tried. Not only that, my right upper arm looked like it got stuck in an industrial press. I eventually settled on a fully lined black number with elbow-length sleeves. Standing in the fitting room, confronted by my mangled butt from three directions, I finally saw the folly of guns. Sure, they looked cool and were fun to shoot, but sometimes they shot wrong things, even innocent behinds. I swore to my reflection that I would donate my Sig Sauer to the poor. They certainly needed it more than me.

The wedding was beautiful, set in the French Renaissance gardens of Mr. Hue's mansion. The grooms wore matching white tuxes and vowed to forever love each other in front of the Hollywood stars, miscellaneous celebrities, and financial heavy-hitters. I had a small nag of self-pity that it was Mark and not me standing there, smiling like a happy idiot. I had to remind myself that being around Mr. Hue was no picnic and that a lifetime with him would eventually ruin memories of any wedding, no matter how kick-ass it was. There was just one little snag in the ceremony when the twins failed to appear with the rings, and everyone ran around like mad until they were found, asleep under a table. They'd gotten into the wedding cake early, but even that did not spoil the day. Only the photographer was not happy, mumbling something under his breath while trying to frame the cake cutting ceremony without showing the ruined side.

Elton John sang yet another version of "Candle in the Wind", this one rephrased to tell the story of how Mr. Hue and Mark had met. I used the opportunity to slip away to the gardens, where I hoped to find some respite from all the marital bliss. What I found instead was my sister and David, hiding in the bushes.

"Oh my God!" I said, quickly turning away. "Are you guys doing it? There's a wedding going on, show some respect!"

"To whom?" Felicity asked. "The husband who lied to me or the billionaire who's trying to steal my children?"

"Don't be so dramatic," I said. "Who in their right mind would want to steal the twins?"

"I wouldn't," David muttered behind her. The first of the fireworks went off, and I could see them both clearly in the colorful lights.

David had changed in the few months since I last saw him. Curiously, the changes were completely the opposite of those I'd seen in Mark - he looked a little sad, stooped lower, and avoided eye contact. In fact, he was starting to look like the old Mark.

"Shut up, David," Felicity snapped. She said it without anger, like a command you'd give to a dog. David sighed.

"That billionaire of yours is trying to buy my children with gifts," Felicity said. "You know that when I come to get them on Sunday nights, they cry and hide from me? Did you know he got each one of them a pony? He has some kind of a plan, I can feel it!"

"Don't give him so much credit - he's not that smart," I said. "Also, he's not *my* billionaire. As of tonight, he is Mark's. They will share unparalleled joy and laughter until their last heartbeat, didn't you hear?"

"Yeah, they will look into each other's eyes for all eternity!" Felicity snorted. "Whatever!"

"I give them six months," I said, and she hugged me fiercely.

My phone vibrated inside my bra, where it was shoved along with the car keys. Ever since I'd decided to forgo guns, there was no need to carry a purse. In addition to saving my life, my breasts provided handy storage for small valuables.

It was Sandra on the line. I could hardly hear her over the cacophony of the fireworks and Elton John. I shoved my finger as far as I could into one ear and pressed the phone against the other. Sandra was yelling something, and after a while I understood that she finally did what she promised. She sold my book to a major publisher, although it wasn't for a hundred thousand dollars.

She sold it for a million.

Probably maybe.

A million dollars. Think about it for a moment. It's not just a large number - it's a symbol of everything we've been told to want in this world. Foreign cars with doors that swing up like magical wings. Houses with in-ground pools and wine cellars. Wines that are older than you, and foods with names that can't be pronounced by mere mortals. A million dollars would open the kind of doors the general public doesn't even know exist.

A million was at least nine hundred and ninety-nine thousand more than I'd ever had in my bank account. It was more than I could have ever imagined, and I *earned* it. It was ironic that I got the money right when I decided that it no longer mattered. I didn't give it back to the publisher, though. It was going to a good cause.

I started my mission by trying to pay back the kindness shown to me by the homeless at The Tip. Strangely, when I arrived on site in Mom's station wagon piled high with bundles of blankets and boxes of fresh fruit, they were no longer there. In fact, the entire Tip had disappeared. I drove back and forth past the spot several times before I had to concede that it was gone. I finally pulled over on the shoulder and wandered around, trying to figure out if I'd imagined it, like one of my crazy dreams.

"Hey!" a rough voice brought me back to reality.

It was an old woman, standing in the open gate of her front fence. She was wearing a Macklemore-style fur coat, despite the sunny day, and smoking a cigarette. She had a lot of swag for a grandma.

"Whatcha doin' here, girlie?" she asked and took another drag from her cigarette. "This here ain't your land."

"No," I said politely and walked closer to her. "I'm just looking for

The Tip."

"Well, The Tip ain't here no more." Grandma flicked the ash from her cigarette. "The city done cleaned it up for good. What's it to you, anyways?"

"I just wanted to help the poor who lived here," I said, and then the woman's face lit up with recognition.

"Say, you ain't that billionaire girl?"

"I'm not a billionaire," I said, although I could hardly contain a smile. That was officially my first public recognition!

"Got yourself a billionaire boyfriend, same difference," Grandma said.

"He's not my boyfriend," I protested. "Actually, he's gay. As a matter of fact, he just got…"

"You wrote a book, didn't ya? How much did that pay?" Grandma wouldn't give up.

"Well, I did write a book," I said with barely contained pride. "But…"

"Say, how 'bout you start helping the poor by giving me a tenner for smokes?" she interrupted.

I resisted commenting on the damage smoking was doing to her lungs and instead fished in my wallet and handed her a bill.

"How 'bout a fifty?" she asked. "For the groceries?"

I gave her a fifty.

"My car is broke," Grandma said. "I reckon another five hundred would do it."

"I don't have five hundred," I said, feeling incredibly guilty.

"Right," she screwed her face up to let me know what she thought of the newly minted rich.

"Well," I said brightly, trying to change the subject. "It was nice talking to you! There's going to be a book launch in a couple of weeks, you can follow me on Twitter for updates…"

She slammed the gate in my face.

*

I didn't let that experience disillusion me, at least not at first. Next I volunteered at the local shelter. It didn't go very well because the homeless were surprisingly up on the latest news, and every conversation invariably ended with "Ain'cha that girl?" and "Gimme fifty". If I pretended not to be "that girl" or worse, didn't have a fifty, the homeless yelled or even spat at me. I longed for more noble and polite poor from some third-world country. They seemed to know how to accept poverty with class.

Sandra discouraged me from volunteering, arguing that my time would be better spent marketing my new book. If I made more money and donated it to charities, she reasoned, I would do more good than serving soup and knitting scarves. As it turned out, Sandra was a genius at marketing. She even explained to me what a marketing strategy was, in terms that I could understand.

"Marketing," she said to me one day, drinking coffee and chain-smoking at my kitchen table, "is all about tricking people into wanting to buy what you've got to sell. Marketing strategy is basically deciding which tricks to use, and when."

"Oh," I said, sipping a Red Bull and making mental notes.

"Say you want a guy to marry you," she continued. "What would you do?"

"Well," I said bitterly. "I would love him and care for him until he decided to date someone else."

"See, that's exactly your mistake."

"Which part?"

"Being too available," Sandra said, lighting a new cigarette. "There's no mystery in that, no challenge. The 'hard to get' concept may be old fashioned, but it's true."

I thought about Harden. "What if you are so hard to get that the guy leaves the country to join the Peace Corps?"

"Ah," she nodded and knocked cigarette ash into her coffee cup, "that's the other edge of the sword. You have to create just the right amount of mystery. Take Lady Gaga for example - does she have a dick? Yes? No? Probably maybe. That's perfect."

"So, what does that have to do with my book?" I asked. "Will I have to stuff a sock down there?"

"No," she laughed. "You're a different type of mystery altogether. A sweet and naive country girl mixed up in high society affairs. Is she pregnant with the illegitimate child of a gay billionaire? Yes? No? Probably maybe. We'll need to stage a few photos of you looking pregnant and then deny it with passion. I can see the headlines: 'Elusive billionaire's mistress is showing off the bump' and 'Sources confirm it's a boy for Mr. Hue'."

"Wow!" I said, excited. "My very own bump watch! Can it be a girl? I always wanted a little girl."

"No, a male heir is better," she said categorically and took a sip of coffee. "Just wait, they'll go apeshit over this. By the way, this coffee tastes like ape shit."

She was right. When an anonymous caller informed a few papers that Isabella Maxwell was going to dine at the Outback Steakhouse that night, the paparazzi went crazy. Good thing I'd studied celebrity bump watches like a scholar - it really helped bring realism to the way I cradled my stomach with one hand and half-heartedly blocked the cameras with the other.

"Good work," Sandra said when we studied the front page photos the next day. "I really like your shocked look in this one. Nice touch."

"That's because I was in shock," I said. "Getting pounced on by paparazzi is not fun. I had no idea how hard life can be for celebrities."

Sandra laughed uproariously. "That's perfect! Just keep up that innocent little girl facade and leave the rest to me."

"I don't feel innocent!" I said, throwing down the newspaper. "I'm lying to them and eventually it will bite me in the butt. And I hardly have any butt left!"

"Nobody's lying," she said. "In fact, I'm vigorously denying it on your behalf and threatening to sue *Star* for defamation of character. It's not your fault if a bunch of half-witted idiots want to look at these pictures and gossip."

I thought back to when I was one of those idiots and sulked, but she was right once again.

Sandra was also tenacious. She didn't stop at the rumors of my pregnancy. There were rumors that I was the mastermind behind the kidnapping, that I was a spy, and that I was not a real blond. There were rumors that the first print of my book had already pre-sold, but that Mr. Hue was planning to sue me to stop it from getting published.

The rumors spread, collided, and gave birth to more rumors. Some were completely unexpected, like the one in which I was romantically linked to Andrew, the sweet old grandpa married to the Lucy Liu look-alike. Lucy, who had since given birth to a little boy, took that one as a cue to leave Andrew and sue him for a breach of the prenup contract. Mr. Hue completely underestimated her.

Of course, all of those claims were passionately denied by Team Isa, while I kept getting caught on camera buying maxi dresses and vitamins. Mom asked me almost every day whether or not I was pregnant, but Sandra forbade me to say anything other than "maybe" to anyone.

"But she's my mother!" I pleaded. "She deserves to know!"

"Not true," Sandra said. "Even if you were pregnant, doctors would advise you not to tell anyone until the second trimester. And remember, it's not a lie if you don't say anything. It's other people's fault for making up rumors."

The other people were hard at work concocting rumors, which were ruminated like cud by all forms of media. I kept avoiding Facebook and Twitter, but Sandra informed me that on Facebook alone there were at least a hundred fan sites and that she was only responsible for three of them. Apparently on Twitter #IsaMaxwell was in the top trending hashtags almost every day.

There were even more invites for interviews, but Sandra spent a lot of time and money hiding me from the reporters. Strangely enough, every time a tinted limo whisked me away, some paparazzo was tipped off by an anonymous caller as to my next location. As a result, my face never left the front pages of the local papers and even some national ones.

The game of cat-and-mouse continued until the day of the book launch. I woke up early on that morning, spooked into consciousness by a wild dream in which I gave birth to Mr. Hue, only he turned out to be a robot. My nerves were shot, and my stomach was upset from all the excitement and build up. I didn't know what to expect, although I was sure there was going to be media mayhem.

The hair and makeup people arrived at eight am, even though the festivities weren't starting until early in the afternoon. Sandra asked them to sign confidentiality agreements, and they did, looking at me like I was an alien from another planet. I tried to make small talk, but the poor girl who was curling my hair with a hot iron jumped in shock and burned my ear. I stayed quiet after that.

It took a crew of three people nearly four hours to get me prepped, mostly because I kept running to the bathroom and throwing up, so they had to start all over again. They persevered until I looked like I had nothing done to me whatsoever. My hair was curled into a messy bun, my nails covered in a shimmery nude polish and, despite constant nausea, I had the natural glow of a healthy country girl. My cute white lace dress and flat white sandals were so adorable I could put Taylor Swift out of business.

"Perfect," Sandra concluded after five intense minutes of studying the final product. The hair and makeup crew released a collective breath.

"I don't think I can do it," I said. I was wobbly and very glad to be wearing flat shoes.

"Yes, you can," Sandra said. "Sit down, relax and try to eat something. We still have a couple of hours before going live. Try to memorize your speech."

She placed a typed page in front of me. I scanned it while nibbling on dry toast and contemplating ways of getting out of the launch. Fainting was an obvious choice and would have been easy, since I already felt dizzy. I looked at Sandra. She looked worried, poor thing, pacing the living room and checking her phone every ten seconds. I sighed. I could not let Sandra down, not after all she'd done for me.

"Maybe a Red Bull would make me feel better?" I offered.

"That's my girl!" Sandra brightened up and produced a six-pack of shiny cans.

My parents were excited and stressed out to the max. Dad was unusually quiet, constantly rubbing his hands together and occasionally giving me the thumbs up. He and Mom sat close to each other and looked like a couple of people who are finally assured that they've done a good job. I had to look away to avoid another bout of nausea.

After one final touch-up by the makeup artist, we piled into a black limo and pulled out of the driveway. Only a couple of paparazzi snapped photos of me through the car windows. I tried my best to look adorable.

"I thought there would be a lot more?" I asked Sandra, but she just smirked and patted my hand.

There were a lot more, all waiting for me at the venue. There were so many people outside of the Barnes & Noble building, you'd think they were there to see J.K. Rowling or the second coming of Christ.

"Are they all here for me?" I asked.

Sandra nodded. Dad gave me another thumbs up, and Mom started crying.

The limo pulled up at the front, and the crowd rushed over, pressing their hands, faces, and copies of my book to the windows. There were a couple of reporters, but mostly just normal people, although their behavior was far from normal. They were shoving and moving around us like the waves of a warm, sweaty ocean. Every single one of them had either a phone or a camera pointed at me, and I was getting blinded by the constant glare of camera flashes.

The crowd was screeching, and it took me a moment to understand that they were chanting my name. It sounded like a set of giant worn-out brake pads grinding to a halt. Just inches away from me, separated only by the glass, a teenage girl seemed to be struggling for breath. It would have looked just like a crowd of Beatles fans if not for a large number of middle-aged men, equally excited and close to fainting.

"What are we going to do?" I asked Sandra.

"Leave it to me," she said. "Just remember to look innocent and answer all questions with 'maybe.' Got it?"

Moments later the Red Sea of people was parted by security guards, who formed a living fence holding back waves of desperate fans. More security came and escorted me through a tunnel of outstretched hands and books. I wanted to get through it as quickly as possible, but Sandra made me pose for cameras, sign books and accept soft toys. I tried my best to smile and say nice meaningless things, but it was overwhelming.

Just as we were about to enter the store, I heard a familiar voice call out my name. I looked up.

"Hey, babe," Brad said.

Months had passed, but the shock of seeing his face again seemed to erase time, as if we had broken up just yesterday. I pressed an armful of teddy bears to my heart.

"Hi," I managed. "What are you doing here?"

He smiled his usual dazzling smile but, surprisingly, I didn't swoon with desire.

He winked at me. "I'm here for you, babe. Look, I even bought your book." He held his copy up for me to see.

Just a few months ago, that would have been enough for me to forgive him. This time, however, it made me suspicious. Brad was a tight-ass and only read menus. Something had changed.

"Oh. Did you like it?"

"I didn't read it," he said. "You look great, babe, like a celebrity or something. What do you say we get back together? Sorry about what I said before."

The paparazzi went mad snapping photos of us together. A news reporter behind me was narrating something about a romantic twist. It was all strange and disorienting, like one of my Mad Hatter tea party dreams.

"What about Tiffany, aren't you guys engaged by now or something?"

"She's engaged," Brad said, and his smile faded. "To some lawyer dude. She's a bitch, just like everybody told me."

"Oh," I said. "Didn't you say you were going to date models once you got drafted?"

"Yeah," he said, "but that's kind of over. I tore my knee up so bad, doctors say it's a wonder my leg hasn't fallen off."

"I'm sorry," I said automatically.

"Nah, it's okay. I got this cool job delivering potato chips. Boss says that if I don't get another DUI by the end of the year, he'll bump me up to twenty-five an hour. Plus, I get to keep all the bags of chips that get damaged in transit, and they do, you know what I mean?" He winked at me again.

I looked him over in stunned silence. He *was* different. His cheek-

SHIZZLE, INC

bones, while still visible, were now padded with a layer of fat. I looked down and saw the beginnings of a pot belly silhouetting against his sweaty polo shirt. Otherwise, he was the same thoughtless jerk I remembered.

Brad misunderstood my gaze. "You look hot too. How 'bout signing a book for a fan?"

I took the book and opened it to the title page. Brad shoved a thin Sharpie into my hand. "Write something special for me, okay? I bet it would be worth at least two hundred on eBay."

"Sure thing, babe," I said and scratched a couple of sentences across the page. I handed the book back to Brad, and he read out loud, "A nincompoop just won't cut it in celebrity circles. I'm doing you a favor."

People snapped photos of the dedication over his shoulder. I heard him yell, as I walked away, "What's a nincompoop? Are we back together or what?"

I didn't answer, and just like that, put Brad out of my mind forever. Well, that's not entirely true, as I'm still beating myself up for putting up with him for so long. But at that moment, I had much more pressing things to think about, like how to survive the pandemonium of belligerent fans.

When we finally made it inside, it wasn't much better. The store was huge, but it was standing-room only, and people must've been waiting for a long time. The air conditioning did little to disperse the odor of so many bodies. *If this is what public transport is like*, I thought, *I'm sure glad we don't have any.* The stale warm air made it hard to breathe, and the pungent bouquet of armpits and lunchtime garlic breath brought nausea back. I handed my collection of fan gifts to Mom and tried to fan some fresh air with my hand. It was no use.

Our little group made it to the corner, where a makeshift podium was erected. It was surrounded by life-size cutouts of me and larger-than-life posters of my book. A huge banner overhead read "Money, power, and violence: Isa Maxwell's story".

Felicity and Tara were already there, draped over their new boyfriends. They started squealing as soon as they saw me and took turns giving me bear hugs. They both smelled like sweat and sex, and my stomach lurched again.

Sandra pushed ahead and went up to the microphone stand. The crowd quieted a bit.

"Thank you, everyone, for your enthusiasm in supporting Miss Isabella Maxwell's breakthrough first book!"

I mistook that as my cue to come up, but she launched into a detailed synopsis of the book.

"Just tell us if she's pregnant already!" somebody yelled from the crowd after a few minutes.

Sandra smiled coyly and shook a finger, "You'll have to wait!"

There was a collective groan from the several hundred people packed inside. I thought for a moment of what would happen if I yelled "Fire!" and had to pinch myself hard to get back to reality.

"I can remember the day I called Isa and convinced her to tell her side of the story," Sandra was still talking. "In fact, if I hadn't called, this book would never have happened. Yet here she is now, Isabella Maxwell, a best-selling author!"

I made another attempt to come up, but Sandra went on reminiscing about all the writers whose careers she'd helped launch, and how they'd all dropped her once they hit the big time.

"But it doesn't matter," she said bitterly, "because there are new and fresh voices to be discovered every day, or at least that's what I have to keep telling myself."

I was looking down at my feet, thinking about how my freshly painted toenails looked like dead fish eyes when someone shoved me.

"It's your turn, sweetie," Mom whispered urgently in my ear.

I looked up at Sandra, who was waving at me impatiently. I climbed a couple of steps and turned to face the crowd. The ocean of faces stared back at me.

"Hi?" I said. Behind me, Sandra whispered something about the speech notes. The notes! I patted my sides and felt a cold shiver of realization that I left them back at the house. I looked back at Sandra, hoping she had a copy. She either didn't have one or misunderstood my mute request and just kept grimacing and gesturing in the direction of the microphone. I turned back to the crowd. They continued to stare.

"Thank you," I said. That was better. It's always a good idea to start by thanking people. Puts them in a more receptive mood.

"Thank you for your support. And thank you, Sandra, for the wonderful introduction and all your help." I applauded, looking back at Sandra, and the crowd half-heartedly joined me. It did wonders for Sandra's disposition.

"Ahm…" I said, trying desperately to remember what the speech notes said. Something about how writing a book is like childbirth…

"Writing this book was like having a baby," I said. "Except, of course, this baby only took a couple of months from conception to birth!"

A few people laughed obligingly. Encouraged, I continued, "I just hope the real birth doesn't hurt as much!"

"Are you pregnant, then?" yelled someone from the crowd.

"No, of course not," I said automatically.

There was a collective gasp from the crowd. Then everyone started talking all at once.

"I mean, yes!" I tried yelling over the noise. "Maybe?"

It didn't do any good. A few reporters were making their way outside, while others rushed the stage, shoving their microphones in my face.

"Ms. Maxwell, can you explain your contradictory statement?"

"Have you engaged in sexual relations with Mr. Hue?"

"Are you, in fact, a brunette?"

Sandra jumped in front of me, screaming "No comment!" over and over. Security guards tried to hold the reporters back while another guard pulled me to the side and through the door marked "STAFF".

The guard went back outside, and I sat down on a box of books in what looked like a storage room. Seconds later, I heard Sandra yelling "No comment!" as she backed in through the door and slammed it shut.

"What did I tell you to do?" she hissed, turning around. "Read from the notes and be mysterious! I remember specifically instructing you to answer 'maybe' to all questions!"

"I did…"

"After you told them that you are *not pregnant*! There is no reason for anyone to buy your stupid book anymore! The whole marketing campaign was based on this one enigmatic secret, and you ruined it!"

That was a bit much. "My book is not stupid..." I tried again.

Sandra was livid. "Of course it is! It's the worst garbage imaginable! You have absolutely no idea about plot structure or even grammar!"

"But you said..."

"I know what I said! I said it would be a best seller, and it would have been. Not because it has *literary value*," she made mocking quotation marks with her fingers, "but because it has best-seller ingredients, like scandal and sex."

She was obviously losing her mind. "My book doesn't have any sex," I said.

"Yes, it does," she said tiredly and sat down on a box opposite me. "I had it improved. You should consider reading contracts before you sign them."

I realized with growing horror that I had read neither the contract nor the actual printed book.

"Did you...use me?" I said, even though I already knew the answer to that question.

"Call it what you want. You were going to make a lot of money, too," she sniggered and patted her pockets for cigarettes. "Except now that dream is all but dead."

My whole body was shaking, and I wrapped my arms around my midsection to hold it together. I felt like I was about to lose it, only instead of the customary tears, a wave of righteous anger came up.

"Maybe yours is," I said, "but don't discount me so quickly. I wrote a book. I don't care whether it sells a million copies. I created something!"

Sandra ignored me and shook a cigarette out of a nearly empty package. "From now on, you're going to do exactly what I tell you. Most importantly, you're going to keep that mouth shut, unless I tell you to read from cue cards. No stupid jokes and definitely no improv, got it?"

I said nothing and just kept looking at her. It wasn't just her attitude that had changed; even her appearance was different. The friendly professional was gone, replaced by a tired hag.

"Do you understand what I'm saying?" she said impatiently, still not looking at me. "Or have you lost whatever little brains you had?"

"I understand," I said. She nodded, put the cigarette in her mouth, and fished around in her purse for a lighter.

I stood up and took a deep breath. There was no way she was going to make me cry.

"There's something *you* don't understand," I said. Sandra ignored me, her arm up to the elbow in purse guts.

"I'm done with this." I felt the weight of the words fall off my shoulders into the space between us. "*We* are done."

"*We* are just getting started," she said, lighting her cigarette. "This fiasco has done a lot of damage, but I can still spin it." She took a drag, blew the smoke up, and addressed the stock shelves. "Young author crumbles under pressure, maybe even attempts suicide. We can get a snap of you with bandaged wrists. That should keep the momentum going for a while. You may have to attack a photographer with an umbrella or something. I'll have a think about it."

"No," I said, confident and terrified at the same time.

"What do you mean, 'no'?" she finally looked at me.

"I mean, I'm not doing as I'm told anymore. I'm not pretending to be pregnant, suicidal, or even some nauseatingly sweet little thing. I want to be myself."

"Being yourself is not going to sell any books, darling, unless 'yourself' is already a celebrity," Sandra said. "And actually, even celebrities fall from grace when they say out loud the stupid shit that's flying around in their heads. Being yourself will make you at best a starving artist or at worst homeless. The rest of us gainfully employed professionals have to pretend, tell lies, and kiss ass. That's how the world keeps on spinning. Just imagine the chaos of everyone saying exactly what they think, let alone doing exactly what they want. We would just kill each other!" She crushed the cigarette pack in her fist.

"That's your opinion. There are people out there who would value me for who I am and not for what I'm pretending to be. I'd rather spend my time with them, and I don't care if that sells any books."

Sandra took a deep drag on the cigarette and said nothing. Little by little, the nicotine seemed to calm her down. She looked me up and down, like a boxer before a fight.

"Let me tell you something else," I continued, fighting hard against the anger and the fear. "I'm done being a pawn in your game. In fact, I'm done being a pawn in anyone's game, no matter how rich or famous they are. What good is it to have millions if you are constantly afraid to lose them or have to lie to yourself and others to get even more? What good are so-called friends if they only want to be with you for what you can do for them? Damn it, God was right! All we really have is friends and family, and at least mine love me and will always love me despite my mistakes. And if I ever do get married, it will be for love, and not for security or even a huge diamond ring!"

Sandra stared at me, the cigarette frozen in mid-air. "What ring? What the hell are you talking about?"

"It doesn't matter. Good-bye, Sandra."

I stormed past her and jerked the door open. My friends and family were on the other side, trying to convince the security guards to let them in. Mom was waving a handful of my baby pictures, Felicity was waving her business card, and Tara was gesturing at Chad's badge. Dad was saying something about his academic credentials and everyone else was trying to yell over him. They all fell silent when they saw my face.

"What's wrong, honey?" Mom asked.

"Nothing. I mean everything. I've gotta go."

"We'll take you home, sweetie!" Mom said.

"No," I said. That was the most times I'd ever said "no" in one day. "I need to be on my own for a while. Clear my head."

Mom started to say something, but I just kissed and hugged her. Sandra appeared in the doorway of the staff room, and I dashed outside, once again thankful for the flat sandals. Our limo was still parked out the front.

I dove into the front seat. "Go!"

The driver obliged. I looked back to see Sandra and my family emerging from the front doors, looking bewildered, and then we were off.

"Where to?" the driver asked.

I thought about it. There weren't any places I could go where Sandra couldn't find me. My phone buzzed, and I turned it off.

"A hotel," I said finally.

"Which one?"

I almost said "Holiday Inn", but stopped myself. It didn't seem fitting for the momentous occasion.

"Which one is the best hotel in town?" I asked.

"Ritz-Carlton."

"Take me there, please," I said and closed my eyes.

*

The driver was right. The Ritz not only looked opulent, but the staff also treated me like a celebrity, which I guess I was. I paid with a shiny new American Express, not a black one, but still good enough to get a luxury suite. Just for one night, I told myself. The rest of the book advance would go straight to the poor.

I asked the limo driver to pick up a few things from my parents' place and allowed a uniformed attendant to escort me upstairs. The suite took my breath away. It had a panoramic view of the city, a proper living room with an elegant couch, a huge bedroom with a bed covered in embroidered pillows, and a bathroom the size of a small apartment. In the center of the bathroom was a giant spa with another spectacular view of the downtown hustle and bustle. It was amazingly quiet, and the air smelled like spring in the countryside.

"Will there be anything else, ma'am?" asked the attendant.

I ordered room service - a steak smothered in creamy sauce and tiramisu for dessert. I was through trying to be a certain weight, too.

My whole body hurt as if bruised. I took a hot shower and scrubbed off the makeup and hair spray. When that didn't seem enough, I filled the spa and soaked in the glorious warm water until the bruised feeling dissipated. My head cleared up. It was time to make another plan.

I dried myself off with a huge fluffy towel and slipped into a luxurious robe. The attendant brought in a couple of bags the limo driver delivered from my parents' place. There was a note from my Mom, something about Sandra's threats and begging me to call them. I put the note away and set my laptop on an elegant desk by the window.

I typed in the log-in password, inwardly thanking Chad for the unsolicited security advice. I resisted the impulse to google my own name and logged into my email instead. The inbox was full of requests for interviews, fan mail, and hate mail. I was scrolling through them, thinking about what to do next, when one caught my attention.

The subject line simply said "Help!" and at first I thought it was one of the homeless, however unlikely it was that a homeless person could get Internet access. I opened the message but had to read it twice before I even began to understand what it meant.

The email was from someone named Prince Amar of Agra. I googled Agra, and it turned out to be a real place somewhere in *India*. My heart skipped a beat.

Amar wrote that his father, Maharaja-something, recently died from a broken heart after losing his wife. As if that wasn't bad enough, Maharaja's will left his entire fortune not to Amar, his only son and rightful heir, but to his two evil, scheming uncles. Amar was sure that the will was forged, as his father had never in his life bothered with the paperwork. The uncles gave Amar a few hundred rupees a month while they spent the royal billions on fast cars and belly dancers.

Amar wanted to sue his uncles and was sure to win back his fortune, which included palaces, private forests, and even an airport. All he needed was five thousand dollars to pay his lawyers. "I am happy to pay your gift back thousand-fold," the email said.

"Is this for real?" I asked my laptop.

I clicked on the attachment. It was a photo of a handsome young man with long black hair and huge gold earrings. Definitely gay. Still, he looked like a bona fide prince.

"Billions," I said out loud. "God, I hate scheming uncles!"

I considered that thought for a moment. I could send the money and help one man, or…

"I could spend that money on a plane ticket, help him win the case, and convince him to use his wealth to help the country's poor!" I said to the laptop. "I could write meaningful articles about his case and the plight of the slums. Slum Dog Billionaire! I could become a real, credible journalist!"

The laptop offered access to travel websites and, just like that, I bought a one-way ticket to Delhi, departing in two weeks. I still needed a ticket from Delhi to Agra and a hotel reservation, not to mention a passport, but I was exhausted. I had just enough juice left in the batteries to get me to the lavish bed and pull one corner of the silky cover over me just before I fell into darkness.

I had another strange dream that night, although it was different from any I'd had before. I was flying through the clouds, high above the rivers and mountains of a beautiful and unfamiliar countryside. It was easy and wonderful, like swimming in a clear, weightless ocean. The gentle wind blew through my hair and caressed my body. I was alone, but not lonely, filled to the brim with wonder and anticipation of what was coming next. I had a destination, although its name escaped me. It didn't matter.

I would know it, once I saw it.